THIS VACANT PARADISE

THIS VACANT PARADISE

A Novel

VICTORIA PATTERSON

COUNTERPOINT ◆ BERKELEY

Library of Congress Cataloging-in-Publication Data is available.

ISBN 978-1-58243-805-4

Interior design by Neuwirth & Associates, Inc.
Original cover design by Gabriel Masón
Printed in the United States of America

COUNTERPOINT
2560 Ninth Street, Suite 318
Berkeley, CA 94710

www.counterpointpress.com

In gratitude

to

C.P.

What loneliness is more lonely than distrust?

GEORGE ELIOT

PART ONE

1

CHARLIE MURPHY WAS on his way to Image Makers, which sold merchandise to those who, as advertised, "have everything." After ascending an escalator from the parking lot (Image Makers was located in the indoor-outdoor shopping plaza Fashion Island), Charlie paused before the picture window of Shark Island, restaurant and bar. In the late-afternoon sun, the glass had a golden shimmer and allowed voyeurs to see directly into the U-shaped bar. It was a one-way window: From inside, the glass looked like a shiny onyx wall.

As Charlie stood at the edge of a walkway, the hurried crowds of shoppers moved around him. His gaze passed over the men and women at the bar. Despite their casual demeanors, he believed they were anxious and lonely.

A man stopped, stood beside Charlie. Snowy-haired and with unruly eyebrows, he wore a black silk shirt emblazoned with miniature pineapples, and tan corduroy pants. "Met my ex-wife," the man said, as if talking to the window, "in there. Bought her a tequila sunrise. A barracuda in hiding, man. She looked like a model. You couldn't pay me a million dollars to go in there—just a bunch of fucking barracudas, ready to eat my balls."

Charlie acknowledged him with a commiserating head nod. The man shook his head; his hands were in his pockets—Charlie heard the faint jingling of car keys and loose change—and then the man shuffled on.

Charlie was about to leave also, but there—in the midst of the fake palm trees and plastic bamboo, the seasonal holiday lights and decorations—were the shoulders and back of Esther Eileen Wilson.

Stunned, trying to make sense, he looked away—past the stores and escalator and parking lot, all the way to the horizon. The late-afternoon sun reflected across the surface of the ocean, like a shimmering sheet. There was the speck of a motorboat and its tiny foam trail.

Esther, he believed, had the capacity to be his barracuda. If only they'd had more time together. She had dated him six months before, for about a month, and he had fallen for her, sure he had, only for her to break up with him for no good reason. Then he'd discovered the reason: Paul Rice, an idiotic man with the advantage of a stunning inheritance, care of the Rice Corporation.

When he looked back, Esther hadn't changed her position. She appeared lonely—possibly because she was alone. Visible through the wicker-mesh barstool, one foot was crossed over the other, high-heeled shoe dangling, ready to slip off.

She was drinking what appeared to be, by the shape of the glass on the bar top, her favorite drink, an apple martini. There was about her figure the subtle look of coolness, but with a pleasing vulnerability and availability.

Considering he was only an appreciative spectator, it seemed silly to feel such trepidation and awe. He was safe, watching. Carried on the breeze was a hint of garlic, the aroma of grilled chicken—it came and went.

And then she did a remarkable thing: Her hand casually readjusted her long hair, back slightly arched—revealing her neck, the hair shifted to her shoulder.

Charlie made himself move away from the window, and his walk to Image Makers was mechanical, forced. At the horizon, the small red sun quivered against the ocean. In his jacket pockets his hands clenched in fists.

He remembered Esther pulling away from a kiss, leveling her eyes on his; letting him (only him, for a passing, terrifying, thrilling moment) witness her fragility. And it had surprised him so much that he'd felt himself open to a deeper possibility between them. But then she'd ruined everything.

AT IMAGE MAKERS, Charlie appeared to be oscillating between the purchase of a step-on glass scale or a foldaway elliptical strider, as any consumer might struggle, if not for a perfect Christmas gift, then for an adequate one.

He needed to buy a present for his parents, something to validate their acceptance and devotion, because instead of showing the slightest interest in the family business, he'd become an academic; and instead of marrying and presenting his parents with grandchildren, at thirty-eight, he was a dedicated bachelor.

But the strain inside him was more profound.

"Do you need any help?" a saleswoman asked, startling him. Her hair was dyed the harshest of blonds—metallic.

He didn't respond, hoping she might leave, but she took his silence as an opportunity to speak about the elliptical strider. She liked him, he could tell. Women liked that he never appeared free from thought, which was ironic, considering they were usually appreciated for having the opposite, trouble-free demeanor.

"I'm looking for a present for my parents."

She nodded and continued her canned speech. "Stainless-steel finish," he heard; "instantly measures heart rate in beats per minute." She appeared to be middle-aged. He guessed by necks and hands. But it was difficult to decide. She might be an old woman who looked young, or a young woman who looked old.

No matter what, he took it as his personal duty to notice and appreciate women.

Her bust was of note: The issue was not whether they were natural—they weren't—but how the artificial could assume the properties of the natural. At what point did the distinction between genuine and imitative collapse? Ample breasts and narrow hips, fulfilling men's latent homoerotic desires: like having big boobs attached to a male essence.

Having had the close and personal scrutiny of both types, he believed there was no substitute for natural, no matter the shape, size, and flaws; he thought of Esther's dark-pink nipples: one in his mouth, the other in his hand. A stirring in his groin followed.

"Would you like a demonstration?" She began to adjust the elliptical strider on the carpet. He didn't answer. "How about the Ultimate Human Touch Massage Chair?" Abandoning the strider, she pointed to a lounge chair. "Memory-foam cushions. Isolated massage pressure points."

He lifted the step-on glass scale—thin and weightless—as if to privately observe its features.

"Why don't you tell me about your parents," she suggested, "and we can go from there?"

"I'll come back another time."

She smiled for him, a private little smile, before turning and walking in the other direction, the T-shaped outline of her thong visible against her khakis.

Setting the scale on the floor, he left. Walking toward the

parking lot, he considered the conspicuous wastefulness at the heart of Fashion Island. A bronze wind chime sculpture, bells hanging from ceiling to asphalt, was a fitting commentary: It was recorded in *Guinness World Records* as the world's largest wind chime, but it was a useless decoration, silent, no whistling, no chiming.

The sky was swathed in reds, air laced with ocean, and something he didn't know how to describe: sweet, heavy air.

And then he was standing in front of the Shark Island window, inwardly conceding that he'd been hurrying, hoping that Esther hadn't left.

Her shoulders were forward, the bulk of her hair on her right shoulder. She lifted her martini glass. He couldn't see her face, but he knew her lips were touching the rim. An empty plate was on the bar top. What had she been eating? She set the glass down, and he imagined her gaze traveling over the other patrons. A group of businessmen sat across from her, powerless; even her seemingly insignificant gestures, he believed, were visual hooks.

A twosome of women entered, greeting two other women—a severity to their hair, makeup, bodies, clothes.

He preferred Esther. Her focus, for a short time, appeared to be on the women, but then her face tilted up, as if acknowledging the ceiling fan and vents, and hair tumbled from her shoulder to her back. As it brushed against her skin, the back of his neck prickled.

Her hands—her fingers—slid up and down her arms (she must be cold!); then she rested her chin on her palm, watching a television in the corner of the bar, with an air of helpless defeat, as if whatever she saw rendered her childlike.

He looked to the screen: A man was surfing, his board's fin slicing through a wave like a knife, opening the water, leaving a peel of white.

When he looked back at her, she was peering over her shoulder. If he hadn't known the glass to have one-way visibility, he would've sworn that she was staring at him, challenging him. Desire and fear came upon him. She was staring right through him. But she was looking at the shiny black glass, a fluke turn of her head, and then she turned back around.

2

ESTHER'S FAVORITE DRINK was the sour apple martini, and as she sipped from the shallow glass, she watched her image in the beveled mirror behind the stacked glasses and bottles of the bar. She saw a corner of her face: lips, cheekbone, eye. This was enough to reassure her, and she set her glass on the palm leaf–embossed cocktail napkin. Her image pleased her, as it did the three businessmen across from her, their ties loosened, watching her while they talked, daring each other to take the initiative. One of them would walk over soon, egged on by the others, and if she played her cards right, she wouldn't be paying her bill. At thirty-three, she was well acquainted with the rules of attraction and commerce.

Esther had come from her four-hour shift at True Romance. Besides ringing up clothing sales, she also offered the women demure praise and encouragement on their selections. Sometimes she wore the luxury clothes as a walking advertisement, but she was forced to rehang the garments after her shifts (even with her 10 percent employee discount, she couldn't afford them); but as consolation, she often overcharged the women and then helped herself to the five, ten, or twenty dollars from the cash register, cosmically fine-tuning the inequities of the universe.

Esther had had many mind-numbingly dull dates with Paul Rice, an overly empathetic man, son of Michael Rice, number 223 of *Forbes* magazine's "400 Richest Americans."

Despite an involuntary tremor in his hands, Paul had been ranked number three among *Orange Coaster*'s most eligible bachelors. He'd come into Shark Island one evening, setting off a buzz up and down the bar: Paul Rice, Paul Rice, Rice Corporation, Rice Corporation. She'd pushed her hair off her back, leveled her gaze. And he'd approached her.

A bouquet of butter-yellow tulips, petals rimmed with scarlet, as if they'd been dipped in paint, had been hand-delivered to her this afternoon. The card had read, simply: "Yours, Paul." Tulips were her favorite—durable as well as delicate. They could decorate a prison cell, if necessary.

Her last date with Paul, he'd steadied one hand on her knee, leaned in for a kiss. She'd hoped that by opening her mouth, letting his tongue play with hers (all the while, his hand inching up her thigh, beneath her skirt, fingertips nosing at the elastic of her underwear), she would feel more natural toward him, more desirous, as woman to man. She let herself be consumed with thoughts of his power and his money. But his tongue had felt foreign, like a child's finger probing her mouth, and she'd reluctantly pulled away, leaned back into the couch. ("You okay?" he'd asked. She hadn't answered, but he'd found an answer that suited him, looking down at his lap, saying, "I didn't mean to rush you, Esther. I'm sorry.")

Esther limited herself to two martinis—this was her first—and breaded zucchini. Years ago, she'd gotten drunk at a charity ball, only to find herself in a hallway closet with a sexually adventurous Tibetan monk who carried a flask in a hidden pocket of his dark-orange–colored robe. Ever since, she had been respectful and vigilant with alcohol.

She was not unhappy, but solitary and introspective.

On one of the three muted television screens, she observed President Clinton taking long strides across a grassy lawn, his hand in the air, waving. She thought he was sexy but she told no one, considering he was so disliked. If Clinton were here, she imagined he would sidle up to her, calculated, daring: "Hey there, darlin'," not even bothering to hide his wedding ring.

Onscreen, Clinton was boarding a helicopter, and as he got closer, his slacks and suit jacket flapped against his body, the grass flattened.

Paul wasn't ready to introduce Esther to his parents, and tonight he was obliged to join them for dinner. Rather than being discouraged or expediting the process, Esther welcomed the opportunity to regroup, as a football team huddled for strategy before returning to play.

Lights in the palm trees and lining the bar top blinked and winked, as if to remind her that Christmas, a week away, held the possibility and probability of a check from her grandmother.

The last two Christmases, Grandma Eileen's caretaker, Rick, at the direction of Grandma Eileen, had at some unidentified point during Christmas Eve, much like Saint Nick, placed seven thin unsealed envelopes amongst the lights and Southwestern-themed decorations on the Christmas tree.

One for Esther; one for Aunt Lottie; one for Lottie's new husband, the former golf pro George Famous; one for Uncle Tim; one for his wife, Mary; and one each for Uncle Tim and Mary's dull-witted but attractive teenage children.

Inside each envelope, without holiday sentiment or card, was a crisp check in the amount of ten thousand dollars and no change. Esther wished for a brood of children and a husband, if only to increase her intake. She owed over ten thousand on her Visa alone and would have appreciated Mary's thirty thousand more; she was jealous of Mary, with her teenage children and new-age piety, although she wouldn't want to look like Mary, a dowdy ex-hippie.

The idea of the Christmas check—all those zeros—lurked behind her emotions like a great shadow. She needed it. *Oh please God*, she thought, *make Grandma Eileen increase the amount.*

But this was unlikely: Grandma Eileen gave erratic gifts of money, and only enough to encourage dependence.

If she were Paul's wife, everything would change: With his money, she wouldn't be beholden to her family, and the check, instead of being a means for survival, would be like a holiday bonus, good for a vacation, perhaps, or a shopping spree.

A tax write-off for Grandma Eileen's estate, the envelope gifts usurped the presents underneath the Christmas tree, and last year Aunt Lottie had had the nerve to sulk, check in hand.

Aunt Lottie was waiting, not so patiently, Esther thought, for the time when her forceful and decipherable handwriting on the pale green checks, not Grandma Eileen's elderly, dismissive scrawl, would direct and ensure gratitude and deference. That day might not be far off, as Grandma Eileen, in her mid-eighties, had been increasingly, belligerently, destructively courting death.

Two women entered the bar, their entrance designed to attract attention. Shrilly, they greeted two other women. Hugs, kisses, squeals of delight, an overwrought display of approval and excitement ended with a purring of small talk. Three out of the four were fake-breasted, and there was a uniformity in the way the women dressed and talked, the way their hair swung at their backs, even the way they laughed.

Why did women act like hyperactive children? Esther hoped that she didn't unconsciously behave like them. But she felt a paternal-like sympathy, knowing that no matter how much money, no matter how much plastic surgery, they would never be as physically attractive as she was at this very moment.

The bar was kept air-conditioned cool, and Esther looked up to the ceiling, adorned with slowly moving fanlights, and saw that she was sitting in the direct path of a ventilator. She slid her hands up and down her arms.

On another television screen, elevated in a corner, a surfer skimmed down a wave, his surfboard creating a foamy seam. She wished to somehow shake off thoughts of her family, but not of the check. She had nothing in common with her family, except a painful past and a tormented, hollow present.

One thing was certain: Aunt Lottie and Mary had better not touch her share of Grandma Eileen's estate. She was owed.

Thoughts of her father entered, and she turned her head to look over her shoulder, with the sense that she could turn away from grief. She stared into the shiny dark glass of a mirrorlike window. The glass gave a blurred reflection of her blank-staring face, the figures of the men and women, and the muffled lights and decorations. She stretched her arms and turned back.

She looked down at the darkened bar top, a smudgy gleam from the overhead track lights. Her resentments acted as a buffer, familiar and safe, and she directed her thoughts back to Aunt Lottie and Mary.

A figure moved behind her, and she took no notice, continuing to stare at the bar top, thinking it was one of the businessmen passing by on his way to the restroom. But then the person came close and she felt fingers on her shoulder.

When she looked behind her, Charlie was already placing his blazer around her. She felt a soothing warmth, but at the same time, a defiance. His skin, smell, and presence were a dead-end temptation.

"I saw only your back"—his glance indicated the window. "I knew it was you."

She recrossed her legs and smiled. Her best strategy was to be simple, not a simple task. But when she met his eyes, she yielded to the desire to allow him to see her—whatever that meant, whoever that was, and for whatever it was worth—like letting out a deep intake of breath.

He slid a barstool out and sat, his knee brushing against her thigh. Her plate was in his way, and he moved it down the bar. Settled, he made a slight gesture with his eyebrows, as if to say, *Now what?*

She stole a glance at the businessmen, confirming that her chances had been lost by his male presence, and, not missing a beat, he said, "Don't worry, I'll pay."

His hand lifted as he attempted to catch the eye of the bartender.

She placed her fingers on his arm, lowering it, and summoned the bartender by raising her forefinger.

The bartender nodded and on cue began preparations for her second and final sour apple martini. "Uh, I'll have a Corona," Charlie shot out, and the bartender eyed him, as if to say, *Maybe you will, maybe you won't.*

Charlie turned his attention to her. "Shark Island?" he asked, as if she were beyond saving, but she knew it was an effort to disguise his attraction, and also to make light of the bartender's likely snubbing of his drink order. "Why do rich people eat at restaurants with no originality? Where the food is as bland and as boring as their conversations."

His glance left her, and she saw that he was looking at the huddle of women at the other end of the bar. She struggled with a need to prove that she was different. Her bust and legs seemed to be her best hope, and she sat more upright on the barstool, to display these to advantage.

He seemed to read something in her effort, and he laughed—a quick burst and then he was serious. She could feel him really looking at her.

Blood rushed to her face and she did her best to hold his gaze, her body slumping into a disobedient ease.

They were quiet, although she felt activity in their silence, as if they were speaking intimately, and she understood that something was vibrating between them. Wisps of conversation, laughter, a televised football game, surf music ("Wipe Out") bombarded them—intrusive, suddenly loud.

He pulled his wallet out, in an effort to lighten the intensity, and his eyes went down. "I don't have the cash"—he paused, as if searching for the right words, and his eyes found hers again—"to get drunk enough to feel comfortable."

Chin on her palm, much like a child, she pretended to ignore Charlie as the bartender poured her martini from a silver shaker.

ESTHER MIGHT NOT have agreed to a walk along Big Corona Beach with Charlie had she not wanted to spend more time with him. She was cautious, knowing how people gossiped. They needed to leave Shark Island before word got back to Paul, and Charlie had suggested a walk along the beach. Maybe it was the sentiments that stirred at Christmas, the lights and music and decorations, and the softening in her gut from her two sour apple martinis. Maybe she was weak, undisciplined, but she didn't care just now.

At the sight of Charlie, two ideas had come to her, one following the other. The first was that their meeting might have been not an accident, but a fateful coincidence; the second, a consciousness that she would allow herself this one indulgence, like eating a carton of ice cream or sleeping all day, before she got back to her hard work. She wore his blazer, a high heel in each pocket, and she walked beside him, silent and barefoot, along the slicked sand. She was tall enough to reach his chest.

Wave upon wave rolled forward, broke, and gathered back—sand hissing. A pattern of fire pits blazed at the far end of the beach. Winter was her favorite season because there weren't as many tourists. The air was dark and misty, an occasional coldness from the larger waves sprinkling her ankles and calves.

She liked Charlie's height, and the way his expression appeared troubled—nobly so. She didn't want to be attracted to him, but it was natural, in the same way that she wasn't attracted to Paul. One of the risks was involuntary intimacy: Charlie drew her in, made her lose track of her priorities.

"My father," she said, stopping to look at the piled rocks of the jetty, "used to tell me about all the people who drowned in the channel before they built the jetties." Her heart gave a bound as she waited for him to react.

His expression was serious and meditative. "Whatever you do," he said finally, "you can't marry Paul Rice."

They both laughed, but there was a stunned quality.

"Maybe I like him," she said.

"That has nothing to do with anything," he said.

She saw a familiar silhouette—compact body—jogging barefoot in the sand, coming their direction, but she was unable to make him out in the dark.

"I know that man," she said uncertainly, peering at him, grateful for the diversion. The man stopped, dropped down, and did a series of push-ups on the ocean-hardened sand. After completion, he rolled to his back, and began a frantic series of sit-ups, elbows hitting his knees.

"What's he doing now?" Charlie asked.

"I think those are calf toners," she said, watching him rise and descend, from toes to flat feet—up down up down—quickly.

After shaking out each leg, the man began jogging again, his looming figure coming closer, closer, his lycra-clad legs swishing, shirtless, until she whispered, "Jesus—Slick Rick: Grandma Eileen's caretaker." Her instinct was to cover her face, but it was too late. If she appeared to be hiding, it would be worse. Slick Rick was Grandma Eileen's right-hand man. "Rick," she said, as he slowed to a trot, his face lighting up in surprised recognition. "It's too late to be jogging."

"She finally let me out," Rick said. He stood before them in a wide stance, arms crossed over his chest. His biker shorts had a padded quality at his groin, and his T-shirt had been tucked into the elastic at his backside. "She's a beast!" he said with a happy face. His chest was nearly hairless, only a fine T of curls arching over his nipples. She didn't trust him, his earnestness and crazy stories—always telling stories. Privately, he talked to her as if she were his confidante. He'd done drugs with her brother, Eric, but with the help of methadone, he'd kicked his habit, while Eric continued to waste away.

Even the way Rick had gotten his job was suspect: Rick's best friend was Aunt Lottie's hairdresser, and in the time that it took for Aunt Lottie to get her tips frosted, Rick's position had been arranged. Did Rick even have nursing credentials?

There was also Esther's suspicion that Rick was gay, and this bothered her the most, not because she was against homosexuality, but because her father had been disowned for this very same shortcoming.

Rick was already talking to Charlie, hand on his forearm, as if they were good buddies; he was a full head shorter. She listened halfheartedly to him telling a story about an elderly woman who had lived along the Big Canyon golf course. While sitting at the steps of the shallow end of her pool, she'd taken a golf ball to the head and had died soon after of a brain hemorrhage. He'd read it in the *Daily Pilot*. He'd also read about the leader of a cult who had died; there had been a scramble for his estate.

"He was Buddhist," Rick said. "The retreat was more like a resort. They played zennis instead of tennis and had massive orgies."

Charlie, laughing doubtfully, cast a questioning glance at her. She suddenly felt tired.

"I'd better get back," Rick said. "I didn't mean to interrupt."

"Charlie's an old friend."

Rick seemed to agree, because he said, "Yes indeedy." He walked a few paces, then picked up his jog, elbows close to his sides.

"That's Eileen's caretaker?" Charlie said.

She nodded. She was accustomed to people's alluding to the bizarre nature of her family. After her father had been disowned, they'd been forced to move, since legally their house belonged to Grandma Eileen. She'd watched her heartbroken father suffer, and had cared for him through a prolonged illness without the aid of her family, until his drawn-out death.

Charlie looked away, toward the receding figure of Rick. Rick was taking long strides up the walkway that led to the beach, and then he was out of sight. Charlie looked back at her, discouraged.

"Don't marry Paul," he said, as if there hadn't been a break in their earlier conversation. She didn't answer. She listened to the long gathering pause of the waves, the crash and rumble, and the collecting rush. Before it was over, another crash and rumble, another collecting rush.

Paul elicited no passionate feelings and, at most, a general ambivalence, but she was determined to fall in love with him, at least on the surface.

And what was love, anyway? She'd been in love with Kelly Toole when she was a sophomore in high school and he was a senior—a water polo player, with a protective smile and a sleek body (he shaved all his body hair, for speed) the same size as hers, so that they were like twins. They spent hours together and she lost her virginity to him, happily.

She thought she would die of heartbreak when he left for Dartmouth. Four months later, when he came home for a visit, he was stubborn and arrogant, with the energy of a bully, and the most passion he had was for the Kappa Alpha Phi fraternity and his equally brutish fraternity brothers. As soon as he kissed her, she knew that he'd been with other women. He even tasted different. He said that instead of being his girlfriend, she could be his "special friend"—translation: He could have sex with her and with other women. They had a horrible fight and breakup.

Nursing her ego, she vowed to see through her emotions next time, to the core of a thing. She cried for what seemed like months, and then, as if on cue, she got the Epstein-Barr virus. The whites of her eyes turned yellow. It took over a year to recover. She'd lost her way a couple of times since then—to no good fortune (literally), but never quite as fatally as with Kelly—as if kicked in the head, out of balance. Love, then, was a broadened irrationality, an amplified susceptibility, and a guarantee of disappointment. She needed to be practical about love, because love was impractical.

And the scales were tipped on the side of men. She believed in equality between the sexes, but she was a realist. Females put so much effort into advancing in a male-dominated world that their looks and personalities suffered. And she'd lost time taking care of her father. Charlie didn't understand the temporal reality of a woman's desirability.

Charlie looked at her, dismayed. "What is it you want?" he asked. There wasn't anger in his voice, only a direct and genuine curiosity.

She wanted to give him a lucid answer, but the question made her wince. Emotions, especially when it came to desire, seemed complicated, and she wondered how anyone ever navigated them.

He squinted up at the sky, as if, since she hadn't answered his question, he might find something there.

"I'm afraid," she said. She hadn't meant to speak.

He stared at her, letting her words settle. She liked that about him—she could tell that he was really listening.

"Of what?" he asked.

She considered. "I'm afraid," she said, "of being poor."

He laughed. Her face must have revealed her hurt feelings, because he launched into an explanation: "It's just that I thought you'd say something like, 'I'm afraid of death,' or, 'I'm afraid of suffering,' or, 'I'm afraid of going insane.' Or maybe, 'I'm afraid of not being loved.' Or how about, 'I'm afraid of not fulfilling my potential'?" He kicked at the sand. "Or, 'I'm afraid of having children or not having children.' God, Esther. I don't know. How about, 'I'm afraid of aliens attacking Earth!' Or even, 'I'm afraid of nuclear war.'"

"I watched my father die," she said. "I watched him suffer."

"I know," he said.

"I'm afraid of being poor," she said, "because then you're uncomfortable and suffer and you can't afford children and they suffer and you might go insane and you don't have the means to fulfill your potential, whatever that means. And if aliens attack us or there's a nuclear war, I'm afraid of being poor because who's going to get away? The rich will be on the first spaceship to Mars. They've already paid for their seats."

He was staring at her. A different kind of look had entered his expression—melancholy and concern.

"How's that?" she asked. "Is that better?"

"I'm worried about you," he said, trying to sound casual, but she could tell that he was startled.

"Well, I'm not worried about you," she said, looking him in the eyes. "Mommy and Daddy already paid for your seat."

He didn't answer and she couldn't resist prodding, albeit gently, almost kindly, "Didn't they? Huh?" She took hold of his hand and swung it lightly. "You're all set, aren't you? First class, window seat."

BACK IN CHARLIE'S Honda Civic parked alongside the curb, Esther lowered her passenger seat and sank with it, resting her head and gazing at Charlie, who watched her in return. He lowered his seat to match hers. His window was cracked so that they could hear the waves crashing in the distance, softly, and he had the heater on low. Her feet were still bare; her toes felt the warm blow of air.

They stared at each other for some time without speaking, a complicated and weighted silence between them. She was aware that there was something in her expression that the darkness couldn't conceal, something soft and desiring, and that it matched his expression.

"You still live with your grandmother?" he said, breaking the silence.

She took it as a rhetorical question, reclined her seat further, as far as it would go, closing her eyes with a feeling of release.

The edge of his hand was against hers, but thankfully, she knew that he wouldn't try to hold it.

AS CHARLIE DROVE her back to the Fashion Island parking lot, she persuaded herself that nothing of consequence had passed between them. Their parting was amicable, and she felt him watching as she unlocked the door of Grandma Eileen's BMW, settled herself inside the car, and started the engine.

3

WHEN ESTHER WAS a girl, the second level of her father's house had an expansive balcony that overlooked Newport Harbor, clear to the jetties extending like two outstretched arms to the ocean. From the balcony on clear nights, she liked to imagine she could fly across the bay, past the jetties, over the ocean, circling the red bell buoy and its blinking ruby of a light—the barking sea lions vying for space on its swaying surface—all the way to Catalina. Her father slept in his bedroom, her brother slept in the room next to his, and often, she would move through the darkened house with the comforting knowledge of their presence.

The banister to the ground floor had a curved mahogany handrail, and she would run her palm along the smooth surface. On the wall behind the staircase was her family's portrait, like a photograph, but with the rougher texture of a painting—she, her father, and her brother sitting on the rocks of Little Corona Beach, waves in midcrash behind them. When she'd posed, the sharpness of the sea rock had hurt her thighs, but she'd smiled directly at the cameraman; and then she'd heard her father: "Beautiful, Esther. Beautiful."

On the cream-colored walls of the living room were oil paintings. One in particular she would pretend was her mother. The background was dark, almost black, and the side of her mother's figure emerged like a phantom. Her mother's face was turned away, her hair gathered in a loose bun. Her skin was milky, with a flushed undertone. She gave her mother different names: Lucretia, Vanessa, Elizabeth. She was sure that her mother was crying, turning her face for this reason, because she'd given up Esther. Sometimes it was torture, or the threat of death, but no matter what tragic misfortunes, she had trouble convincing herself that her mother's reasons were valid.

She never told her father. He claimed that he'd been fortunate to adopt her; she was special and different. She was better than anyone, and she should never forget it. He gave similar explanations to her older brother, Eric, who coped by caring less. He hated their father, for no reason.

She made up for it by loving their father even more. She didn't mind that he was not married and that he didn't have girlfriends, was beyond that. Besides, she wanted to marry him—she wanted to be with him always.

When she tried to remember her first two years, before he'd adopted her, she saw nothing but a dark red color, and a vague emptiness expanded in her chest and stomach, unending. The feeling terrified her. She resolved not to try anymore.

Sometimes when she looked at her father, a burning sensation would catch at her throat, dissolve through her body, as if traveling through her blood. Later, when she was old enough to understand, she knew that this was because she loved him.

SHE WAS EIGHT years old, crouched underneath the family portrait late one evening, peering between the rails of the stair banister, when she witnessed her father kissing his tennis instructor, Scott. She pressed her face between the rails, her silky nightgown gathered between her legs.

Darkness hung around the men, blurring their bodies, but she could see that her father's hands were at Scott's arms. She was aware, even as she watched, that what she saw was secret. Her father said something in a hoarse whisper, his voice barely rising to her—it sounded like *I need you.*

The men were near the front door, and she wanted Scott to leave. She wanted her father to be talking to her. When the men's faces came together, for a shocking second she thought they were trying to eat each other. When she realized they were kissing, she bit the inside of her cheek, making it bleed.

Back in her bedroom, she wanted to squeeze the image from her mind, but it was etched permanently inside her. She tried to understand. No one had told her that such a thing might be possible.

Later, she woke and staggered to the bathroom, her feet cold on the tile. Her stomach was turning, as if filled with jelly, and everything around her seemed ominous and unexplainable. It was this image of her father and Scott kissing that came to her as she vomited over and over into the toilet.

Her father came to the bathroom—she must have woken him. "Sweetheart," he said. He looked helpless and sad, and she wanted to tell him that she'd seen him make a mistake. Because that was what it must have been—a mistake. Her real father was separate from the man she had seen in the doorway. It was as if some other person, a stranger, had possessed her father.

4

IT WASN'T MUCH warmer sitting at the bench of the bus stop, though the bus stop shelter did cut the breeze. The silvery sun gone, it was just beginning to get dark, and the streetlights and the Christmas decorations and the noises of traffic made Eric Wilson think it was like being at a movie—no, that his life was inside a film and he wasn't really here, he was just acting his part.

With his eyes closed, the lights and visions and noises passed through him, strangely comforting. He slumped lower, the side of his body leaned against the backdrop of the shelter, his chin tapping against his chest.

"Hey there," he heard, and he opened his eyes and straightened his frame to find that Rick was walking toward him, his hand doing a sideswiping, hip-level hand wave. Rick wore a purple sweatshirt with the word PEACHES in yellow cursive across the chest, and Levi's.

Rick seated himself on the bench next to Eric. It had been simple and easy to be friends with Rick when they had been active drug addicts together, united by the intimacy of procuring and injecting heroin, drugging their senses, nodding off together; but now, underneath the bus stop shelter, cold and hungry, Eric did not want to speak, knowing that if he did, he might reveal the hideous emotions that he felt for himself, and for Rick, who he knew was sober.

Rick had a grease-speckled paper bag from the nearby Winchell's. Eric's stomach did an excited flip, but he wouldn't eat anything in front of Rick. Rick might imagine that it was a concession or an admission of defeat.

Rick began unfolding the opening, and Eric shook his head, indicating that he did not want a donut or a Danish or whatever else might be in there. Rick shrugged, placing the paper sack to the side of the bench, and Eric knew that he would leave it for him to eat later. They were silent, and then Rick reached out and gently touched Eric's shoulder.

Eric flashed him a hint of a glare and then looked away.

"You remind me of your sister," Rick said, and Eric returned his stare. Rick seemed to be in thought. "I want to help her," he said, "but she's like you."

"Okay," Eric said. Years ago, Rick had overdosed and Eric had driven him to the ER, sat beside him while his stomach was pumped, lied to the police about everything that had happened when they came to make their obligatory report, waited the whole thing out. Ever since, Rick had taken it as his duty to pay Eric back, and although he didn't like it when Rick wanted to save him, he didn't mind the thought of Rick helping Esther. "Okay," he said again, and he knew that Rick wanted more from him: to eat a donut, ask for help, go to an NA meeting.

Rick laid it out almost every time, asked him the same types of questions. Eric gave him a full glare, hoping to stifle what was coming. But it was no use.

"Eric?"

Eric closed his eyes, faced the other direction.

"Do you want help? Are you ready?"

"No."

"Is there anything I can do?"

Eric didn't answer.

"Do you want to talk?"

"No."

"What do you want?"

"Nothing. For you to leave."

"All right," Rick said, and then Eric felt Rick's fingers spread across his shoulder, and despite everything, Eric's heart lurched with tenderness and affection. A shifting of shadows and the soft rustling of clothes indicated that Rick was standing and leaving.

When he was sure Rick was gone, Eric leaned forward and held his hands together, eyes still closed. For a second, he wondered what he looked like—if it looked like he was praying. Words floated in his head, without his speaking them. *Leave me alone*, he thought. *Everybody just leave me the fuck alone. Go away.*

He was getting no answers, he wasn't feeling anything, and then he was ashamed. But the feeling didn't overtake him, because it was as familiar as his own breath.

After eating the donuts (one glazed, the other chocolate iced with rainbow-colored sprinkles), sucking the excess sugar from his fingers, and then wiping them against his shirt, he got up and walked to the corner, where there were four coin-operated newspaper machines.

The first two had nothing inside, but when his index and middle fingers slid into the coin-return slot of the third, he felt the ridges and the cool firmness of two quarters against his fingertips.

5

ON THE INDEX finger of Grandma Eileen's fleshy and wrinkled right hand was a luscious ten-carat radiant-cut diamond set between two tapered baguette diamonds. On the middle finger of her age-spotted left hand, she wore an eleven-carat cushion-cut pastel-blue sapphire. Sunlight slicing through a crack in the balcony curtains reminded Esther of the diamond—how a fiery blaze could exit the crown and be seen as a ghostly flashing across a room. The rings looked better on her young fingers. She'd tried on the jewelry more than once, fishing the rings from the sudsy-slick jewelry cleaner in Grandma Eileen's bathroom, after making sure the bathroom door was locked.

Esther turned her head from the wedge of sunlight. She lay in bed with a headache. Was it a hangover from her two martinis last night? Was it emotional residue from her dream? She'd dreamed of Grandma Eileen's death. She would get money, maybe even one of the rings, but her relief had turned into a melting of sorrow, and she'd woken sweaty and crying, her silk pillowcase damp and cold. She was not a crier.

Because it was the Sunday before Christmas, she was expected to attend the late service at Maritime Church, and afterward visit her great-uncle—Grandma Eileen's brother-in-law—at the convalescent home, along with Grandma Eileen, Aunt Lottie, and Mary. Women's duty.

Esther lived with Grandma Eileen in her one-of-a-kind three-story home, which, curving forward from the cliff edge, bottom deck secured by sea-discolored metal columns, balanced over rocks and ocean. Grandma Eileen had taken Esther in after her father had died. She'd been broke and in debt.

Aunt Lottie and George Famous had their own two-story home in Newport Shores but visited Grandma Eileen often, under the noble guise of "taking care" of her, though they could usually be found from morning till afternoon on a nearby golf course, and in the evenings at one of their favorite restaurants.

Rick had been hired over two years before for the less agreeable responsibilities, such as toilet duty. He lived in an apartment in Costa Mesa, commuting in his dusky-green Mercury Grand Marquis, but he might as well have lived with them, since he was in the house from early morning until late at night.

Esther's bedroom on the first floor was an afterthought, converted from a playroom long since unused by Mary's teenagers. Her room had a separate bathroom and kitchen and extended from the house, with its own door to the outside.

As Esther rose from bed and made her way to the bathroom, she felt the familiar vulnerability of living off her grandmother. She paused to part the balcony curtain, and the view was level with the sea, as if she existed on the ocean's surface. Grayish whitecaps, threadlike clouds, and a brilliant morning sun . . . the beauty was corrupted by the detail that it could be taken from her. Her life was provisional. She let the curtain swing back.

What had started as prostate cancer had progressed to bone cancer, but the rumor was that her father had died of AIDS. The tangle of emotions she had for Grandma Eileen was reinforced by the fact that her father had never truly blamed his mother for disowning him, even at the end, when all his savings had gone to paying hospital bills. And despite everything, Esther had affection for Grandma Eileen, and not only because of her impending death and will. She might not have fallen sway if she hadn't had the sense that she was necessary and important: "Nobody else understands me," Grandma Eileen liked to say, to the mortification of Aunt Lottie and Mary. She would've liked to hate her grandmother, and at times hatred *was* the clear and prevailing emotion, but she appreciated Grandma Eileen as her father had, and she was aware of the great power she had in Grandma Eileen's reciprocation.

While she showered, she thought about how she wanted to come upon age like Grandma Eileen: no longer dependent on being beautiful, slim, or gracious, and with enviable influence. But she wouldn't be prejudiced and cruel-hearted. She would enjoy her wealth and spread it to the deserving.

Grandma Eileen's husband, Grandpa Gurney, with the financial backing of his family, had made his fortune in real estate, and he'd let his brothers in on the business and all its gains. But there was no question that Grandpa Gurney was the financial genius and their superior.

In the late sixties, at the height of his success, Grandpa Gurney had unexpectedly and inconveniently died from a brain aneurism, sending shock waves through the family and inciting a scuttle for control. Grandma Eileen had surprised everyone by taking the reins, firing disingenuous lawyers, and fortifying her role, as if she'd morphed into her husband.

There hadn't been a challenge since, although Aunt Lottie watched her mother closely, waiting for clear proof of dementia or Alzheimer's disease. But when it came to business, money matters, and the various details of her will, Grandma Eileen remained as sharp (even sharper, Esther believed, though most wouldn't admit it because she was a woman) as Grandpa Gurney in his heyday.

As Esther began her grooming routine, her headache lessened. She felt a resolve, a reinforcement of her goals: a future full of the things that she loved, with no one to take them from her. Blow-drying her hair, feeling the silky length along her bare arms, witnessing her beauty in the mirror bolstered her. She wore a nude-colored Chantelle French bra and panties, and she admired her breasts.

Peering closer to the mirror, she noticed the lines forming at her mouth, the familiar sense of time moving in on her. She set the adjustable lighted mirror to a less critical notch, a happier glow. Newport was full of women desperately clutching youth, well beyond menopause, and one of her fears was that she would become one of them. But by worrying about it, she would only hasten the progression.

She thought of Charlie—how strange that they would have talked so openly—but it was best that she not see him again. Her thoughts centered back to her objectives (Paul Rice), leaving Charlie behind.

After deliberation, she decided on a turquoise cotton skirt and a white blouse, humble and womanly, knowing that her appearance should please Paul, whose attendance at Maritime Church was a given. She slipped flat sandals on her feet. Boring and feminine.

"Horrible, horrible," she heard, knowing that Grandma Eileen was coming, hearing the *thunk* of her cane against the stairs. Grandma Eileen's voice was deep, like a man's. She was alternately lucid and delusional, and sometimes the two were mixed. She talked about herself in the third person, which was unnerving. When she was in her element, she was as sharp as a knife slicing through the soft flesh of a melon, and could do as much damage.

It wasn't a good sign that she was making her way to Esther's room, as she did so only when agitated. Esther's indulgent behavior had backfired. Her suspicion was that Slick Rick was sent out into the world as a spy. She would have to come up with a plausible explanation, as Grandma Eileen considered Charlie a failing, and Esther wasn't quite sure if she disagreed.

Her door was pushed open, and Grandma Eileen, stooped forward, leaning on her black walnut cane, scrutinized her with a direct gaze. She wore her deceased husband's sleeveless vest-jacket, with fly-fishing patches covering the front, over a peach-colored polo shirt, and her pale-cream polyester slacks embroidered with miniature lemons. Along with her rings, at her neck, hanging beneath the wrinkled lump of her throat, was an eight-carat princess-cut diamond.

"So what's this I hear," she said, with sharpened eyes, "about your romantic evening with the Socialist?" She began her heavy tread across the room.

"Charlie's a sociology professor," Esther said, knowing that this wasn't better. Any kind of academia, especially those of the humanities and social science varieties, were deeply suspect. "We took a walk."

"He's a Communist." Grandma Eileen tapped her cane against the floor, hand clutched at the brass golf-ball knob. "That's what he is. And from what I've heard, he likes to screw married women." Her body was soft and pillowy, spread with wrinkles. "His poor parents," she continued. "Ungrateful bastard, turning away from his family's business. Screwing married women. Clinton-loving liberal philandering piece of shit."

Esther was silent, waiting for Grandma Eileen to finish. Charlie's parents were fellow members at the country club, and she knew that this was where Grandma Eileen garnered most of her information.

"Frank and Karen are good kids," Grandma Eileen said, referring to Charlie's older siblings. "But they got a bad seed with that Commie-lover." Her legs, unaccustomed to supporting such girth, had become bowlegged. Standing defiantly, she breathed heavily, waiting for an explanation. "What about Paul?" she said when none came.

"Paul and I are dating; we like each other very much."

"Do you think he appreciates that you took a romantic stroll?" Grandma Eileen's tongue popped out, made a brief, grotesque appearance, and went back inside its cave. "Don't waste your time," she said, "on losers."

Rick's familiar steps could be heard as he made his way down the stairs. He was never far from Grandma Eileen. Wearing faded Levi's and a white T-shirt, he leaned against the doorway, an indulgent pout to his mouth.

"This gives a whole new meaning," he said, fingering a $100 bill, "to money laundering."

Grandma Eileen was known to carry sizable amounts of cash on her person, and often some of the bills went through the washing machine. Grandma Eileen had been making the accusation that someone was stealing her cash. Esther believed that Rick, more than providing a play on words, was ensuring his trustworthiness.

"You have to be more careful," Rick said, crossing the room and handing the bill to Grandma Eileen.

"I'm missing two hundred," she said, folding the money and slipping it into the vest-jacket pocket. She yanked the zipper shut. "George took it, last night." Aunt Lottie's new husband, George Famous, was an easy target, and for that reason Esther believed him innocent. While it was obvious that Grandma

Eileen was paranoid, someone was probably stealing from her. Esther herself had recently taken $300 from a roll of cash, rubber-banded and left thoughtlessly on the kitchen counter.

"Did you take all your pills?" Rick asked.

Grandma Eileen moved two more steps, so that she stood directly in front of Esther. Long lines streamed from her nose to the corners of her mouth, as if carved in her skin. She had fine silvery hairs on her chin and her upper lip. "Looky here," she said, thrusting her arm forward, arm fat swinging. She fisted and unfisted her left hand, leaning with her right on the cane. Her eyes were a transparent blue, ambiguous as they opened themselves to Esther, taking her in like empty pools. "I took my pills. No pain," fist; "no pain," unfist; "no pain," fist. "Not bad for Eileen Marie Wilson. Huh? Not bad for Eileen Marie Wilson."

"Not bad," Esther agreed, if only to get the fisted arthritic hand away from her face. But in truth, she felt privileged, as she always did when Grandma Eileen allowed her to truly see, holding nothing back, as if to say, *Here I am. This is me.*

EVER SINCE GRANDMA Eileen had failed her driver's test, unable to bribe the woman who handled the vision chart, her driver's license had not been renewed, and Aunt Lottie had become the official Sunday driver. Grandma Eileen saved her worst venom for her daughter, badgering and cruel, and Esther sometimes wondered if Grandma Eileen was preparing Aunt Lottie for an eventual takeover—to become savage in business—but she knew that she was giving her undue credit.

"That's a yellow light," Grandma Eileen said, "not a red light. Slow, slow. Not stop!" Esther, sitting in the backseat next to the heavily perfumed Mary, could feel the way Aunt Lottie struggled to maintain her cool, her hands gripping the steering wheel as the Mercedes idled at the signal. Aunt Lottie's shoulders rose and fell in a sigh. A seagull was perched in the red light of the stop signal, its dark outline visible, and when the light changed to green, Grandma Eileen said, "Green! Go! Go!"

"I know, Mother," Aunt Lottie said. Even from the back, she looked like Grandma Eileen, her hair cut short and curled in a helmetlike manner. She wore a vest covered with patches of U.S. license plates.

Grandma Eileen's spacious Mercedes was the preferred means for driving to Maritime Church, and the parking attendants, also know as Parking Pastors, wore Hawaiian-print short-sleeve shirts and waved white-gloved hands, directing Aunt Lottie to the handicapped-parking spaces.

"That way, that way," Grandma Eileen said, and Aunt Lottie shot her a disgruntled look. "I've got to go where they tell me," she said. Grandma Eileen made a reach for the wheel. Aunt Lottie slapped her hand away. "Stop it!"

"That way! That way!" Aunt Lottie made an unexpected sharp turn, a Parking Pastor waving frantically and trotting after the Mercedes. Mary, nudging Esther on the thigh, whispered, "Here we go," as if they were on an adventure together.

Esther smiled, her face tight with effort. "How are Caitlen and Bailey liking high school?"

"Caitlen is adjusting, trying out for cheerleading, but Bailey, with his dyslexia, is having some trouble; he'll do fine in water polo and golf."

It was most difficult for Esther to be gracious with Mary, since Mary's home had rightfully belonged to her, having once been her father's. She remembered every detail but avoided the street, so that she wouldn't have to see it or think of it as being occupied by someone as revolting as Mary. She imagined Mary smothering the wall with generic watercolor paintings—dull landscapes and seascapes—or, even worse, her framed psychedelic Grateful Dead posters, as confirmation of her hippie past. Mary covering the hardwood floors with thick cottony carpet and festooning the kitchen in some appalling theme, like ducks or pigs. An awful plaque hanging above the sink: WHEN MAMA AIN'T HAPPY, AIN'T NOBODY HAPPY.

The women walked to the church auditorium, more like an office empire. Motionless clouds, thick and claustrophobic, loomed low. Mary, hair curly and loose at her shoulders, wore a floral-print dress, cinched at the waist with a conch belt, and as she walked beside Esther, her clogs made a sucking clop sound. She was always reading New Age books, talking as if she were some kind of guru, indulging her children with all sorts of diagnoses: sugar and wheat allergies and rare learning disorders. Mary feigned a motherly concern for Esther, and Esther's resentment had been cultivated over the years with the understanding, reinforced time after time, that in truth Mary did not give a lick about her well-being.

A divinity scene beside the parking lot, with life-size replicas of Mary, Joseph, and Jesus, caused the women to pause. "Jesus is the reason for the season," Grandma Eileen said definitively, before continuing toward the church. Grandma Eileen often used broad religious declarations, her most frequent being "The Bible is God's word breathed." Not long ago, she'd claimed Mikhail Gorbachev was the Antichrist—proof being the purplish birthmark on his forehead.

Aunt Lottie tried to help Grandma Eileen up the stairwell with a hand to her shoulder, but Grandma Eileen shrugged her off. "Leave me alone," she said. "I know how to walk."

"Why is it," Mary asked rhetorically, so that only Esther could hear, "we reserve our worst behavior for those closest to us? We save the worst of ourselves for them."

Esther, watching the large upside-down heart shape of Grandma Eileen's ass, didn't answer. Aunt Lottie's backside was a smaller version, and it gave both women an appealingly vulnerable quality.

"One of the true signs of character," Mary said, "is the ability to love a person regardless of differences."

"What's that?" Grandma Eileen said, turning with a scowl. "What'd you say?"

"I'm talking about the Golden Rule."

Grandma Eileen flapped her hand at Mary.

The women sat in the second row; a special reclining chair had been set up on the aisle for Grandma Eileen, and Esther was chosen to sit next to her. The darkened auditorium began to fill with people, most dressed casually. The choir and band assembled onstage. Purple-bluish lights filtered through the auditorium, and two large screens lowered. The drummer, blue spotlight on his glass-enclosed drum set, started the service with a steady beat, and the lights filled the stage, revealing a smoky atmosphere.

The choir was mostly women, three visibly pregnant, and they began grooving to the beat, their arms on each other's shoulders. The only clear sign that Maritime was a church was the small wooden cross in a corner of the stage.

Esther watched the video montage on the screen: African American children, smiling and happy. Some crazy Jesus actor making his way through his disciples. A shot of the Earth from space, and then the camera zoomed in on a throng of Chinese people walking down a street. Inadvertently, she felt as if she were part of one great cosmic Christian universe, but whatever small grains of belief she had were best cultivated in private. She didn't trust spiritual showmanship.

The couple in the seats ahead of her held their hands in the air. The man wore flip-flops and jeans and the woman's hair was in need of a dye job, with silvery-gray roots.

Pastor Ken walked to the center of the stage, smiling and holding a microphone. He wore khakis and a Hawaiian-print shirt, like the Parking Pastors.

"There's Ben," Grandma Eileen said. She called him Ben and had done so for years. Esther wondered if Ken had tired of correcting her, or whether he allowed the name change because of Grandma Eileen's financial contributions.

Esther searched the faces, looking for Paul. She thought about how close he was to proposing. A few more months. She remembered her father saying, "You'll do well. You'll marry someone rich."

Ken's sermons were affable and innocuous, making the audience chuckle. She didn't believe in the church, but she pretended to. His voice provided a calming backdrop and her thoughts drifted. She remembered her father: his thinning hair, his half-crooked smile, a look of laziness. She remembered a cruise to Alaska when she was seven, her first taste of crab; a trip to Spain; excitement and travel and her tennis lessons and golf lessons and piano lessons. There was always enough money. And then the constant presence of Scott; she could see his lanky body in his shorts and Izod shirts, a windbreaker that he wore, his arms making a whispery noise when he moved. The skin separating his nostrils was chronically chafed; his cocaine habit was beginning to wear through the thin flesh. She could see him rubbing the skin, his fingers pressed there. And the quarrels. They took another trip to Europe, away from Scott. Scott, in retribution, paid a visit to Grandma Eileen, bribed her for money.

Strange that what Esther remembered the most about the afternoon that Grandma Eileen had told them to leave their house was Grandma Eileen's matching gray pantsuit. "Do what you have to," her father had said, and then he'd put his foot on her coffee table. "That's a polished surface," Grandma Eileen had said.

After her father's death, Esther became fascinated by a photograph of him that Grandma Eileen kept framed on the mantel in the living room. With curiosity, she would study his competitive, leering grin. He had just finished a meal at the country club and was leaning back in his chair. He must've been in his late twenties. The picture seemed at odds with who Esther knew her father to be, and she wondered why Grandma Eileen kept it. His elbow was on the table, his jacket sleeve slouched down, revealing a hairy forearm, and he held in his fingers, pointed outward, a fat cigar. The image was potent with entitlement, self-mockery, outward mockery, satiation, and it contrasted with all those years as a child she had spent with him—cracking eggs with him into the big blue bowl, to make cookies; holding her face still while he applied her makeup on Halloween, so that she could be a princess or a cat or a clown, his face hovering over hers, gentle and patient; sitting with him in the big reclining chair ("our chair," he called it), when he let her stay up late to watch *Saturday Night Live*.

If she looked at the photograph long enough, her point of view seemed to shift into her father's, feeling the situation, defenseless against himself, pretending to be someone else—a mockery of masculinity. She saw that shame lurked beneath his expression—close by, waiting—and she felt the protective motions of his mind and instincts as he hid, further away from himself. *I'm not gay*, the photo said. *Fuck you. I'm not gay.*

The church schedule was at Mary's knee, and Esther read what Mary had scribbled in the margin: "Don't have the right to judge. God expects us to be loving. God wants us to know He is good all the time. You need to trust me. I'll be good and you need to be loving. Never pay back evil with more evil. Do things in such a way that everyone can see you are honorable. Dear friends, never take revenge. Romans 12:17–21."

Grandma Eileen leaned forward, and Esther saw that her eyes were directed at a man and that she was agitated. The offending person had clipped his sunglasses at the back of his collar. With relief, Esther saw that the man had a really dark tan, and Grandma Eileen noticed as well, leaning back into her seat.

Esther didn't want to be racist, and of course she wasn't homophobic, but when she was with Grandma Eileen, heterosexual Aryan Christian uniformity made life less problematic.

After the service, the congregation assembled with their steaming cups of coffee near the glowing lawn. Kids played inside a big hollow plastic whale in the middle of the lawn, and the grass was covered with giant balls and tubes for them to climb through.

She saw Paul from a distance, near the bookstore and café, recognizing his baggy chinos, his dress shirt tucked in slackly at his waist. She knew that he bought his clothing by catalog from J.Crew.

Pity warmed her, thinking of his shaking hand lifting the Styrofoam cup to his lips, coffee sloshing. She would make sure that he saw her at least once before she and her relatives left, but she wouldn't force a conversation—her image would be more effective.

The dark clouds had merged to a uniform gray, the sky dull. She saw that Brenda Caldwell was making her way through the crowd, her husband, Sean, close behind. Sean was a lawyer who specialized in corporate takeovers, and he and Brenda had married young, while sophomores at USC. Brenda had been pregnant, and their harried wedding had been arranged without fanfare but with the approval of both families, since their fortunes would merge. Three children and great financial success later, both were unhappy in their marriage, and Brenda was known to have engaged in at least two affairs, her last with Charlie. Everyone, including Esther, seemed to like Sean and sympathize with him. Sean had once told Esther that he secretly pined for her, and she appreciated the small power this gave her.

A hand to the elbow along the way stopped Sean, but Brenda continued her course. Esther admired her beige slacks and white tailored blouse. Her clothing, her face—everything about her—spoke of money and privilege, of careful and exacting attention, in an effortless, carefree way. She was fulfilling her inherited obligations—to dress well and look beautiful. And her affairs were a family legacy, extending as far back as her great-great-grandfather, a well-known philanderer.

Esther felt a smile come to her face as Brenda's eyes met hers. After hellos and small talk, including affirmations of each other's clothing and of Ken's sermon, Brenda paused. Her hand was at her waist, fingernails filed in soft ovals and coated with a shimmery, translucent gloss; she seemed to be in thought.

When she looked up, her expression was beautiful in its emptiness. "I'm not sure how to ask," she said, "but I was wondering if you want to come by, and I can give you some of my things that I was going to pass on?"

Things, Esther knew, included handbags, designer sunglasses and clothes, and all the other items she pined for while working at True Romance or window shopping in Fashion Island.

She felt herself submitting to Brenda's goodwill while at the same time chafing against it, understanding that there must be something behind the offer, some knowledge or gain for Brenda.

"I'll call you this afternoon," Brenda said, instead of waiting any longer for Esther to answer, and her lovely fingers came forward and gently squeezed Esther's forearm. "Same number?"

Esther nodded, in a shaming admission that her domestic situation had not improved. Her forearm was squeezed again.

"Okay," Brenda said, releasing her grip.

"Thanks so much," Esther said, thinking that one day she would not live off the castoffs of others. One day *she* would be passing things down.

EVEN UNCLE RICHARD, living at New Horizons Senior Care off MacArthur Street, was a lesson to Esther in what might happen if she was not vigilant. Without money, without power, without influence, he'd been relegated to a convalescent home, while Grandma Eileen would spend her final days in the familiarity and comfort of her house, nurses and doctors and caretakers at her call.

"Where's the bar in this place?" Uncle Richard asked as Esther entered his room, as if it hadn't been a year since she'd last seen him. He was trying to be funny—it was the same thing he'd said to her last year before Christmas, but it made her feel worse, as if he'd planned the quip far in advance.

"I've been looking all over for the bar." He sat on his bed, his legs crossed at his ankles, his burgundy-colored socks matching his cashmere V-neck sweater. He looked sad and resigned, as if he'd been waiting for them all morning and now that they'd finally arrived, it was a disappointment.

"Now, now, Richard," Grandma Eileen said, smiling horribly. She clumped forward with her cane, a Christmas present clutched to her chest. She set the present on his bed, and he ignored it.

Mary set a smaller present alongside the other, and Esther knew that inside the box was probably catnip or a wind-up mouse for Uncle Richard's old cat, Captain Ahab, who had accompanied him to the pet-friendly convalescent home. Uncle Richard liked to tell the story—probably untrue—of how he'd rescued Ahab, finding him in the Mojave Desert, fending for his life against a rattlesnake.

Esther glanced around the room, looking for the cat, but she couldn't find him. The only visual clues were the wisps of cat hair that covered Uncle Richard's sweater.

Grandma Eileen paid for Uncle Richard's care, as Grandpa Gurney had had to provide for him in life. He'd been happy to live off his brother, and he'd settled into old age in an alcoholic daze. Esther's father had called him a useless drunk, and she'd grown up thinking of her great-uncle as expendable.

Now, Uncle Richard's liver was shriveled and decayed. His gaze was on the wall. "What is good for me," he said cryptically.

"Gurney," Grandma Eileen said, "was good for you and to you, and don't you forget it."

He ignored Grandma Eileen. With a pained, wistful expression, he turned his attention to Esther. "Did you know that you are the most beautiful woman I've ever seen in my whole goddamn life?"

Esther only looked back at him. Emptiness expanded in her stomach—a sad, empty nothing—and she cast her face down so that the others wouldn't see. She sensed Mary's eyes on her, and then she heard Mary's voice: "Suffering comes from confusion, and its purpose is to awaken our true natures."

A silence fell over the room, and although Esther kept her head down, she had the appeasing sensation that Uncle Richard was glaring at Mary.

Uncle Richard coughed, and it sounded as if he were clapping his hands. "Someday," he said, "someday, someday."

"Don't talk in riddles," Grandma Eileen said.

There was a silence, until finally, in a hoarse whisper and with his head down, he said, "I'm not."

"Riddle me this, riddle me that," Grandma Eileen said.

"Here," he said, thrusting a piece of yellow lined paper at Grandma Eileen.

"What's this?" she said dismissively, passing it to Esther without a glance.

"My roommate is crazy," he said, a quick jerk of his head in the direction of another bed. "Get me out of here."

A man, his face extended from his tightly tucked-in sheets, skin yellow and withered, slept with his mouth open.

Outside on the patio, Esther saw Captain Ahab—the size of a dog—sauntering toward his plastic domed litter box.

"Don't be silly," Grandma Eileen said.

As Esther silently read the paper, she knew that Uncle Richard was making a point to the others by watching her.

Recorded Conversation of my roommate Jim talking to himself on 12/13/1994:

They all love me.
I didn't want to yell.
Let's go home, Helen.
I want to go home.
Undecipherable mumbling—and suddenly he yelled, Take a shovel to his head!

Esther looked up from the paper to Uncle Richard's frantic eyes. "That's what I'm talking about," he said, but she understood that what he was really trying to tell her was, *Whatever you do, whatever happens, don't you ever, ever end up like me, in a place like this.*

6

"I MEAN, HE'S just so obviously guilty. It makes me sick, absolutely sick. Do you know what I mean? Someone needs to take that man, tie him up, and kill him. That's right—kill him. He's a murderer and he needs to be punished."

They were at The Palms, and Charlie had been listening to Jennifer Platt, his former pupil, fill him in on her life, post–community college. And now that Jennifer had finished telling him about her newest passion for sports medicine, she was expressing her obligatory outrage over the upcoming O. J. Simpson trial. Behind her was a tinted window with a view of the bay, and he found himself gazing absentmindedly over her shoulder.

A side benefit of his profession: former admiring female students (between ages eighteen and twenty-two) who, post-graduation, nostalgically dug up their old notebooks and syllabi, his phone number placed squarely on the front page of his course outline; in a burst of impulsiveness, they called. All it took was a suggestion—"Would you like to meet for a drink?" His former pupils executing their student-professor fantasies. As far as he was concerned, it was an ethically evenhanded, win-win situation. The young women quickly understood that he had nothing more to offer than an escapist night or two, and he had the pleasure of their company.

They usually came to him at a thought-provoking transitional juncture—after a breakup or before settling down into marriage—and he thought of himself as a conduit to their futures, a quick spark of connection, nothing more. No hurt feelings.

But tonight as Charlie listened, he was ambivalent, knowing that it wasn't just her choice of subjects or that she'd described a public lynching or that she talked on and on and on.

He was trying not to think about Esther—she'd been monopolizing his thoughts. He'd even sought her out at True Romance, although she'd been on Christmas vacation, and her manager—a well-dressed, slightly bedraggled and masculine woman, probably in her late forties—didn't appear too happy about it.

The sky was black, freckled with stars, and a slim white moon looked like a backward *C*. Their plates had been cleared. Jennifer was on her fourth Corona; he was on his third Heineken. She was young and beautiful and willing; she smelled like jasmine and vanilla; she'd alluded to a roommate-free apartment. At a certain angle, she looked like a younger Esther, with fuller lips. She wore a low-cut, blue-and-white-striped jersey, and her breasts loomed above the cotton material in a pinkish-tanned *m*.

A light off the pier cast a clear spotlight over the bay; under its reflection, the water was green and oily. At the other side of the pier was *Chocolate Pleasure*, a sleek red motorboat. Earlier, they'd watched it sidle to the dock, thumping with the bass of music, four young women dancing at the bow, and Fred Smith, the retired black basketball player, with his fingertips at the wheel. Charlie had felt a pang of excitement, and then he'd been embarrassed by his reaction. Fred had tied the boat along the dock, and the assemblage had made their way up the pier. The group had since established themselves along the bar, Fred at the center.

Charlie wanted to believe that he had an affinity with Fred. Although he wanted to blame it on social circumstances, lack of opportunity, he'd never had a real friendship with a person of dark skin color, only two superficial acquaintances.

"The man is a sociopath. He put a smiley face in the *O* of his signature on his so-called suicide letter. I can't believe he went to USC. He's giving football a bad name. Do you know what I mean?"

A nerve pulsed below Charlie's temple. His liaisons had normally contained a blameless quality. Never before had he blatantly used someone to clear his mind of another. A canopied Duffy motorboat moved slowly across the surface of the bay, leaving a calm wake.

In between the silences of her three trips to the ladies' room, this was what he'd learned about Jennifer: She'd sat in the first row of his Introduction to Sociology class, even though the subject matter mostly bored her ("Sorry! I was only trying to get done with my prerequisites, but I always thought you were cute and kinda sad, like a puppy dog."); she was twenty-two, an Aquarius, although she didn't entirely believe in astrology, and she hated her name. ("Everyone around here is named Jennifer—I want to be *different*—and what kind of last name is Platt? I want to get married, so I can change it!) Jennifer Flat had been her nickname in high school, due to her lack of cleavage (although she'd obviously remedied that with solid C-cup implants); she had trouble with her demanding stepfather; he was "in real estate" and a member of the city council; he'd been more like a father than a stepfather, supportive, even paying for her apartment, but he was a "total perfectionist"; she'd been engaged briefly to a successful stockbroker and businessman, but had broken it off when she'd found him cheating with her best friend and roommate (leaving her apartment roommate-free); she wasn't bitter, because the breakup had forced her to decide what she really, really wanted to do with her life; now that she was going to eventually go back to school for sports medicine, she felt more fulfilled than ever; she'd always been interested in her body and what she ate and health and sports, and how great was it that she could combine all her interests and share her knowledge with the larger world, giving her life purpose; and if that didn't work out, if the math and science proved to be too much, she'd been thinking about massage therapy or communications.

"He's a sick man. Do you know what I mean? Sick, sick. 'Absolutely one hundred percent not guilty, your honor.' I mean, who does he think he's kidding? The whole thing is wrong. If you just look at his eyes, you can tell. His eyes are *guilty*." She paused to sip at her Corona, a lime peel submerged at the bottom of her glass.

The way she studded her monologues with "You know what I mean?" saddened Charlie, made him more a professor than a man enjoying a beautiful woman. She was insecure and needed constant reinforcement.

"I hope he goes to the electric chair," she said, and she took one last sip, finishing her beer, as if to finalize her statement.

He was accustomed to communal expressions of indignation over O. J. Simpson. It was a way for people to bond. But he wanted O. J. Simpson to fade away; he was weary of hearing people barking about it. Bark, bark, bark! Guilty, guilty, guilty! It would be useless for him to express the larger racial and sociological implications. She hadn't received the usual corroborating head nod, and this made her uncomfortable.

He let his eyes meet hers. "I don't believe in the death penalty."

She was startled, fingering her cocktail napkin, creating little tears at the ridge. Her eyes dropped to the table. "Not right."

She shook her head so that wisps of her blond hair brushed against her shoulders. "The Bible says, 'an eye for an eye.'" She was duplicating someone else's words, probably her stepfather's. A flushed patch of skin at her throat, extending across her collarbone and down into her low-cut top, caught his attention. He wanted to put his lips there, reassure her.

There was an awkward pause, and he felt the certainty that he'd spoiled her evening. After receiving a negative response concerning the possibility of dessert, their waitress set the check on the table in its faux-leather holder, ingrained with THANK YOU in gold letters.

Jennifer gave a small sigh and looked dismissively over his shoulder, taking in the restaurant. He pretended not to care, becoming engaged with calculating the accuracy of the check. He set the case on the table with his American Express card tucked inside the clear plastic pocket.

"Do you believe in the male-female thing?" Jennifer asked out of nowhere.

"What?"

"My fiancé and I were seeing this therapist. Everyone goes. It was a premarital package. She believes in the male-female thing, and maybe I don't do it well enough." The flush at her neck had extended to her face.

"I don't know what the male-female thing is."

Her eyes were wide and young. "I'm supposed to be submissive and he's the head of the unit. He's the spiritual leader and my job is to guide from the background. The man needs to be in charge and that's the way God intended. The woman needs to *honor* her man and the man needs to *cherish* his woman. You know? Women are the *gatherers*. Except now, instead of gathering berries and tomatoes and things, we gather shoes and clothes and knickknacks for our homes. And men are the hunters, right? But now, instead of hunting deer and buffalo and stuff, you're out hunting big bass on your boats or something. Well, I think maybe I was too forceful. Maybe I talked too much, had too many opinions. You know what I mean? Maybe I didn't let my fiancé be the *man*. And Denise, you know, my roommate, well, she's so quiet and pretty. And she just knows how to be submissive *naturally*, where I really need to practice."

There was a long pause as she waited for him to answer, and her eyes were wet and pleading.

"I believe in the human-human thing," he said at last.

"I don't know what that means," she said, but he could tell that she was pleased; that without meaning to, he'd said the exact right thing.

He saw an opportunity and began to talk. He started with an anecdote, and from there he ventured into a philosophical discourse concerning *Schindler's List*. He veered slightly into the Whitewater investigation, Kenneth Starr, and the various conspiracy theories linking Hillary Clinton to Vince Foster's suicide, but he quickly saw by her grim-mouthed reaction that he should refrain from all political topics; she was especially offended by the mention of Hillary Clinton, having drunk the "Hillary is a big fat lesbian/feminist/Communist" Kool-Aid, and he steered himself to safer terrain: sporting events, the weather, movies. And a story about losing his favorite "blankie" as a child, cooling it off in the wind outside the moving car window (they were on the freeway), only to have it slip from his fingers and flutter away. His mother had tried substitutes (an exact replica, a bathroom towel, a strip of her sweater), to no avail.

Jennifer looked at him as if he were still just an adorable boy, flapping his blankie out the car window. She was beckoning him with her expressions, allowing him to be in charge. It was similar to when he lectured, a feeling of his audience's admiration, and he reminded himself to not cover any territory that she might've already heard as his pupil.

He spoke self-deferentially about his profession. Her eyes glimmered in appreciation and she remained attentive. As he spoke, his thoughts wandered. The key, he decided, was to benefit from a relationship, to remain comfortable. He took his freedom seriously. His parents had provided him with the means to freedom, as long as he kept in line.

His parents' beachfront home had two USC flags (one above the front door and the other, slightly smaller, at a second-story window), and the only time they appeared distressed was when USC and UCLA battled each other on the football field. His parents had an easygoing acceptance, demanding only that he not burden them with his ideas and politics.

Instead of looking into the vast, fathomless abyss called Life, his father had tried to instill in him the consolation of making a great deal of money. Although Charlie had not complied, instead choosing a life in academia, his father had not punished him financially. By receiving monthly dividend checks signed by his father, he was able to travel and to maintain his membership at a gym, his sailboat, and his weekend golfing expenditures, not possible on his professorial salary.

He was grateful and sought to please his parents (married forty-seven years), yet by not adding to the gene pool with grandkids and by refusing to participate in his father's business (while at the same time accepting monthly profits from it), he couldn't shake the knowledge that he was failing.

His mother, in particular, was urging him to "pick a good woman, marry her, and settle down."

If only he were able to pick and choose the women he fell for. His last "relationship" had been an affair with a married woman. Brenda had smelled like gardenias and limes and maybe a hint of ginger. She was impulsive and sexually adventurous. He'd rationalized his affair as a favor to her husband: She was too much woman for one man. He'd tried to keep the relationship secret, but being with Brenda was like plugging into an electric current: He would feel more alive for days, as if the cells of his skin were open, the molecules hungry. They were like animals—there weren't exactly human emotions involved. Their bodies seemed to want to erupt in violence. He had ended the relationship at its passionate zenith (three-hour sexual "sessions," heightened by screaming fights; she'd even hit him with the back of her hand and then shoved him against a wall) intuitively protective, like hunkering under a table during an earthquake.

He thought of Nora—noble, intelligent, funny, thoughtful, sensitive, forthright—her hair some indistinct shade of brown, her pale skin that splotched so easily with emotion. Her face had too much of everything—too much forehead, nose, and lips—so that her every expression was loaded. Sure, she was no beauty, but Nora exuded virtue. She leaned forward when she listened to him, squinted a little, as if making sure she didn't miss a thing. She was interested in the world, she was *interesting*—she'd been in the Peace Corps; she'd started Clothing for Change, for underprivileged women; she could hold a conversation on any subject: philosophy, politics, you name it. Sometimes he even learned from her!

Yet he wasn't attracted to women who made little effort to be attractive. Nora wore these awful gray sweatpants, and her clothes never seemed to fit quite right: a little too lumpy here, a little too tight there. She didn't shave her armpits. She'd yawn, lifting her arms, and he'd see the silky mouse-brown hairs twisted around each other—dewy—peeking through her sleeve holes. He had supposed that this European convention would be erotic in a base, woman-is-from-the-earth kind of manner, but he found it almost pornographic in the wrong way, like accidentally seeing an old woman's vagina, or his sister's vagina, or his mother's vagina—not that that had ever happened, thank God.

And Nora gave off the faint (very very faint) smell of spoiled milk, even after she had showered. He wondered, at times, if he were imagining the smell, but when he got close to her, there it was, albeit just barely, as if it came from her very essence. Pheromones were a scientific fact, not some made-up bogus selling point for colognes and perfumes. All he had to do was take a long, strong whiff of Nora as proof.

Besides, women like Nora weren't interested in societal conventions such as marriage. She was smarter than that. She was like him—a female version of Charlie (although Nora was a better Charlie than he was; she was more ideologically pure). And God knew he wasn't interested in the restrictions of marriage. Despite everything, he experienced a gut-thrust of guilt (Nora was his best friend), as if he should be attracted to her, but the forces of desire were beyond his control.

And then his thoughts instinctively sought refuge in Esther, specifically in the bold pink half-dollar–size areola of the nipple on Esther's right breast, when he had stroked it (with her permission) with the back of his hand.

Esther had surprised him in his car, at the end of their date, when he had made his request in jest ("Let me say goodbye to you here," and he'd touched her chest), by unbuttoning her shirt, turning on the car's interior light, unsnapping the back of her bra, and dislodging the glorious appendage from its shelter: The rim of the areola was surrounded by little ridges, barely visible, and the nipple was a beauty. "Oooh," she said, "that feels so good," and as she closed her eyes to heighten her pleasure, he was already dreading the loss of that nipple, and what that loss meant in terms of future losses, knowing that he didn't meet her fiscal requirements and that she was humoring him, taking her gratification one last time.

As he continued talking to Jennifer, he thought about how Esther trailed complications; she was guarded, enigmatic, unpredictable, and when she spoke, there seemed to be an undercurrent of the unspoken, a scrambled intricacy of meaning.

He felt a tingling of desire, his heart hammering, and he made an attempt to relocate his yearning in the general direction of Jennifer's impressive physical attributes, but his lusty wishes seemed to linger around him, amorphous and without a course. His concentration began to fail.

Jennifer seemed to notice and take pity, her hand crossing the table and touching his knuckle. He sensed that she appreciated him but that she had decided—probably around the same time he'd stated his opposition to the death penalty—that she would never bring him home to meet her step-father.

Briefly he saw her as an adolescent with her tyrannical step father, a man she'd never been able to please. A man who'd forced her to run track or play volleyball or swim laps every day. She'd been able to hold his attention through her developing body. She probably had an eating disorder, anorexia or bulimia or a combination. Or maybe she forced herself to use a StairMaster for two hours after any food indulgence.

"Oh, God," she said, directing his attention to her breast, "look—I'm peeling." Her fingernails brushed at a pinkish patch of skin above her left breast. Her gaze lifted.

He sidled across the booth, touching knee, hip, and elbow. He turned her hand palm up and traced his finger along her wrist.

He let his breath come close to her ear. "You smell so good," he said.

She let out a sigh. "Okay," she said. "Hmm."

"You're very beautiful."

She moved an inch or two away, as if to regain composure—but she was smiling. He poured the rest of his Heineken into her glass and she took the glass, lifted it to her lips, and finished his beer, her eyes on him. Then her eyes stared somewhere over his shoulder.

"Oh, God," she said, setting her glass on the table. "Fred Smith is coming. What do you think he wants?"

Charlie turned and saw that Fred was walking to their booth, hands deep in his pockets, with an amused smile. When he reached their table, his right hand left his pocket and he set his fingers on their table, his fingernails a soft pink against his skin.

"How was dinner?" he asked.

Jennifer's expression cleared into a hospitable smile.

"It was great," Charlie said, his smile mimicking hers.

Fred leaned forward. His hand slid over the faux-leather check case. "Music to my ears," he said. His skin was dark brown with a golden undertone. His hair looked shiny, flat, and curled close to his head.

Fred walked away slowly, casually passing the credit card to a woman near the cash register without looking at her.

When he reached his space at the bar, cleared open by the women, his fingers bordered the rim of a short glass at the bar top. But he didn't take a drink. His gaze was on a basketball game on the television screen.

"Do you think he owns this place?" Jennifer's voice was a grating attempt at indifference. Charlie didn't answer, his eyes lingering at the bar, fascinated by Fred Smith, and he could sense Jennifer's mounting frustration.

BUT ALL WAS not lost. When Jennifer invited Charlie back to her apartment, he said sure, why not? He opened the restaurant door for her, and her shoulder grazed his as she passed. "Have a good night," said the hostess, an alluring brunette, and he smiled, reaching for a toothpick in a small brass jug at her podium, his other hand still at the door.

He caught one last glimpse of Fred, fingers at his short glass. Fred was a man who would not forfeit an opportunity like Jennifer Platt, and Charlie was a man who would not forfeit an opportunity like Jennifer Platt.

The Palms was located along Mariner's Mile, a length of Pacific Coast Highway studded with yacht brokers and restaurants, and as they waited for the valets to retrieve their cars, he took in the lights and saltwater smell and money of it all.

The night was cold and sobering, and he had only enough cash to tip the valet for his car, but Jennifer didn't mind, her hand dipping into her purse.

He drove his Honda behind her red Volkswagen Rabbit convertible (personalized license plate: HAPY4ME) to 31st Street, her apartment above the boardwalk, waves crashing somewhere in the night, but all he could see was dark sand, the outline of a lifeguard stand. And the next thing he knew, he was following her swaying hips in her tight little skirt up the stairway, admiring her calves, the backs of her thighs. She fiddled with the key at the door, giggling because she was shaky and having trouble.

"Here," he said, helping, his hand over her hand.

And then they were in the hallway, the lights off, front door closed; she turned to him and he put one hand at her hip, the other at the small of her back, and moved her closer.

Her face came to him, and his hand tucked under her jersey, up, up, fingers crawling beneath the underwire of her bra, on her breast, at the hardened sweet tip of a nipple. Her mouth was open and yielding when it reached his, and she made a groaning noise. He plunged into the kiss, but it felt like a black hole, his mind falling into space.

He brought himself back, feeling for her teeth with his tongue; her cheek pressed against his, sweaty. Her breast was warm, cupped in his hand like a kitten, but with the firmness and ripple of silicon, and then the underwire of her bra pressed into the skin of his knuckle.

They were moving in one stumbling jumble toward a couch, when his thigh hit the corner of a side table, stabbing him. His mouth pulled away. "God," he said, but she seemed to think he was expressing his exultation, and her mouth came violently back at his, a gleaming flash of teeth.

And it was all wrong suddenly, all wrong. He didn't know how to tell her, so he tried to kiss her softly, gently, slow down, slow down, and then get to the end, hand releasing from her breast, pulling outside her jersey.

They were sitting on a leather couch where she'd led him, and she was leaning in a prone direction, but he kept her at a sit. His head rolled back and forth a little, trying to pull away. He tried to get a look around him, but all he saw was a corner of her eye, flashing in something like alarm. A chill rose inside him; she had a hold of his bottom lip, like a hungry bird.

"Thtop," he said.

She pulled away, and even in the dark she looked like a little girl who had gotten her feelings hurt; guilt crept at the back of his neck.

"What?" she asked. "What's wrong?"

"I'm sorry; it's me."

"What?"

"You're a beautiful girl." He set a hand on her forearm. "I'm not the one for you."

She stared at him, and in the darkness her eyes appeared wide and blameless. “I know that; we’re just having *fun.*”

He should’ve been glad, but he felt a nick at his pride. Guilt and disappointment and embarrassment took him by the throat. Why wasn’t he the one? Why was she so sure?

◈ 7 ◈

NORA GIVENS WAS happiest when she abandoned herself to fantasies about Charlie. Besides jogging six laps around the high school track each Sunday, they spoke by phone nearly every other day about everyday things. The general nature of their conversations furthered her illusion of an unconditional love, a connection that did not rely on profound and consequential discussions, or on the physical facets that other intimate relationships needed to exist (although she wouldn't mind crossing *that* road, and often deliberated over it). Theirs was a sacred and unconventional connection, full of respect, existing beyond boundaries, a spiritual telepathy.

Most people wouldn't understand. Like when her friends had warned her about Jake, a fellow Peace Corps volunteer in Honduras, telling Nora that he was using her. Late one night, her second week in Honduras, he'd come to her room, smacking his palm against her window. He'd passed out on her mattress, smelling of pot and booze, and rather than trying to wake him or sleep on the floor, or wake and upset her Catholic host family, she'd taken off his old Adidas sneakers (size 14) and slept with him. The warmth of his body, the bulky extent of him, his steady breathing, calmed her. At some point during the night, they both woke, one thing led to another, and he performed cunnilingus on her. Although she received the traditional orgasm reward, when his face appeared from between her legs—mouth and chin glistening—she felt like she'd been doing him the favor.

When they woke in the morning, she was pressed against him, her legs cupped behind his. He began coming over most nights. She gave him a key. As soon as the mattress dipped with his weight, she felt herself release. And it wasn't the sex. He called her his "sleeping buddy" and she called him her "sleeping twin." He curled next to her, fitting his knees behind hers, his lips in her hair, his breath at her neck. Their positions changed with a nudge or a sigh, turning as a unit: her knees hooked behind his; later, turn again, his leg scissored between hers. She was tall and gawky, and he was a lumbering man, limbs like leaden blankets; rather than making her feel trapped, he made her feel safe. They forgave each other the unavoidable embarrassments—a slipped fart, or the times when he was so drunk and stoned, he peed on the mattress. And he was privy to her menstrual cycle because instead of sleeping naked, she wore her gray sweatpants.

Her dream life, whether remembered or not, became entwined with his. And never before (or after) had she had an absence of nightmares. Last she'd heard, Jake was married, three kids, a mortgage broker living somewhere in Oregon. When she thought of him, it was with tenderness, an inner knowledge of his fallibilities, his innate sensitivity. But she'd never thought that Jake might be The One.

Charlie had sexual relationships with other women—Brenda Caldwell, for instance—but those entanglements weren't a real threat. Charlie had even said, "Don't ever confuse sex with love or love with sex." If she was honest: Yes, she wanted to marry Charlie, to bear his children, to grow old with him. And she was sure that it was a signal that he signed her birthday cards and Christmas cards: "Love, Charlie."

But when Charlie had called her at 10:42 PM, distressed over a "date gone bad," she'd been disappointed. She was there for him, always had been, always would be, but these sporadic occasions were tiresome. It wasn't so much what he'd told her as it was the tone of his voice. She knew that when he arrived, her job would be to listen, mentally preparing for pauses where she would reassure him. Her active role would be to placate him. She looked at her alarm clock. It would probably take fifteen minutes for him to arrive.

These late-night discussions promised for intimate revelations and left Charlie feeling "a whole lot better," but left her with lingering bad feelings, sometimes for weeks, because she did not have the kind of relationship with Charlie that she wanted (she wasn't completely stupid) and, unlike Jake, Charlie *was* using her. Worst of all, she was letting herself be used.

But this time would be different, this time she would be prepared. He needed to know how she felt and make a decision. There needed to be reciprocity. She should have spoken up long ago, and this time she would not falter.

As she waited to hear Charlie's Honda pull up at the curb, she squinted at herself in her bathroom mirror. A pimple at the rim of her nostril—nose too wide. She underwent the usual turmoil: If she picked, it would only get worse—reddened and irritated and spreading—but it was a habit that soothed her.

She settled for lip balm, a little blush.

She was no beauty, had known since kindergarten. She didn't want to fight a losing battle (average women pretending to be beautiful). Her acceptance was as familiar and comfortable as her gray sweatpants, providing a suspension of vanity, a freedom to focus on her inner life. She was different from the competitive females vying for attention. If only men (Charlie) could get over their (his) preoccupation with the visible aesthetics of women (her), the way she had.

Her eyes passed over the Martin Luther King Jr. quote taped to the corner of her mirror: "A man who won't die for something is not fit to live." Each month, she changed the quote, hoping to be inspired and/or changed.

November was Mohandas K. Gandhi, and she still had it memorized, despite its length:

> I do dimly perceive that while everything around me is ever changing, ever dying, there is underlying all that change a living power that is changeless, that holds all together, that creates, dissolves, and re-creates. That informing power of spirit is God, and since nothing else that I see, merely through the senses, can or will persist, He alone is.

She moved through her living room, bedroom, and kitchen, tidying for Charlie's arrival, setting loose clothes in the laundry basket and throwing away an old banana peel in the trash can outside so it wouldn't stink. She filled her teakettle with water and turned the stove knob with a hiss of gas.

Looking in her refrigerator, she didn't find much for him to eat. Cottage cheese, carrots, two tomatoes (on the rotting side), a package of corn tortillas, a package of orange and yellow shredded cheese, three cartons of leftovers from restaurants (all needing to be thrown away), and a carton of eggs.

She took a Coors with her to her small balcony. Looking over the twinkling lights of the other houses and apartments, the telephone wires, the wind in the palm trees, she opened the can and drank. It was dark and cold, and the wind shuddered through the hairlike glittering ribbon wrapped around the palm trunks.

The long increasing scream of the teakettle brought her back inside. She turned the knob of the stove and listened to the kettle's dying wail.

She lived in a one-bedroom, one-bathroom upper unit of a bungalow duplex in Costa Mesa, owned by Mrs. Elizabeth McFadden, former president of the Junior League and current benefactress and president of the board of directors for Clothing for Change. Nora's title was executive director, which meant that she did the grunt work while Mrs. McFadden simultaneously kept her manicured hands clean and received all the credit and awards and write-ups.

Nora and her indigent female clients (parolees, drug addicts, the homeless) were expected to express their eternal gratitude to the board of directors. Nora filmed clients' "testimonials" for fundraisers, and they'd become so rote ("In these clothes, I feel like I can accomplish anything! I have a newfound confidence!") that she fantasized about allowing her clients to speak openly, allowing herself to speak openly, a type of reverse scrutiny.

But she kept her disillusionment with the nonprofit world private: Mrs. McFadden was her landlady, and her rent, along with her salary, was contingent on Mrs. McFadden's goodwill.

When Nora had returned from the Peace Corps, in order to make good on the principle of promoting her community's understanding of people in developing countries, she'd set up slide shows at churches, high schools, and the homes of accommodating philanthropists.

She'd been having trouble readjusting (for instance, when she'd stood in the produce-packed aisle of a Pavilions grocery store, weeping), and her slide shows weren't helping to lift her morale because of their low attendance.

Charlie had been one of the only people to express a genuine interest. Twenty-six of his students had also come, and it had been her most crowded, successful slide show—hands raised in the crowd, full of questions. (Later, he'd admitted to offering extra credit, even more so if his students asked questions.)

She'd noticed him right away, a fluttering in her stomach. Tall and handsome, he had an aura of gloomy meditation. He wore faded jeans and a suit jacket, and his dark hair was long for a man—thick, with a touch of gray—but not too long. With a hand, he brushed it from his eyes and it surprised her, reminding her of something a teenage girl might do. When he looked over at her, perhaps sensing her interest, his eyes had a flicker of amusement, as if they'd known each other for a long time.

After her presentation, he came over, waited while a woman she didn't know—plastic-surgery face, midfifties—held her hand and said, "You look so skinny, Nora! Maybe that's what I need to do to lose weight: go to a Third World country!"

And then Charlie approached, and even before he was sure that the plastic-surgery woman was safely out of earshot, he leaned forward and said, "What's wrong with these people?"

Charlie often commented on her altruistic choices, first the Peace Corps and then Clothing for Change, saying that he held such respect. "I don't get it," he'd say. "You grew up here. How'd you turn out so different?"

She didn't tell him her theory, preferring his baffled awe. And besides, her attempt at an explanation would be long and convoluted and humiliating and probably wouldn't make much sense. She might say something like:

Her father, a chiropractor, had been a religious man of the David Koresh variety; Armageddon had been his constant preoccupation, and instead of bedtime stories, he had told her of the second coming. She hadn't seen him in over twenty years: he'd left for a communal-style farm in Montana with a "bunker," remarried, and had three sons: Luke, Jonah, and Peter.

Her mother, a secretary for a wealthy capitalist, had remarried her employer, thus providing Nora, six years old at the time, with a stable home life and a superior education in Newport Beach, but the fatalistic die had already been cast.

Despite her privileged upbringing, her costly Stanford education, her two years in Honduras, her pragmatic rationality, and her three years of intensive psychiatric therapy and "self-betterment," her father's religious mania had bled into her, proving that childhood was—as the experts agreed—a formative experience.

Although she told no one apart from the psychologists and psychiatrists, she had a deep inner certainty that the world was ending, and that before that happened, things were going to get very, very, very ugly. Her thinking, she believed, was probably genetic, embedded in her DNA.

She wasn't so much concerned for the state of her soul ("Blessed is the one who stays awake and is clothed, not going about naked and exposed to shame"), but the fleetingness, randomness, and meaninglessness damaged her.

Nearly all were doomed, including the people she loved most, and her inability to stomach an exclusive country club–type heaven had soiled her vision of an afterlife, whether she was a member or not.

Her decision to join the Peace Corps and to birth and develop Clothing for Change came partially from a desire to remedy the flagrant injustice: If most people were going to hell, she wanted to make life better for the ones who already lived there. No one deserved a double hell.

She dreamt apocalyptic nightmares with black smoke and fire demons and "foul spirits like frogs coming from the mouths of dragons," and her waking hours were streaked with a substantial morbidity.

She stayed current with world affairs and local affairs, prolific and biblical in proportion: Iraq and Kuwait; Israel and Palestine; the passing of Proposition 187; the Whitewater scandal; Newt Gingrich; O. J. Simpson—not to mention the earthquakes, hurricanes, and famines.

The main thing that continued to console her, year after year, was the continued survival of Earth and its populace.

WHEN NORA OPENED her front door, a visible sadness in Charlie proved irresistible, and despite how she'd been preparing, her heart softened at once. His movements had a thoughtfulness, as if he balanced everything in his mind before taking action, before speaking. It gave him a pensive, slow quality—but it seemed to Nora that it was always worth the wait. Only when nervous did he chatter, but she'd become proficient in deciphering what he really needed to say.

He sat on her couch, his top leg held out at an angle, foot resting on his thigh. He had an enviable manner of making himself instantly at home.

"I don't know," he said, shaking his head. "I can't stop thinking about her."

Nora was not at ease with the topic of Esther, and she knew that "her" equaled Esther. Charlie had had infatuations with beautiful women, but this was different. Call it female intuition, call it ESP. Her best chance would be if Esther died—a car crash, choking, suicide. Then she would have to console Charlie.

"I went on a date," he said, "to forget her, but it didn't work."

She'd already made Tension Tamer tea, and she went to the kitchen, pressed out the tea bag with a spoon, and added a tablespoon of milk and sugar, the way he liked. Within minutes of being with him, she'd lost her presence of mind, and she now wished she could get him to leave so that she might recover it—or not slip further down the rabbit hole of love-stupidity.

She set the mug on a cork coaster at her coffee table and sat next to him.

"Even if I want to be with her," he said, pausing to take a sip. His lips tightened as if he'd burned his mouth, and he set the mug back on its coaster.

"What were you going to say?"

He looked at her blankly. It annoyed her when he began to tell her something and then stopped midway, midsentence—as if what he had to say was so delicate, so profound, so intimate, that he was reconsidering, deciding whether or not to share. Usually, after a long buildup of anticipation, he'd tell her anyway.

"I want to hear the rest," she said.

"What?"

"Come on," she said. "Tell me."

"I can't afford her anyway," he finished.

He stretched out his long legs underneath the coffee table, and at the same time, he supported his head at the back of the couch, tilting it so that he appeared to be contemplating the ceiling.

Nora's hands were clasped in her lap, and she ran her thumb against a hangnail. She was aware of the blood in her veins. She watched Charlie take a sip of his tea; he had a sputtering, coughing reaction. He shook his head, his face pinkening. He coughed violently, hand fisted at his mouth.

They were quiet, and he appeared to be staring at a spot on the carpet. Her heart drumming, she decided to take a risk.

"You need someone with similar goals," she said. *Someone like me*, she thought. *Me. You need me.*

She willed him to understand their relationship through the

prism of her emotions. He was staring at his spot on the carpet, but she hoped that he was absorbing the information. She imagined his epiphany, her longing acknowledged.

His head lifted to look at her. He uncrossed his legs and leaned forward. She waited. And then waited some more.

"I can't stop thinking about her," he said, his face soft with amazement.

Her embarrassment and shame were surpassed by a sudden wave of hatred. If the man she wanted to marry, the man she loved, was this inept an interpreter of her feelings, then her loneliness would not change.

She felt stirrings of grief, an acknowledgment of loss; she pulled the tiny ridge of skin from her fingernail, creating a stinging speck of blood.

He continued to speak about Esther, commenting on what he knew about her history. All her character deficiencies, he insisted, could be linked to her past. Could Nora imagine growing up in a family that acknowledged success according to financial gain only? Could Nora imagine if her only access to this success was through her womanly traits, which she'd been trained to employ with manipulation and deception?

Nora agreed that it was tragic, but she pointed out that most people had to deal with their share of tragedy.

"And let's not even talk about her father," he said, his eyes widening at the injustice.

"Yes," she agreed. "Awful. No one should be disowned for being gay—as if it's a lifestyle choice, rather than a genetic trait."

Charlie was uncomfortable discussing the origins of homosexuality. He changed the subject, as she expected.

"Not only that," he said, "her family's dishonest and cruel."

"Her grandmother's the one with all the money?" Nora asked.

"A scary woman," he said. "Fierce. She dangles money and

then pulls it away. Esther's trained—like a monkey, a trained monkey. But she's smart, fighting for her very life."

Against her will, Nora found herself listening gravely and nodding her head.

"Paul Rice," he said, spitting it out. He was silent, as if the name said everything.

"How old is she?" Nora asked. "Does she want kids?"

He didn't answer.

She tried changing the subject—but he was trapped.

He continued to discuss Esther, the problem of Esther. Esther this, Esther that. After he was finally done, his head lowered and, despite everything, her heart beat in commiseration.

"She doesn't want to marry him," he said.

The next few minutes were infused with a kind of solemnity on both their parts, as they each pondered their respective fates, until finally he spoke: "Did you know that Fred Smith owns The Palms? He must've bought it."

She wanted to tell him that people usually purchased things by buying them, but then he changed the subject.

"Do you have anything to eat? I'm starving."

While relaying her meager food choices, she felt that, once again, she'd given more of herself to Charlie than she'd intended to. She resigned herself, like taking a punch: a quick, sharp initial pain, and then a lasting ache.

◈ 8 ◈

AFTER HIS FOURTH failed drug rehab—what was it, nine, ten years ago?—Esther's family no longer acknowledged her brother, Eric, as if by ignoring him, they rendered him (and thus his upsetting and tiresome and implicating heroin addiction) nonexistent; but, just as Grandma Eileen considered a yearly visit to Uncle Richard a sibling responsibility, Esther paid monthly visits to her brother (without her family's knowledge) to give him money, with, she believed, the blessing of their deceased father. She'd been doing so for about two years. She drove slowly, watching for Eric, driver's-side window down on the metallic silver BMW she'd borrowed from Grandma Eileen. In the usual inundation of holiday cheer, the streetlights in Santa Ana were decorated like giant candy canes, tied with glittery ribbon, flapping softly in the night breeze.

Tonight, along with her monthly payment, she was adding a Christmas/birthday bonus of $50; Eric was thirty-six, three years older than she was. She remembered their father's toasts on Eric's birthdays, before the fights and the constant running away from home and the confiscated baggies of marijuana and Ecstasy. "To Eric and Frank," he'd say (December 12, Frank

Sinatra's birthday also), wine glasses of grape juice lifted, *clink clink clink*; and then Eric's sidelong glances, his shy, responsive, and rare smiles.

The little fucker, she thought. *He'd better not be homeless. Again.* Aside from her credit card debt, Eric was the greatest hindrance to her gaining financial equilibrium—forget about plain and simple autonomy.

Until I marry Paul Rice, she thought. *And then everyone can kiss my ass.* She had a premeditated destiny—it had been drilled into her for years. When she was twelve (sometime after she'd gotten her period), her father had taken her to Castaways Park, to the peak, which looked out on Newport Beach. There it lay beneath them, all the mansions and yachts, the biggest mansions at the rim of the bay, with docks and yachts and boats of their own, and, going up and up, more homes and Fashion Island—a circle of shiny buildings and palm trees.

The Back Bay looked like twisted fingers of green water, spreading through bridges and land and stretching underneath a ribbon of Pacific Coast Highway, where she heard the buzz of cars and the occasional thunder of a truck rolling past. Catalina, at the horizon, was under a veil of haze—barely there. Instead of taking in the view, her father was looking at her. "I love you so much," he said. "It's almost over for me, but it's just beginning for you." He pulled the hair back from her face, stroked her cheek. "You're gonna show all these motherfuckers," he said.

ERIC WASN'T HARD to find: If she drove long enough, she'd see him walking along a street or leaning against a wall. Or she'd find him at the Olive Pit, sitting in the back booth, the one with the splitting foam cushion—each time, it was opened up and split a little more, like a sideways foaming mouth. There were no windows and it was dark and it smelled like stale beer, urine, and hay. But at least there weren't many people inside, and the ones who were there rarely acknowledged her, not even bothering to look up from their glasses. Eric called the booth "my office."

Last time, he'd even cracked a smile for Esther, after coming upon her, pretending to surprise her: "Boo!" And for Eric, she'd pretended to be surprised, even though, with his cough, sniffle, and tread, she'd heard him moving toward her.

And then, as they sat together in the booth, he'd turned the tin ashtray over and over and over in his shaky hands while she'd filled him in (in a general way) on her life; and then she'd asked him questions (in a general way) about his: Is your cold better? Are you sleeping? Have you got enough money? (All answered with "yes," whether or not they were really nos.)

"Are you living the dream?" he'd asked. (A long-established question—she couldn't remember when it had started—between them. An inside joke. That, and "Keep your eye on the ball. Keep your chin up. Is your eye on the ball? Chin up?")

"Yes, Eric," she'd answered. "I'm living the dream. How about you?"

"Oh yeah," he'd said—ashtray turn-turn-turning in his hands—"I'm living it, all right."

At some point (this part was horrible for the both of them), she slid the envelope of money across the table and he took it without looking at her. Rick had told her that he'd spotted Eric at a bus stop near a Winchell's, and as she turned a corner, she saw the bus stop shelter, a billboard advertisement for *Forrest Gump*—Tom Hanks sitting with his knees together, awful haircut, hands at his knees—and beneath the stone bench, a huddled figure.

How odd that she could tell it was Eric, even without seeing his face. She slowed the BMW even more, and the car behind her let out a shrill and sustained honk. *Asshole*, she thought, as a Jaguar sped up to pass her, thump and bass of Huey Lewis and the News's "The Power of Love"; a face stared back at her, indistinguishable behind the tinted-glass window, the silhouette of an uplifted, jabbing middle finger, and then the Jaguar accelerated in an angry engine roar and was gone.

One gray sock—this detail stayed with her, even as she made a U-turn to go back around to the bus stop. Where were his shoes? Where was his other sock? Then she saw Eric again, and, to her dismay, she saw herself—in the curve of his back, the angle of his legs. When she'd asked her father if they were biologically related, siblings beyond adoption, he'd said, "Are you sure you want to know?" And the answer was already there, in his eyes.

Once, when she was very young (even before she and her brother had been officially adopted) and her father thought she was napping, she had overheard him talking to someone on the phone. She'd stood at the door to his bedroom and listened, but his voice was muffled, so she pressed her ear to the door.

"Yes, yes. That's right. I know. I know. Things had gotten out of hand long before. They'd been neglected—personal hygiene, nutrition." He was quiet for a minute or so, and then his voice came back so angry that it frightened her. "No! I'm not going to tell them. Accidental overdose or not, Esther's the one that found her. Jesus. Can you imagine? That's not something—that's not something I'm going to talk about." Another pause, and then his voice was calm, sad. "That's not something; it's not something I want to talk about. Still in diapers, and, well, there's your mom, dead—it's just too much."

She heard him moving toward the door, and she went back to her bedroom, lay back in her bed and waited for her father to appear at her doorway, signaling the end of "quiet naptime." And the wall was sliding, so she shut her eyes and listened to the birds and the ocean and her heart, until the noises finally faded to a shared hum inside her head.

ESTHER PAUSED OVER Eric, unable to wake him with the nudging of her hand. In her other hand she held a tightly folded envelope; inside were fifteen $20 bills paper-clipped with an old receipt from her purse, on which she'd written a to-the-point note: "Happy Birthday. Merry Christmas. Love, Esther."

The yellow light above them made a buzzing noise. There was a long, red, pus-filled scrape at his arm, and the concrete evidence of his addiction, from the needles puncturing workable veins: the *x*-shaped nicks with their halolike bruises. One hand was tucked protectively between his legs, but the other was flapped out at his stomach, his fingernails leathery-looking and split apart at the tips.

As she slipped the money inside his front Levi's pocket—pushing, to make the envelope go deep, where hopefully no one would steal it—she kept her face turned, but she could smell him anyway: pungent, like bad BO mixed with honey.

She fought an instinctive gaglike response, her neck angled uncomfortably, and she looked past the bus stop's canopied roof at a parting of dark clouds, a fraction of moon.

He might buy drugs, but she didn't care anymore—at least, that was what she told herself. She was practiced at guarding herself against Eric, safeguarding her love. Everything he did seemed to hurt her, though she knew that he did it unconsciously.

Impulsively, she took off her coat with its fur-trimmed collar and put it over his body, tucking it under him, so that it would be more difficult for someone to take; and this time (holding her breath), she looked at his light brown eyelashes, the slanted scar on his forehead from when he'd run into an opened oven door when he was six or seven. And there she was again, in the angle of his cheekbone and the slant of his mouth. What had they been playing, anyway? Hide-and-seek?

All that blood—normal for head wounds, her father had said. In the emergency room, as the doctor had stitched Eric's cut, they'd made her wait behind the extendable curtain—she sat in a plastic chair, so small, her feet were unable to reach the floor, an untouched paper cup of apple juice on a side table. She'd believed that it was her fault, for chasing him, and when she'd heard him screaming behind the curtain, she had felt like she was screaming, as if they were really and truly one person; she'd pressed her palms against her eyes, her stomach tightening, imagining the nurses holding his legs and her father holding his arms. A chanting in her head: *Please, please, please, let him (me) be okay. Let my brother (me) be okay.*

Accident-prone, born with a death wish, Eric was often in emergency rooms and there were many hospitals, but she never got used to it. She was a witness, an unwitting participant. Fourteen stitches at the back of his head, from when he was trying to pull her up the brick wall in their backyard. ("Come on," he said. "No, no, I can't," and she let go, so that he tottered for a second, his face morphing into surprise, and then fell backward, cracking his head on a rock.) Riding his bicycle, he caught his bare foot in the spokes—a quick *thut-thut-thut* noise, and then it was over, but the metal had slashed through his heel, leaving a steady stream of blood (twenty-four stitches). Hit by a car when he was nine—"Look both ways!" she shouted, Eric running across the street to get their ball, the sound of car brakes screeching, the smell of rubber from skidding tires, and Eric rolling up the hood like a sack of bread, and then back down, plopping onto the street (his appendix had been removed, leaving a long jagged scar down his stomach, like a train track).

She remembered approaching Eric's room when he was eleven, a few days after she'd seen their father kissing Scott. She was determined to ask Eric about it. He was lying on his back on his bed, his legs extended upward at full length, and she paused and stood in the doorway, already wary of his moods. He slowly bent his knees up and down the wall, watching them move in the lamplight, making bars of shadow.

"Can men marry men and women marry women?" she asked.

For a long time, he ignored her. But then he turned his face in her direction, and his look made it clear that he would not answer, and that she should never ask him again.

Although others couldn't see it, she perceived a deep knowledge in Eric that seemed connected to their past, to what he remembered. But he guarded his knowledge fiercely, as if he had some secret awareness of the way the universe worked and would keep it to himself, and when she looked in his dark eyes, she saw a glimmer of his uncertainty and his fear, his vulnerability and sensitivity, and she understood how incredibly fragile he was; she believed that if she ever let on that she knew, even for a moment, or asked him the wrong question, he might quickly unravel. So she didn't usually ask him questions.

She searched in the book their father had given them, *Everything You Need to Know about Sex*. The completion of the sex act was described as feeling similar to a sneeze, and whenever she sneezed, she would think, *This is like sex?* She was astonished to discover that milk came out of a woman's nipples and that the testicles of the man contain the sperm. She was amazed at the size of an unborn baby's head, at the upside-down position of the baby in the womb, at the rendezvous of the ovum and sperm (which seemed to her an exciting race), and at the fact that babies were born to all women essentially the same way (she had the notion that the procedure differed with different women). But there was nothing in the book about men kissing men.

Not long after, Eric's bedroom door was cracked open, and she looked in and saw him. He was nude, having just taken a shower, and his skin was pink from the hot water (he took only very hot showers). His hair was slick and wild from a towel-dry, and he was seated on the side of his bed, staring at a pubic hair. He extended it with his fingers, and it looked to be about a quarter of an inch long. His face had an abstracted, rather wondering look.

She shut his door quietly and went to her own room. But despite the space between them, she felt as if she were still in the room with her brother, sharing his loneliness, his wonder at his developing body, and she understood that she would always be connected to him, as if by an invisible line.

AT LEAST THIS way, with Eric passed out, she didn't have to attempt conversation; she didn't have to watch his face while she talked: twitching, nervous, cheeks sunken, his hand passing through his greasy hair, as if the motion soothed him, his thoughts beating around them, hounding them.

And she didn't have to pretend not to care that he'd lost his shoes, that he'd lost more weight, and that he hadn't showered in days or weeks. But her heart was loose, unsettled, shredded. She wondered if her visit with Uncle Richard had made her more emotional. She wasn't usually this close to tears. Maybe it was Christmas—people were prone to depression during the holidays.

It wasn't until she was back in the warm safety and new-leather smell of Grandma Eileen's BMW, at least three blocks away, that she realized she'd spent over $200 on her jacket, the one that she'd just given Eric. But she didn't go back to get it.

ESTHER PAUSED OVER the jewelry in the glass case. *Take me, take me*—the items on display hummed. But she wouldn't take anything over $100, knowing that these were the items that would get her caught. There was a satisfaction in even the lower-priced goods, the earrings and bracelets and necklaces hanging from the racks. Huey Lewis was stuck in her head: *That's the power of love—Can you feel it?* A nervous energy, but she took her time, glad that the stores in Fashion Island had extended their hours for the holidays.

As promised, Brenda had called her, and they had made plans to meet at the central location of the Fashion Island Christmas tree at 9:00 PM and to decide what to do from there; Esther had about fifteen more minutes. She recognized herself as superior to the women clutching multiple shopping bags, who struck her as comparatively stupid. She was prettier, smarter. They didn't appreciate the beauty of the world they inhabited, and the items they purchased she deserved for free.

The image came to her of the little lemons covering Grandma Eileen's polyester pants, and then of her brother's one gray sock, a hole at the bottom; she dropped the small gold hoop earrings she'd been fingering into an opening in her purse.

Immediately, there was perspiration on her palms and along her hairline, but when she saw her image in a mirror, she looked calm. Huey Lewis was gone.

She watched herself in the gleaming glass and mirrors as she moved through the store, and she experienced a numb and soothing equilibrium; for a moment, she allowed herself to imagine what it might be like for Eric: heroin blending with the blood, expelling everything life-related, a dreamlike, deadening euphoria. She thought of the earrings in her purse, along with the lipstick and bracelet that she'd already stolen. She started for the exit. The two or three times the detectors had sounded as she'd crossed through them, she'd continued walking, heartbeat racing, and no one had run after her.

And it was the rush of anticipation, adrenaline spreading through her, that made her feel powerful, a conviction returning that life was once again somewhat contained, and a willingness—a desire—to continue living it.

But later, alone in her bedroom, she knew her power would deflate, sifting through the items that she'd stolen or thinking back on her actions, the inklings of guilt and remorse, and an awe at her inability to cull the impulse, knowing that when she entered a store or worked at True Romance, whether she wanted to steal or not, she probably would.

FASHION ISLAND HAD carted in a twenty-thousand-pound white fir tree, 115 feet tall. Specialized cranes had lowered the tree, suspending it midair and placing it directly on flatbed trailers. Finally, the cranes had lifted the tree to its present, erect state. Decorating the branches were seventeen thousand color-coordinated lights and ornaments and bows—silver, gold, and red. Esther had had to memorize these facts, a job requirement for Fashion Island employees, in order to satisfy inquiring customers.

Underneath the tree, on a huge, circular red felt blanket, were large plywood fake presents with gleaming plastic bows. Esther and Brenda were outside, standing near the Christmas tree, watching children climb the presents and smile for pictures.

"How are your kids?" Esther asked, unable to remember the specific names.

"Thank God for Maria," Brenda said and sighed wearily. Her eyes met Esther's with an amiable blankness. "It's Sean that I can't stand," she said. "Why can't he leave me alone?"

Brenda's hair was a rich dyed blond, shoulder length, tucked behind her ears so that her diamond stud earrings were visible. She wore a tangerine-colored sweater. Her waist was small and her breasts round and polite. Her legs were her best feature, which, whether exposed or not, were long and defined. She carried herself with assurance and elegance, and a halo of sexual energy surrounded her.

Esther understood why Charlie had succumbed to the pleasure of not only being in contact with near perfection, but also being physically devoured by it. She envied Brenda, able to dismiss her husband, to take lovers, and to buy whatever pleased her.

She knew that Brenda went through hobbies as quickly as she updated her wardrobe. Her affair with Charlie had been during her academic phase, which had extended beyond her Jazzercise phase and her foray into the culinary arts.

Brenda was taking painting lessons and had told Esther, "Sean told me to paint landscapes, but I told him that I'm creating tiny foldout vaginas from tissue paper—just to bother him."

Even though (or more likely because) she was established and surrounded by money, Brenda somehow managed to make it seem unimportant. She had a way of making Esther feel that she was relaying things about herself in confidence, things that she'd never told anyone before. But Esther knew that she gave this impression to others as well.

There was dampness in the air, a hint of fog and drizzle. A yawning hunger came over Esther, and she realized she hadn't eaten since that morning.

"You must be freezing," Brenda said, looking at her disparagingly. And then, "Where's your jacket?"

A little rain blew, wetting Esther's face. She thought of Eric wrapped in the jacket. "I'm okay," she said, rubbing her hands along her arms.

Brenda smiled, and her eyes showed that she didn't believe it. She laughed. "I don't know why," she said, fishing in one of the shopping bags at her feet, tissue paper rustling, "but I just remembered something: Charlie used to call me a 'blueblood.'" A gleam came to her eyes, a first hint at emotion. "He told me I used the word 'bedlam' too much." She broke the tags off with her hands and handed Esther a black cashmere cardigan.

THE SMALL GOLD hoop earrings Esther had stolen hung from her earlobes, the bracelet she wore on her left wrist, and the lipstick—a little too orangey—was smoothly applied on her mouth. Brenda had invited her to The Palms for cocktails and a late dinner, and her acceptance had been influenced as much by the chance at a free meal (and two sour apple martinis) as by anything else.

Her empty plate had been cleared—grilled salmon with a wedge of lemon, a side of steamed vegetables ("God," Brenda said, "you were hungry!").

Brenda had only picked at her gigantic Cobb salad, and Esther had toyed briefly with the idea of taking home the leftovers, but the thought of having to voice her desire had made her decide against it.

Large tinted windows overlooked the bay, Christmas lights muffled and swaying on the water, stars and moon invisible. An occasional sprinkle of rain splattered against the glass.

The Christmas boat parade had finished, and Esther saw one

lone sailboat, red lights strung along its mast, motoring its way home, making a smeary, bloodlike trail on the water.

For a moment, she concentrated on listening to the monologue of the man at the table next to theirs, speaking to his male friend. ("I told her, 'If you look nice, it's because I made you look nice—from your hair to your nails, right down to your underwear. These other people don't really care about you. Not the way I do.' I told her, 'You want new breasts, I'll get you new breasts.'")

The Palms was fishing themed, with nets tacked on the walls and schooner models set inside glass cases. Esther still wore Brenda's cashmere cardigan, and as she rose from their booth to use the restroom, she followed Brenda's eyes to the bar, where she saw Fred Smith standing, his hand at the rim of a glass. His shoulders were wide in his blue silk shirt and his bicep muscles, unflexed, were the size of grapefruits. Mingling around him were women, but he ignored them, his concentration on a televised golfing event.

"What's he doing here?" Brenda asked, in such a way that Esther knew that she was both thrilled and appalled.

Fred Smith, a retired black basketball professional, had had the impudence to retire to a multimillion-dollar beachfront home, almost single-handedly constituting Newport's less than 1 percent African American population.

Esther was well acquainted with him, as he'd approached her a number of times at Shark Island. The quickest way for Grandma Eileen to disown her was for her to take up with Fred.

"He doesn't look as tall," Brenda said, "as he does in those American Express commercials."

Fred's bullet-shaped deluxe speedboat was bumping against the dock outside the restaurant. He threw loud and boisterous parties that required police intervention and made for front-page stories in the *Daily Pilot*.

Sexy. But not her type. There was his problematic skin color, the tattoo that crept up the back of his neck, the diamond stud earring in his left earlobe, and his irrefutable ladies'-man reputation (although she was confident that she could be the woman to break him of that habit).

And she knew that while Brenda and the like would find amusement in his presence, and that he'd gain a certain acceptance with his money, he'd never crack their inner circle. If he were included, it would be only at the margin, as token proof of their open-mindedness.

Fred confused her: His millions rivaled Paul's inheritance, but his money was less significant than his person. Hesitation and doubt prevented her from seriously considering him as a possible love interest. She knew that it was connected to her fear of being associated with a black man—she couldn't cross that threshold, and even in her imagination, she wasn't that brave.

Fred seemed to understand all this, so his flirtations carried a challenge, a thrusting at her beliefs, and a hostile, teasing quality, as if he were daring her to acknowledge the weaknesses in her character.

Her interactions with him had a cathartic quality, especially when they were antagonistic. All the coarse prejudices of her family, everything she'd been brought up to believe about black people, seemed to be brought into the light of day and ridiculed with his attentions. Sometimes she teased him back, participated, but usually she was cold and direct, and he seemed to appreciate this about her.

As Esther began to make her way to the restroom, her eyes met Fred's assured eyes, and a smile came to his face.

She kept her face blank and continued her walk, straight past him. She was aware of the effect her appearance had on others, accustomed to attention when she moved through a restaurant. She knew what it meant to look beautiful, even when the conditions inside her were ugly, and she was satisfied by Fred's attention.

As she reapplied her lipstick in the bathroom mirror and scrutinized her image, observing the lines around her mouth, a ripple of fear passed through her. The bathroom was lit in a soothing darkness, except for the harsh lighting above the mirror, meant to assist women in makeup application. The light drew out her worst features: face pale and garish with foundation, lipstick, and blush, each pore open for inspection. She pondered the loss of her power, inevitable through age and decline. She wouldn't depend on plastic surgery—the results were shocking and perverted, rather than ageless.

As if to prove her point, a woman exited a bathroom stall, looking very much like Jack Nicholson as the Joker. When she smiled at Esther—a fat, red lipstick–enhanced, ear-to-ear congenial grin—it seemed that her face might split.

"I love that color on you," the woman said, referring to Esther's newly pirated lipstick. Her eyes shone, and her face was shiny and stretched.

"Thanks."

"Chanel?"

"Mm-hmm," Esther confirmed, reading the tiny print at the base: "It's called I'm Not Really a Waitress."

The woman's smile continued to radiate in alarming disproportion to her other facial features. "Well, it looks fabulous," she said. With concentrated effort, she began reapplying her own lipstick in the mirror, and in the lighting Esther saw the tiny, parallel face-lift scars at the beginnings of her left ear: //.

BACK AT THE booth, as Esther and Brenda waited for their check, Fred crossed the restaurant, his long legs moving slowly, hands deep in his pockets.

"He's coming," Brenda whispered.

As Fred got closer, Esther saw that he was staring at her. She saw the challenge in his eyes, and she knew immediately that he would provoke her.

His hands came out of his pockets, and he briefly rubbed an elbow with a palm.

"I've got this one," he said, his hand moving to their table—graceful fingers, filed nails.

Esther was irritated, wishing that her free meal with Brenda had been extended to two free meals, rather than one.

Brenda was delighted, not so much because it made a difference to her pocketbook, Esther knew, but by the novelty and the story she could tell her friends later.

"Really," Brenda said, in compulsory hesitation, "it's not necessary."

"Not a problem," he informed his listeners. "I bought The Palms last week."

Brenda thanked him and introduced herself, and her amused and dismissive tone was proof that Fred was a carnival curiosity, nothing more; by Fred's blasé reaction, Esther realized that he knew it as well.

"When," he said, turning away from Brenda and casting his full attention on Esther, "are you going to marry me?"

She looked at him very straight and very hard. A silence while he stared back, the awareness of Brenda watching them. Then he laughed, and she wanted him to leave, her cheeks burning, knowing that Brenda would pass along an anecdote, and that she'd already become the brunt of a joke.

"Fred likes to tease," she said, moderating her reaction for Brenda, but her voice had an edge. "He's not serious."

He continued to look at her.

"Why did you decide to buy The Palms?" Brenda asked.

He ignored her, continuing his smiling appraisal of Esther.

Esther repeated Brenda's query, since his concentration was focused on her and she had a better chance of getting a response. But even before he answered, she knew that he was going to say something to embarrass her.

"Aren't you ready for the love of a black man?" he asked.

Esther heard Brenda laughing, but she kept her gaze on Fred. "You," she said, "are crazy. You've got plenty of women, so leave me alone."

"And you," he said, his laughter lingering in his eyes, "my sad and lonely friend, are equally crazy." He paused. "But you're also a beautiful, beautiful woman, even if you're not ready to accept my love." He tapped at his heart to emphasize his sincerity. "Can you blame a Negro for trying?"

9

AT BEAUTIFUL NAILS, two female employees of indeterminate Asian ethnicity and age—*probably Vietnamese*, Esther thought, *early twenties*—led Esther and Brenda to the glass display selection of nail polish bottles. "I'm not used to these vampy colors," Brenda mused, her fingernail clinking against the bottles of purples and reds, "but Charlie doesn't like women to paint their nails a trashy color, so there"—she selected a bottle—"ha! See, I'm so over him."

Esther selected a pale, creamy color called Bunny Nose, in agreement with Charlie's aesthetic, and the employees led Esther and Brenda to their spa chairs, side by side. While the employees worked—efficient, examining cuticles and preparing soaking solutions—they spoke to each other in their native tongue. They sat on small stools so that they appeared to be squatting, positioned at the feet of their clients.

The one who was taking care of Esther had shiny black hair, a cascade hanging across her shoulder, and she said something that delighted the other, whose hair was braided down her back. They laughed, covering their mouths with their hands.

"I wonder what they're saying," Esther said.

"Oh, they're making fun of us," Brenda said. "You can be sure of it." She wore a turquoise velour tracksuit, and the zipper jacket was a softer color at her rounded breasts, where the material was stretched.

The employees seemed indifferent, at best, and it made Esther uncomfortable. And their language sounded brusque, no matter what they were saying. She looked down at the woman who held her wet, sudsy foot; the woman began scraping at her heel with a pumice stone, and her eyes looked back up at Esther—through her.

Brenda said, "I used to go to Nail Emporium—it's so nice and clean inside—but it got so bad. The employees are very, very rude."

Esther nodded in agreement while the woman placed her foot back in the tub of sudsy water and lifted her other foot for examination. She had also had a bad experience at Nail Emporium, involving a shy and ostensibly gentle woman, also of indeterminate ethnicity, who had butchered Esther's pinkie with a cuticle trimmer, accidental or not.

"They would find anything to make fun of clients," Brenda continued. "You couldn't understand what they were saying, of course, but you could tell. I saw them make fun of this woman who was getting her upper lip waxed. They were laughing—'hee hee hee'—and this woman got so mad. They tried to stop her—'Oh, no, miss, we no laugh at you, no, no'—but she left."

The employee took a small brush to Esther's toes, and as she worked, she continued to chat quietly with the woman who was scrubbing Brenda's heel—but then Brenda's foot was set down for a second so that the employee could say something back to her friend, with full attention.

Brenda looked at Esther in complete alarm and disgust.

"Talk, talk, talk, talk—jibber jabber," Brenda said loudly. "Sooo annoying!"

The chatter between the employees ceased abruptly, and before they knew it, the older woman who manned the phone and the cash register—probably their boss or manager—was at their side. "Everything okay, Mrs. Caldwell?" she asked, her face directed at her employees, severe and angry, letting everyone know her familiarity with Brenda, as well as her position in the matter.

Three clients sitting across from Esther and Brenda watched with sympathy, and one gave Esther an acknowledging smile, as if suggesting that the current crisis was all part of the hazards of beauty.

"Fine, Diana," Brenda said, graciously suppressing her anger in empathy for the trouble Diana had in keeping her employees in line.

"Okay, Mrs. Caldwell," Diana said, her eyes still on the two squatted before them, "but you let me know if any more problem." And then she spoke angrily in her native tongue for several awkward moments, while her employees kept their heads down in shameful displeasure.

"Well, that's that," Brenda offered, as the older woman resumed her post at the phone and the cash register.

For several moments, all was quiet, the *thrum* of the spa chair vibrating against Esther's back.

The employees had been appropriately chastened, and now they peered at their clients' feet with fierce attention, as if it were a life-and-death matter.

Esther closed her eyes, enjoying her gentle foot massage. Fingers pressed into her calf, back down to her foot; a soothingly cold emollient was spread on her legs. The fingers of her left hand were directed to a bowl that contained a warm, gel-like substance, so that she had to lean a little to her left.

"Whatever happened to Daniel, what was his last name?" Brenda asked.

"Logan," Esther said, opening her eyes, feeling a pinch of shame.

"Logan, that's right. Daniel Logan."

"I'd rather not go into it," Esther said, examining the cover of a *Cosmopolitan* on the side table. The woman on the cover—her bosom thrust forward in a low-cut leopard-print swimsuit—radiated a trouble-free, voracious sexuality.

"I heard that he wanted to marry you, but that his stepson from his second marriage came home from college to visit and you ended up flirting with *him*."

Esther didn't speak, remembering the sagging, pelicanlike pouch of skin below Daniel's chin and his obsession with the saxophonist Kenny G.

"How could you do that?" Brenda asked, delighted.

"Daniel Logan was sixty-three at the time," Esther said, flipping through the magazine with one hand. "Besides, I was just flirting." She paused, glancing at an article titled "Seven Bad Moves to Take His Climax to the Max."

"And whatever happened to that other one—Scott Blakefield?"

Esther made a face at Brenda, conveying her opinion of Scott. She directed her attention back to the article. *Guys are wired to respond to even the slyest feminine wiles*, she read. *With these sexy suggestions, he'll be aching for you.*

"He's a little stupid," Brenda agreed, "a lot stupid. But doesn't he own an airport? Isn't his nickname Two-Yacht-Scott? And he's not that bad looking—if you take away his potbelly and that weird thing he does with his mouth." Her eyes went googly and she twisted her mouth in a sideways smirk.

"He's diabetic," Esther said.

"God, Esther! So what! What were you thinking? It's

almost like you set yourself up for failure. Have you thought of seeing my therapist? I'll give you her number. In fact, let's call her right now!"

"That was a long time ago," Esther said. *Find out everything you ever wanted to know about sex*, she read. *What pleases him, how to mix up your sex routine.*

She thought about Jeff Tyler—now, that was a handsome man. When she kissed him, his lips had been soft and lovely. And he had a sizable inheritance. But along with his health-food obsession, he had indulged in a cocaine habit, insisting that Esther participate; he would snort a line and then chatter endlessly about a limited range of overexhausted topics (his workout routine, his dietary needs, his unhappy childhood). Their breakup had proved fortuitous, as he had become a recurrent attendee of the Betty Ford Center.

"Well, all I can say," Brenda said, "is that you better not mess up with Paul. I mean it."

"Paul and I are very happy," Esther said.

Brenda's cell phone made a muffled squeal from inside her purse. Brenda shifted to wipe her hand on a towel and reached for her handbag. As she sifted through the contents, extracting a wallet-size black phone, Esther found herself pining for a cell phone, if only for the aura of importance it ascribed to its owner.

"I was just thinking about you," Brenda said, and then, for Esther's benefit, she pointed to the phone and mouthed, *Asshole*, so that Esther knew that it was Brenda's husband, Sean, on the line.

Brenda paused and then said, with emphasis, "I said we'd talk about it later." She heaved a sigh. "I don't care," she said, and then, "Yes, yes, I know what I said. Yes, I'll be there. Can you just shut up for a second?"

As Esther's left hand was lifted from the bowl and replaced

with her right hand, Esther looked at her nail lady, whose face was a mask of professional indifference.

"I don't *care*," Brenda said, and then she hung up, placing her phone back in her purse.

The lyrics of the theme song from *Aladdin* played softly: "A whole new world, a new fantastic point of view. No one to tell us no, or where to go, or say we're only dreaming." Even with the music, Esther could hear the air straining through a vent above her, and when she looked up, she saw that a piece of string had been tied there, shaking as proof.

For several moments, no one spoke, as if in deference to the gravity of Brenda's situation.

But then Brenda's nail lady queried, "Same color for hand?" She held up the bottle of blood-red polish that had been used on Brenda's toes. When Brenda didn't answer, she asked again, with measured deference, "Same color?"

"I don't care," said Brenda, echoing her recent phone conversation. Her hand was on her forehead, as if all the pleasure of decision making had been taken from her.

ALTHOUGH BRENDA AND Sean had met through the fraternity system, had shared the same goals and ideals, had experienced the same Christian upbringing, had both recently declared a renewed enthusiasm for Jesus Christ as their personal savior, and had agreed to raise their three children in the tradition of "family values" espoused by Maritime Church, they hated each other.

Brenda had gone as far as to make "empty" threats to leave Sean ("I told him that I would take him for everything, just to scare him."). Being devoted Christians fortified the bonds of marriage as impossible to break (divorce was referred to as "the

Big D" and was not an option, because of its implications of failure and sin).

They belonged to the segment of the upper class in Newport Beach that settled into what was expected: a pipeline from USC and back again, never straying far from their hometown. Wealth maintaining its wealth, at all costs. Everything was in service of the continuum, especially marriage and reproduction, the birthing of more like-minded souls. Raised secure in affluence and having never experienced the misfortune and upheaval of poverty, they were disciplined to steer clear of anything out of the norm.

And so, Esther thought, they would stay married, and they might possibly destroy each other—hate rising and increasing, spinning out of control.

"She's changed," Sean had jokingly said one evening, in relation to his wife, who was present and in full audible range, despite his pantomime of speaking to Esther in confidence.

Brenda expressed her reaction with a full grimace and a shake of her beautiful head.

"Really, she didn't used to be this mean."

"Fuck you," Brenda proposed, "you fucking asshole," and she left Sean and Esther for her bedroom, so that they spent the next few hours together, watching television and snacking on popcorn.

Remote and sarcastic, full of fury, and ready to demolish her husband, as well as anyone who stood in the way of what she wanted, Brenda had changed and was continuing on her path. Beauty and wealth had fostered high expectations, and she was constantly being disappointed.

The more time Esther spent with Brenda and Sean, and the more time she spent in the Caldwell household, the better she understood that her role was to be a buffer between husband and wife.

Later that afternoon, after her nail appointment, Esther met Sean at the Newport Beach Golf and Country Club for a short round of golf, in Brenda's place, at Brenda's behest.

"Brittany fell off the swing," Brenda said. "Maria called. Brittany's fine. Don't worry. She's not hurt. I think more than anything it scared her, really shook her up. Would you meet Sean for me?"

Esther had not yet witnessed the maternal instinct displayed so abundantly in her friend, and so was pleased to help. And besides, she had the advantage of Brenda's calling the pro shop, instructing that Esther should select the golfing attire of her choice ("Put it on our tab.").

Esther chose an outfit that could succeed outside of a golf course, gaining a favorable wardrobe addition from her small favor. It occurred to her only as she was trying on spiked golf shoes that Brenda might have exaggerated her maternal flair for the opportunity to be away from her husband, knowing that Sean wouldn't complain about Esther as a replacement.

Despite being hairy, Sean had lost most of his head hair in his early twenties and was compensating with a mustache and a trimmed beard around his wet, pink, poutish mouth; as she approached him sitting at a table in the country club bar, his lips pursed into a smile and he rose and opened his arms.

"Esther," he said, leaning in to kiss her on each cheek—"like the French," he explained—his hands at her biceps.

Something about his breath wasn't fresh: cocktail peanuts and alcohol and a general neglect of oral care. He'd gotten fat—sturdy—like many of her male peers. The marrieds were the ones who tended to gain weight, feasting on meals as a main form of entertainment or adding sympathy pregnancy pounds.

The men he'd been drinking with at the table observed them keenly. One had a wiry and nervous presence, and the other was fat, a patch of sunburn at the back of his neck where his hair had recently been cut short, sunblock neglected.

Sean introduced her, and she understood that despite their both being lawyers, they weren't adept at small talk with the opposite sex—all blustery bravado and attempts at cool detachment. She didn't have the patience or inclination for the conversation, and, fortunately, Sean led her away within a few moments.

"Your friends are"—she was going to say *nice*, but it was a lie, so instead she opted for the universal and non-committal—"interesting."

"Oh, yeah, Esther," he said, "sure. Most of my friends, I don't even like."

THE GOLF CART whirred and buzzed along the path, clubs rattling. The golf course was sparkling and unreal, like a fairy tale, and Sean spoke philosophically while he drove: "I used to think that golf was a cruel joke on the upper class," he said. "Think about it, Esther: Who would be dumb enough to spend money on a sport that is more like a strange form of torture? Hitting this little ball with a club, and then you can't even see it. Half the time, you're searching for your ball. But now I understand."

"What do you understand?"

He paused, in deep contemplation. His left hand steered the cart, fingers balanced at the wheel, and his right hand rested on his bulky, hair-covered thigh.

"Myself, Esther," he said. "I understand myself. You know, you're not competing with anyone. And it's an honor code. You can cheat all the time, but you don't." He flashed a fierce look in her direction, and she wondered if he was alluding to Brenda's infidelities.

"Because the game is always in my heart." With his free hand, he tapped his chest, where, tucked underneath his rib cage, the symbolic love organ existed. "It's really beautiful and complex."

Esther smiled warmly, knowing that Sean was entering a state of bliss at her attention. In the distance, the ocean looked like a shiny steel blade.

"Do you like to golf?" he asked.

"I used to take lessons," she said, "but not lately."

"Why?"

"Funds," she stated simply. But in truth, she found golf dull.

After a long pause, he said, "Money is a different kind of prison."

His statement prompted her to laugh. He parked the cart along the path and looked at her questioningly.

"Only a person with money would say something that stupid," she said, in an uncharacteristic rupture of irritation.

He studied her for several painful moments, and she felt her face heat up at the intimacy of his stare.

"I'm sorry," she said.

"Not at all," he said. "Not at all. I want you to be able to talk to me like that, Esther. It makes me feel"—he paused, searching for the word—"useful," he concluded.

"You're already useful," she said. "To your kids, to Brenda. In business."

"No, no," he said, shaking his head. "That's not what I mean. Useful—like you need me."

She saw that his eyes had misted with emotion. Birds twittered in the tree above them, unseen. The branches and leaves were parted just enough to let sunlight glitter through, landing on the pond water, speckling it with gold. She could hear the water trickling over the rocks from the man-made waterfall.

"Let me ask you something," he said, and she had to wait several moments while he grappled with how to word his question. A heron landed in the pond, sending long ripples across the surface.

"If you were a woman—wait, no, no. You are a woman, of course, that's not what I mean."

He tried again. "If you didn't know me as a friend . . . if I weren't your friend . . . and let's say I wasn't married to Brenda . . ."

He stared down at his thigh, struggling. She saw that the skin near his ear had colored, fingers of red.

Finally, "Would you ever think of me that way? You know? Would you ever want to be with me?"

In a burst of sympathy, Esther threw caution to the wind. "Yes," she said. "You're a catch. Young, sexy, smart, funny. A real catch."

"Really?"

"Of course," she said. "I wouldn't lie about that."

"Really?" he said again, but he was smiling, and she didn't have to answer.

Sean's subsequent relief and good humor made Esther sure she had responded appropriately. How easy it was to stroke the male ego, and Sean's was dry and thirsty. One little droplet was enough to satisfy—no harm in that.

On the second tee, a short three-par across water, Esther swung the driver and missed the ball. The workers, two of them, had cut the engines on their fairway mowers, hunched in their seats, instructed to disappear as much as possible for the convenience of the golfers. The bills of their baseball hats were lowered, as if they weren't looking. She reteed her ball, took a deep breath.

"Take your time," Sean instructed from somewhere near the golf cart. She moved away from the ball. Three practice swings later, she positioned her feet in the soft grass and bent her knees, peered at her ball. Her swing started smooth, fluid, but it jerked at the end and she squeezed her eyes shut. She heard the crack of her club making contact, and then a *thunk*.

"Oh my god," she said, her hand going to her mouth. "Did I hit him?"

She looked at the workers through the glare of the sun, to see if they were okay. Both workers stared back at her; the one who was closest to her was hunkered very low in his seat.

His dark hand went up, his shoulders unfurled. "Is okay," he called out. "I okay. The ball no hit me. Almost. But no hit me."

ON THE THIRD tee, Sean became distracted from his titanium Callaway driver selection. They stood beside their strapped and belted golf bags in the golf cart, and Esther soon discovered the cause: Fred Smith, in a red-and-gold Ferrari-style golf cart, was whirring down the path, coming their direction.

"Isn't he going the wrong way?" she asked.

Sean didn't answer, instead observing, "And apparently the speed limit doesn't apply to him."

Fred wore an Irish patchwork tweed cap and a matching vest. One long leg was extended rather recklessly, and his foot seemed to skim the ground; instead of accompanying his right hand on the steering wheel, his left hand appeared to be enjoying the feel of air coursing between its fingers.

He swerved past Sean's golf cart at the last second, leaving them in a rush of wind, and he called out, "How about it, Esther?" and then they heard him laughing, and a final, "Whhhoooooheee!"

She knew her face was red, but when Sean looked at her, she saw that he did not hold her responsible.

"At least he's having a good time," Sean said. And then, after a long pause, he added, "I hope to God he's not a member."

10

ESTHER, MARY, UNCLE Tim, Aunt Lottie, George Famous, Grandma Eileen, and Rick sat around the pinewood dining table at Grandma Eileen's vacation home in Palm Desert. Uncle Tim and Mary's oblivious teenagers were skiing in Mammoth, and Esther was glad they were gone, since their sheltered innocence made her disdainfully jealous.

Rick leaned across the table and lit Grandma Eileen's cigarette with a cupped hand around a match, even though they were inside and there was no breeze, and then he lit himself a cigarette as well, shaking his hand to extinguish the match. He wore a T-shirt stenciled with puppies cavorting in a patch of flowers.

Esther wondered if other caretakers smoked with their clients, but she understood that their relationship was unusual, and that Rick acted more like a companion. Earlier in the week, he'd taken Grandma Eileen gambling at a nearby casino, but they'd had to leave, after Grandma Eileen's mishap. ("She didn't want to go to the bathroom," Rick had told Esther. "'Not yet. Just one more,' she kept saying, 'just one more,' at the slot machine. Then she sent me to cash in her chips, and I heard a security guard's walkie-talkie thing, and I knew immediately: 'Uh, there's been an accident'—static-*shhh-shhh*—'we need to send a janitor'—static-*shhh-shhh*. She almost made it. They put up these orange cones to mark off the spot.")

Grandma Eileen sat at the head of the table, using an empty crystal wine goblet as an ashtray, sharing it with Rick. Turkey, mashed potatoes, yams, coleslaw, salad, rolls, and assorted pies brought in from the country club had been assembled on the fine china, giving the appearance of a home-cooked meal. Six long green and red candles at the center of the table, set in wreathlike holders, cast a soft, flickering light. But no one had an appetite besides Rick, who, between smoking his cigarettes, ate heartily. He reached across Esther for the silver water pitcher and refilled his wine goblet with ice water.

Grandma Eileen's desert home was on the seventh tee, where golfers hit golf balls into the pond. The golf course was strictly maintained and reseeded every December, sprinklers set on timers, and Esther momentarily watched the whisk and turn of five sprinklers outside the dining-room window—*chhh chhh chhh clack; chhh chhh chhh clack*, silver wings of spray.

At five-second intervals, water splattered against a corner of the window, leaving a sliding trail of droplets. In the distance, the mountains looked ominous and unreal, the brownish red of bricks. For a moment, nothing mattered. More and more, she'd been losing herself in melancholy reveries, and by letting herself go, she felt that she was becoming less alert, but she couldn't help it. Her attention returned to her family and her situation.

"I don't like," Grandma Eileen opined, cigarette between thumb and forefinger, "that all those Orientals are scoring higher in math and science. I saw it on *60 Minutes*."

"They work so hard," Mary said, eyes squinting as if the smoke caused her physical pain. She'd been agreeing with Grandma

Eileen, nodding her head, and displaying such premeditated consideration that Grandma Eileen silenced the dinner table by saying, "I'm not a little child, Mary. Leave me alone."

Mary's expression for a passing second was despondent. She wore Christmas ornaments as earrings, tiny red balls, and a sweatshirt bearing a sequined angel.

Esther picked at her meal, with the prongs of her fork molding her mashed potatoes into a mountain, a trail of gravy like a waterfall. She didn't exactly have sympathy for Mary, but she understood that her overbearing goodwill was compensation, as they'd all been disappointed by the absence of envelopes on the Christmas tree that morning, with no hint as to why.

Esther had rehearsed for weeks in preparation for her check; she'd been counting on it. Characteristic of someone who had once had money, she had the habit of freely spending it. Although she went without the facials, waxings, and weekly hair salon appointments of her peers, she had the added responsibility of her brother. All she wanted was $10,000 of relief.

Even before her family had woken, Esther had made her way to the Christmas tree, under the pretext of getting a drink of water, and with the sun rising, casting a dark pink glow across the living room, she'd seen the blinking lights and the Southwestern ornaments mocking her—no check, no check, no check—reminding her of what it had felt like as a girl to be crushed when she'd learned that Santa was a myth, an invention, and a lie that grown-ups used to manipulate children.

While her need was a practical necessity, the others were frightened because it proved that they didn't know what was going on inside Grandma Eileen's white-haired head, and thus what alterations she might make in her will. She could feel them questioning: *What does she mean by this? What could she possibly mean*? Adding to the mystery, in place of the checks, Grandma

Eileen had given them identical clay football-size sculptures: a vagabond wearing a top hat, his pants belted with string, leaning over to feed a bluebird from the palm of his hand. Possibly a mass purchase from the Home Shopping Network.

The distress was palpable, and Grandma Eileen, surly and impatient, provided no explanation. She cast a discouraging glance at her family. Her head dropped and she stared at the table. She wore a snowman brooch that at the slightest touch jangled out various Christmas melodies, and she kept touching it accidentally, sending it into a lighted frenzy. While she usually gave Esther preferential treatment—at the very least, a signal to the others that Esther was favored—she was aloof.

The family was expunging its fate with wine, and had already killed three bottles. Rick was the only one not partaking; he had already made plans to borrow Grandma Eileen's Mercedes so he could attend one of his Narcotics Anonymous meetings later in the evening.

"They're not called Orientals anymore," Aunt Lottie said bitterly, way after the fact.

Grandma Eileen's head came up, but she didn't say anything. In the candlelight, her rings and necklace shed a soft brightness.

Aunt Lottie was a little slurry. "You should be more worried about all those Mexicans."

The flap of wrinkled skin at Grandma Eileen's throat looked as if it had grown. Her mouth opened and closed, opened and closed, as if she were making sure it still worked.

George placed a hand on his wife's knee as a show of support, but Aunt Lottie made a point of removing it. When angry, Aunt Lottie could be as cruel as Grandma Eileen. Esther was sorry for George: he'd married Aunt Lottie with aspirations of an easy, moneyed life, unprepared to contend with Grandma Eileen's viselike grip on her daughter. He looked from one face to the next, not knowing what to say or do, and finally settled for staring at a candle flame at the center of the table. His body shape, large lower extremities, thickened ankles and thighs, narrowing all the way to his head, reminded Esther of the Weeble Wobble toy she'd had as a child, and she thought of the song from the commercial: "Weebles wobble, but they don't fall down."

Uncle Tim was quiet, as usual, and when he stood to pour Esther more wine, his crotch was in the direct line of her vision; he tottered before steadying himself with a hand on the table. She knew that as a result of prostate cancer, he wore an infant diaper under his briefs to guard against loose urine splatterings; it created a soft, unisex pouch. By being Gurney and Eileen's eldest son, he'd been in line to take over the business, but everyone understood that he was a failure ("One gay, the other useless"), and that Aunt Lottie was the one with a talent for numbers and how to increase them. He'd taken too many drugs in the sixties, and his vocation was to live off his family's fortune, as those before him had. His wife, Mary, was the greedy one, not to be trusted.

Uncle Tim sat back in his chair and lifted his wineglass, filled to the brim. He took a long sip, his eyes directed at George. "Sorry for being a shit on the golf course this morning," he said—but he didn't appear sorry, his eyes hard and direct. By being the newest arrival, George was the brunt of the family's antagonism.

Grandma Eileen responded by sucking on her rose-tipped cigarette. "Why don't you just shut up with that crapola," she said, smoke spiraling from her nostrils. "I'm just so tired of this life," she continued, and then she said something else, but she mumbled it so that no one could hear. She stubbed her cigarette in the crystal goblet, and it continued to give off a sharp-smelling smoke. Rick poured water into the goblet to kill it.

Grandma Eileen's hand rose from under the table; she reached it across the table and set it on top of Esther's, like a cape, and then she sighed heavily. Her diamond was turned under, cool against Esther's skin.

The others watched, their communal disappointment aggravated. When Esther was a child, she had wanted to change her name to Eileen. When she and Eric would visit their grandmother, they didn't have to knock on the door or ring the doorbell. (She met Grandpa Gurney only once; he was never there, and then he was dead.) Their father would open the door with his key.

Eric would hang back, but she would run into the house, looking for Grandma Eileen, and then, upon spotting her, she would run even faster, her heart drumming with love, inevitably knocking against the sofa or a table. "Clumsy-Wumsy," Grandma Eileen would say, but her arms would stay open to receive Esther.

Once, after such a greeting, locked safely in Grandma Eileen's arms in a prolonged hug, Esther looked up at her and asked, "Why are people so afraid of you?"

"Who's afraid of me?" Grandma Eileen said, letting her go and turning to get her cigarettes and lighter from the coffee table. She seemed genuinely shocked and hurt.

"Everyone."

"I'm not scary," Grandma Eileen said, lighting up a Pall Mall. She paused, thinking. "I don't know," she said, and then she inhaled her cigarette deeply and gave Esther a crazy grin. "Maybe because I have so much money," she said, waggling her cigarette-free hand, as if to spook Esther, while letting the smoke come out of her mouth.

Esther looked out the window to the pink-and-silver sunset, the colors spread across the pond. Why did she crave family, even when family hurt her? The sprinklers clicked off, misting to an end.

Grandma Eileen stood, inadvertently knocking her snowman brooch, which lit up and jingled "Deck the Halls." Rick stood on cue and placed a palm on Grandma Eileen's elbow.

"You barely ate," Aunt Lottie said. Ignored by Grandma Eileen, she turned her attention to Rick. "She barely ate."

Rick appeared to commiserate, but his allegiance was to Grandma Eileen, and as she moved her chair aside and clamped her way with her cane toward her bedroom, he followed close behind.

The door that separated Grandma Eileen's half of the house from theirs slammed shut, as if Grandma Eileen were making a final point, and for a moment, all those left at the table stared at each other in hurt wonderment; then, as if providing the soundtrack to their situation, they heard the familiar music from *Jeopardy* from behind the closed door: *nee nee nee nee, nee nee nee . . . bump badamp bump bump.*

11

LYING IN A fetal position on the white leather couch, trying to watch *It's a Wonderful Life* on the enormous flat-screen TV, Esther heard Aunt Lottie and George arguing in the kitchen. Over the noises of their washing the china (water slopping in the sink) and storing the extensive country club leftovers (cabinet doors, refrigerator being angrily opened and closed), she was having trouble concentrating. She'd already turned the volume up twice with the remote and didn't want to risk Grandma Eileen's wrath.

Esther used to watch the movie with her father, and he'd quote from it ("You want the moon, Esther? I'll give you the moon."). She was doing her best to sink into the relief, the feeling it used to give her. But after hearing Aunt Lottie—"You bastard. You bastard, bastard"—and then, minutes later, the sound of George's Jeep Cherokee, wheels peeling against the street as he made an angry exit to who knew where, Esther decided to abandon the movie and retire to her bedroom.

A half hour later, while the others no doubt slept, Esther sat on her bed, wearing her silk robe, lightheaded and slightly intoxicated, listening to the soft *thump* of the washer and dryer near her room, and considered the aftermath of her spoiled Christmas.

With Grandma Eileen, the equation was simple: Money equaled Love. The only way Grandma Eileen would be generous was if Esther's actions were in alignment with Grandma Eileen's wants—but what did Grandma Eileen want?

And then Esther tried to remember what she'd received last Christmas from Grandma Eileen, and what she'd given—a bottle of perfume? A gift certificate for Neiman Marcus?—but all she could remember was the check.

On her dresser was the sculpture of the cheerful homeless man. She thought of Eric, stooped below the bench at the bus stop, his one gray sock, the bruises, the scrape along his elbow, his smell.

She opened her drawer and set the sculpture inside, its back to her, the bluebird obscured. The drawer wouldn't shut because the sculpture stuck out.

She remembered watching *It's a Wonderful Life* with her father while he was in the hospital, and how everything had flipped: how she had seen him in his illness, his poverty, his uselessness, his clinging to a mother who had disowned him, his conformity (even in his rebellion), and his aching need to be loved. And how she'd become the parent, looking down at him in his hospital bed and grieving for him.

The check was payment for being in this family—appropriate reimbursement—and she'd been robbed.

She didn't want to fall into a hopeless despair, and attempted to concentrate on her resentments, but she had the sensation of being buried alive, consumed by her family.

One consolation: She was meeting Paul's parents at the country club for brunch tomorrow, for which she'd already selected a modest dress and shawl, hanging from a cushiony hanger on a hook outside her closet—a definite move in the direction of marriage.

She imagined soaring beyond her daily humiliations: the friction of unpaid bills, the invariable temptations to spend, and the constant servitude to those who didn't deserve her. But she didn't want to think about Paul either.

As a diversion, she channeled her thoughts to Charlie. By becoming Brenda's friend, she'd become her playmate: accompanying her on errands and getting manicures and pedicures together (paid for by Brenda). Because Brenda was still interested in Charlie, it was natural that he would be a frequent topic, as they discussed what concerned Brenda.

Brenda's frequent vocal analysis of Charlie—his various character deficiencies, as well as his positive qualities—had rekindled Esther's imagination.

"He's deeply sensitive," Brenda had said, as if still working out the puzzle of their breakup. "He couldn't reconcile being with me. He doesn't feel at home in the world."

Brenda dwelled on the minutiae of Charlie: his hair ("Have you noticed how when he's nervous, he flips it from his eyes?"); his body ("Even with his clothes on, you can tell he works out."); and his eyes ("When I look into his eyes, that's when I can tell he experiences things more deeply than we do.").

And while Brenda spoke, Esther remembered her walk on the beach with Charlie, the way he had looked at her in his car.

And she remembered how when they had dated, she had allowed his hands to explore her breasts, an energy radiating from his fingertips. Their long kisses, his mouth indistinguishable from hers.

She could spend hours kissing him. And at night as she lay in bed, she touched herself, her hands his hands.

Everything took on an inspiring component, enhanced by the

fact that she was keeping information from Brenda. She found herself thinking about certain things Charlie had said, or what Brenda had said he'd said, or even what she anticipated he would say.

Unlike with Paul, when Charlie talked, she was surprised, challenged, frustrated, upset, amused, and rarely, rarely, rarely bored.

"Don't underestimate," he'd once told Esther, "the sheer hatred behind class envy, the disillusionment it can bring when, despite what the American Dream tells us, the discovery is made that class can't be crossed because of certain inevitabilities—the color of our skin, the social class of our ancestors."

And another time: "We live in a small, privileged enclave, Esther. Monotonous, rigidly limited, no interest in art or literature or music. A well-to-do, well-ordered, conformist, exclusive, safe, unimaginative little world. We're concerned not with our fellow humans, but with beating out our fellows—winning, appearing to be the best. Selfish entitlement and mediocrity. The appearance of wealth is primary: You don't have to be wealthy, but you have to look like it. I'm interested in what false values do to us, the limited possibilities and the loss that success means—both for women and for men."

And of his own profession, he'd said, "Professors are some of the biggest cowards and class climbers I know, Esther. Don't be impressed."

But she *was* impressed. Her preoccupation had to do with the light he shed on her own situation. Once, he'd asked her: "Who are you? Who are you, really?" And when she hadn't answered, he had told her that she was selling herself short, even if she couldn't see it yet.

Having been trained for a life of privilege, she began to understand that her maturity might have been stunted and her existence limited. This was mixed with her growing sense of an alternative that seemed possible only through Charlie.

Most of her life, she felt, was spent trying to learn how to be brave. She'd been raised to believe that her worth was her beauty, marriage her ultimate goal, but Charlie offered a wider perspective.

Although she longed for something different and tried to imagine it, she couldn't see it. She was thrown off, vacillating between questioning the premises she'd always held and longing for security. And a romantic vision was developing, a belief that Charlie could liberate certain undeveloped powers within her.

The dryer emitted a long buzz, and she heard Rick, home from his NA meeting, moving through the hallway. She wondered what he had to say, and beneath her curiosity was loneliness, aggravated by her lasting inebriation.

Her bare feet were soft against the carpet. As she approached Rick, she saw that he wore a Santa hat. Because of the darkened hallway, there was a furtive quality to their meeting. He smiled when he saw her. "George's car is gone," he said, complicit while soliciting information.

She told him about Aunt Lottie and George fighting in the kitchen and George's sudden departure.

His mouth pursed in concern, but there was a light in his eyes. Then she decided to change the subject.

"You must miss your family," she said. "I mean, especially at Christmas."

His expression was blank, and for the first time, he had nothing to say. He took off the Santa hat and placed it on the dryer.

She wondered why he didn't talk about his family. They were quiet as she helped him fold and stack towels, the tree lights providing a blinking glow. Their positions were similar, when she thought about it, in that he lived off Grandma Eileen, but he got a monthly paycheck for his trouble.

"Shh," he said, pressing a forefinger to his lips, letting her know he was about to tell a secret. And then, "Don't tell anyone"—he smiled—"I'm Jewish."

She felt a quiver down her spine, knowing that she could get him fired. Grandma Eileen wouldn't stand for it. It occurred to her that he might be lying.

"Eric saved my life once," he said. She disliked when he talked about her brother. When she didn't say anything, he explained in a deeper voice, "Those were my bad drug years."

She smoothed her hand along the towel, refusing to comment. The towels that she had folded were in a lopsided stack. She wasn't accustomed to domestic chores, having been raised with maids, and she was continually aggravated by the amounts of labor needed to produce even the most rudimentary surroundings.

She noticed that he had a book with him, and he took it from his jacket pocket to show her: *How to Win Friends and Influence People.*

"I read it once a year," he said.

"Why?"

"'The more you get out of this book, the more you'll get out of life!'" he said, reading a blurb from the back of the book. He could see that she wasn't interested, so he put it back in his pocket and continued to fold.

"Tell me about yourself," he said.

She told him nothing—nothing of her past; nothing of her father's illness; nothing of her grief; nothing of her hopes. But the silence wasn't strained.

"I want you to know," he said, pausing in his folding, and with great concern in his demeanor, "that Grandma Eileen is going through a really, really, really rough time."

Alarm spread through her, but she wasn't sure why. "What

can I do?" Her alarm became an annoyance that he would be a Grandma Eileen expert, as he was not even a family member.

"I just want you to be aware," he said enigmatically, his eyes filled ostensibly with his emotion for Grandma Eileen.

Grandma Eileen needed to hurry up and get it over with—die—so that they could all get their share and get on with their lives. Esther had no illusions: As soon as Grandma Eileen expired, Esther would be dismissed, as smoothly and as efficiently as Aunt Lottie had terminated the gardener last month, when she'd caught him and his bong behind a wall of bougainvillea. They were "family" for only as long as Grandma Eileen was alive. She was tired of watching her grandmother finish herself off incrementally with booze and drugs and cigarettes. And she was being dragged down, as if her grandmother had an irreversible hold on her—a death grip.

They continued folding, and, after a long pause, Rick asked, "How's Paul?" She resisted the temptation to confide. "I fall in love all the time," he said, proving that her nonresponse wouldn't impede their intimacy.

She felt herself nod and grimace.

"I want the person to see me," he said. "I try so hard."

His revelation was absurd, and she chose her next words so as not to indicate sexual preference: "When was your last relationship?"

"The last one"—he crossed his arms over his chest and leaned back on his heels, his eyes narrowing—"was a long, long time ago." He brightened. "It was the kind of love that takes four to five hours a night to take care of. You know what I mean? I'm still getting over it."

She wasn't sure she knew what he meant, and she found herself thinking about Charlie.

"It must be hard for you," he said. Her head went back; her

eyes squinted in irritation. "To be so pretty," he continued, and then, as if sensing her confusion, he launched into a long-winded explanation: "I was working out at the gym," he said, "watching Phil Donahue on male sexual hang-ups and insecurities, and then I came home and watched Oprah's fortieth-birthday special: a surprise party and even her boyfriend—I can't ever remember his name, can you? Sted-something. Stedwall? Stedly? Well, that's not the important part. He carted out this big cake." He paused, set a stack of towels in the hallway cabinet. "Oprah's guests were all past forty," he continued. "They were singing 'Happy Birthday,' passing around a microphone, and it got passed to Cheryl Tiegs, and you know what she said? You'll never guess what she said." Esther shook her head and shrugged, admitting that she didn't know. Rick took on his version of Cheryl Tiegs's voice: "'I'm sorry, I don't sing; I just look pretty.'"

She didn't know what to say, but then a blare of noise came from behind the door to Grandma Eileen's half of the house, and she followed Rick to Grandma Eileen's bedroom.

Grandma Eileen sat against the pinewood headboard of her king-size bed. The Southwestern decor appeared to have climaxed in glory all over the walls of her bedroom: a glass enclosed feathered-arrow display; paintings of horses and sunsets and cacti in chalky grays and oranges and blues; an exhibit of antique rifles; and a large plaster gecko hanging clock, purple tongue flicking in and out, in time to the ticking seconds.

Grandma Eileen was watching television, the bluish-colored lights from the TV floating over her. She had a remote and a cigarette, and there were four Heineken bottles on her bedstand dresser, next to three vials of prescription medicine and a glass of some kind of murky cleansing liquid that contained her dentures.

When Rick reached for the remote, she clutched it against her nightgown, near her floppy breasts.

On the screen, a televangelist raised his hands ("Let us praise Him! Let us praise Him! Let us praise Him!"), and his wife cried beside him, orange hair piled on her head, tears and mascara streaming down her cheeks.

"I'm wathing a movie," Grandma Eileen said, lisping without her dentures; the lower half of her jaw continued to move, as if she were rubbing her gums together.

Rick reached again, but she hugged the remote tighter. He managed to take her cigarette from her fingers and extinguished it in one of the Heineken bottles.

"Mothsly," she said, remote hidden under her breasts, "Eileen Marie Wilsthon liketh the movie."

Esther went to the television and lowered the volume.

"She's loaded," Rick said, and then he directed his words more loudly at Grandma Eileen. "You're drunk."

"I'm wathing a movie," Grandma Eileen said, but this time she was defeated. Her lips were slightly parted and tucked over her gums, so that her mouth looked like a small black hole.

Rick sat beside her and stroked her arm.

"Last time," he said, looking away from Grandma Eileen to Esther, but continuing to stroke her arm and managing, at the same time, to dislodge the remote from her grip, "she was watching the BET channel. A rap video."

He looked back to Grandma Eileen with what looked like affection and pride. "You remember?" he said, his voice sweetening. "You said that was a movie, too. God, it was so loud. *Thumpa, thumpa, thumpa—boom boom.* You wouldn't even let me turn it down. You're just a little bit confused, aren't you? But that's okay. That's perfectly fine. Because Rick is here now. And Rick is going to take care of everything."

Grandma Eileen blinked, slowly.

◈ 12 ◈

A MAN QUIETLY played the piano in a corner of the country club, as if hoping to fade into the background. The buffet brunch was set on eight tables, with an ice sculpture of a swan at the center, and the display made Esther queasy, contributing to her hangover. In a slim white vase at the center of the table where she sat with the Rice family were three waxy red tulips. At the other tables, families chatted amicably, and she noted that they didn't have tulips, confirming that Paul had brought them.

Certain habits of Paul's genuinely bothered Esther, although she did her best to hide it. Paul had slim fingers with neat nails, and his hands fluttered madly but steadied when he picked the skin behind his ears, along his hairline. He then examined his bunched fingers, close to his eyes, looking for what? At first she had believed this to be an infrequent habit, but the more time she spent with him, the more she understood that whatever bothered him behind his ears—imagined or real—was a continuing ailment, and that she'd better get used to it. Also, there was the way he tried to communicate with the waiter and busboys that he was the same, as if he didn't have money, which only amplified his differences.

She was panicked now that she'd finally met Mr. and Mrs. Rice, mainly because Mr. Rice was the type of male over whom her beauty held little sway. She'd been aware that this kind of grim man existed: one oblivious to her, armored against her appeal. A man with tunnel vision. Mr. Rice cared about business; he was a serious man. After he made a point, he smiled, not a real smile, but a lips-only smile. His eyes remained dead.

His Canadian bacon was gone; he only picked at his French toast. He had the same albinolike coloring as Paul, same flaking along his sideburns.

Esther wasn't able to flatter Mr. Rice or flirt with him; her knowledge of business was limited, and while she faked interest and improvised, listening intently and asking questions, she knew that what he wanted was to be alone at his desk, expanding his empire.

"Miguel," he barked across the room. "My wife needs more water."

Mrs. Rice was an extension of her husband, business partners more than companions or (God forbid!) lovers, and as she sipped at her Bloody Mary, celery stalk on her bread plate, she contributed little to the conversation. Her plate was stacked with honeydew melon and cottage cheese and a side of unbuttered wheat toast, but she had focused her attention on the finger-size sausages, cutting them into niblets and then eating the pieces one by one. She had a postmenopausal and sexually neutral appearance, with her boxy figure in a dark blue pantsuit and her hair sensibly coifed, pepper gray. Her only signs of femininity were a string of pearls wrapped tightly around her neck and her sturdy fingers decorated with diamond, ruby, and emerald rings.

When Esther had first entered the country club, while Paul and his father had stood to greet her, Mrs. Rice had continued to sit, her eyes traveling over Esther's sandals, dress, shawl, ring, necklace, and purse (in that order) before landing at her face. Unimpressed.

Then Esther had caught Mrs. Rice staring at Paul, hard and searching, taking him in from inside to outside and sparing nothing, and in observing Mrs. Rice's staggering stare, Esther had shuddered, understanding that Paul had to habitually and continually face his mother's scrutiny—that he was always having to live up to her expectations, every hour, every day, and that by bringing Esther to the brunch, he'd disappointed in some fundamental way.

Esther used her fork to cut tiny fragments off a crab-and-Gruyère cheese omelet, made for her by the chef as she had waited by his table in the buffet line. She set her fork on the plate, prongs entwined with yellow egg matter. She clutched her shawl tight, drew it 'round her body, as if huddling for security, and sipped her mimosa.

Despite Paul's tulips, thoughts of her future crowded in her head, intolerable: married to a man who picked at his ears and would not once surprise her. A father-in-law who cared nothing for her; a mother-in-law who despised her.

She watched Paul's coffee being refilled, a brown syrupy arc issuing from the thin spout of a silver coffee pitcher, steam rising from his glass mug, and the smell was unbearable. For a fleeting instant, she thought she would throw up, but she swallowed the rising tide.

Paul's eyes met hers from across the table. She attempted a smile, but her mood was dark and foreboding, and she wasn't successful.

Paul's condition, what he called Essential Tremors, worsened in response to strong emotions. His hands were under the table. His knife and fork were crossed over his plate, although he'd barely eaten his mushroom-and-cheddar omelet. There was a blush to his cheeks—two pink streaks, as if he wore makeup.

In high school, Paul's twin sister had died in a drunk-driving accident, and the tremors had developed soon after. Paul had explained that his parents continued to grieve, as if a shroud had been placed over them; Esther hadn't quite understood the gravity until meeting Mr. and Mrs. Rice, and now she was convinced that there was no chance of light cracking through.

What had seemed nobly sad in theory—a family forever in mourning—was in reality disturbing.

She took a bite of her omelet while thinking of death. And then, against her better judgment, she imagined performing the sexual act with Paul while his parents and twin sister (an exact replica of Paul, but with long hair and breasts) watched like referees, and she felt the egg matter turn both rubbery and liquid in her mouth. She could neither chew nor swallow. Saliva pooled in her mouth.

She forced herself to swallow, and then she washed everything down with her mimosa. But the food and drink wanted to climb its way back out. She set her napkin to her lips, swallowed again. Her skin was hot, prickling.

She excused herself to the restroom, and when she stood, Paul half-stood, his chair dragging against the carpet. He crouched before the table, hands shaking, his linen napkin crumpled at his thigh like a small white animal pausing on its way up his leg. She implored him with her eyes to sit back down, and he complied.

Mr. Rice—grimly engaged with his fork, extracting crescents of oily onions and red peppers from a side plate of grilled potatoes, and then setting them on the rim of another plate—ignored her, but she caught a glimpse of Mrs. Rice, who was staring at her with obvious dislike.

Walking the long hallway to the women's lounge, she observed the hanging portraits of the country club's presidents, from its founding (1932) until now. The faces—white, male, old, grimacing—blended together, and by the time she arrived at the women's lounge, she was convinced that they were a horrific conglomeration of Mr. Rice; she didn't want to return to the table, much less marry into the family.

Her queasiness released itself into the toilet, prompted by two manicured fingers down her throat, bits of crab and egg and pulp from the orange juice, until she was left with a few last nasty dry heaves and some floating bile.

She heard a woman coughing near the sinks, as if to alert her that it was rude to vomit at the country club, and she wiped her mouth with toilet paper. The piano music was being piped into the bathroom through hidden speakers, barely audible, a melancholy interpretation of "My Favorite Things."

The bathroom door opened and closed, whoever had coughed her disapproval thankfully leaving. Esther's body had a cold-sweaty and tingling relief after vomiting, but the panic would not leave. She flushed the toilet twice more, appreciating the aggressive sound of the water swirling and rushing down the porcelain bowl, carrying away any last filmy evidence of her sickness.

At the sinks, along with the black combs in the blue-sanitized water, hairbrushes, a large wicker basket with folded hand-drying towels, and the various hand soaps and body lotions, were tiny bottles of Scope mouthwash, and she rinsed her mouth. She spat the greenish-blue into the sink and watched it run down the drain. When she looked at herself in the mirror, she had the sensation that she was observing someone else—a woman with a stunned expression, skin pale.

She sat on the couch in the women's lounge, in a separate room, near where the old women played poker and bridge; but this morning the peach-colored, womblike, windowless room was empty, the wall lined with yellow lockers, little padlocks on each one. The piano music was shut off from the room, making it strangely peaceful and stagnant.

In a numb stupor, Esther breathed deeply, knowing that she was decreasing her chances of marriage with each passing minute—but she sat and sat, until what seemed like an hour had passed. During this time, she thought about many things, including how her father had told her that she was an "easy" child.

"You'd float in the pool for hours," he'd said. "I'd put you in the pool so I could read. Yellow floaties on your arms, and your ducky inner tube. Your fingers tapping at the water. Humming a little, singing a little. I had to make a conscious effort to remember you."

"Was I happy? Was I smiling?"

"No, not really. But you weren't unhappy."

She tried to remember the feeling: her feet swirling beneath her, float-drifting. Hands flapping against the surface, bumping against the tiled edge of the pool, drifting back to the center, like being nowhere and everywhere at once.

She thought about how when Eric was twelve or thirteen, she saw him at the balcony, pressing a lit cigarette into the palm of his hand.

"Stop!" she said, and he seemed to wake up, pulling his hand back.

How long would he have continued if she hadn't seen him? At the center of his palm, a blister formed, surrounded by a bright red circle. When it popped and deflated, he showed her the wrinkled, saggy pouch. A scar remained, a perfect concentric outline, and Eric claimed he could tell when it was going to rain by the way it reddened beforehand.

She remembered seeing her father cry when she was a kid. Only once. She heard him first. A low moaning noise coming from the kitchen. When she walked through the door, he wiped at his face and turned away from her. She saw his spine shuddering, seeming to collapse a little.

"I'm sorry," he said. "I don't want you to see me like this."

She was wearing her pajamas with footsies, and he turned and hugged her, lifting her so that her padded feet left the floor for a second.

And while she sat and remembered, there came to her images of Paul's parents waiting at the table. She saw them discussing her rudeness, her strange behavior, her lack of a college education, her job at True Romance. And she could feel Paul's mother feeding off his shame, refusing to look for Esther in the women's lounge, to make sure she was okay ("She's a grown woman, Paul; she can take care of herself.").

She knew that Paul's father would be contemptuous, his cheek quivering with disgust as he summoned the waiter for their check.

The image of Paul waiting was too painful—but she could feel him pulling at her, urging her to return. *Please, Esther. Don't do this to me. Don't leave me here. Come back, Esther. Come back.*

But the part of her that remained herself, that part that she had tried to submerge when she was with him, would not disappear, and she felt that it was this small and nebulous part that kept her body weighted on the couch.

As time passed, her despair, anguish, and panic dissipated. She sank further and further into nothingness. Once, she imagined she heard the ocean thundering—but it was her own blood in her ears.

At one point, panic threatened to return, but she decided that it wasn't real, and because she decided this, she wasn't as afraid. She was pleased by this ability to see through her fear, to gauge it as a nonthreat.

Instead of fear, she discovered a great unwillingness to participate in the life that waited for her beyond the lounge door. The part of her that dreaded the consequences was stilled, until she felt that she could take a long nap. She was weak and tired, as if the emotional labor she'd been through had been physical as well.

She felt like she had been awake for days. When she turned off the light, the room was filled with an amniotic darkness. She made her body comfortable, using the couch as a bed. Her shawl became an improvised blanket.

ESTHER DOZED AND woke and dozed again. Images came and went. She was half-present, aware of her surroundings and then unaware, as if drifting through space. In this dreamlike state, she composed excuses for Paul—varying from the self-flagellating to the humorous to the charitable to the long-winded and psychological, and to the purely factual—but none was satisfactory.

Briefly, she imagined Paul kissing her, and while she allowed herself to be touched and kissed in her imagination, she was filled with revulsion, detesting his tongue, his teeth butting against hers, the smell of his breath, and she wondered whether he had ever guessed what was going on inside her. How could she continue to fake it? She understood that she could not force herself to love him.

Already through the youthful portion of her life, she had decided that any intelligence and thoughtfulness and philosophizing on her part had only hampered her achievement. But she continued to ponder. It was a curse.

For women like her, ambition was a series of self-denials: not to be with a man if he wasn't wealthy; not to be unpleasant; not to be loud or opinionated; not to be indecent; not to be promiscuous; not to be unfeminine; not to get fat; not to get old; not to have wrinkles; not to be poor; not to end up childless; not to pursue an identity separate from her family; not to be different; not to be herself; not to question; not to think too much; not to be too educated; not to be too smart; not to be stubborn; not to be defiant.

She decided that hers was the worst deception: pretending to desire Paul—the worst shame. A flare of self-hatred and self-disgust rose inside her, and then, just as quickly, it died back down.

She heard women coming and going from the bathroom, but, thankfully, no one entered this part of the lounge. A woman blew her nose three times, each consecutive blow louder, and then it was quiet again.

Her sleep deepened because, by this time, she believed that Paul and his parents had left the country club, left her life, gone for good.

She felt the physical sensation of allowing her mind to go further into a cavernous slumber—like a dark shadow moving across her, spreading over her—and then it stayed dark and quiet and still.

WHEN ESTHER FINALLY woke, her body was rested and her hangover was gone. She left the women's lounge for the bathroom and turned on the faucet at one of the sinks, washing her face three times with cold water, as though somehow she could rinse everything that had happened off her skin.

She would have liked to continue sleeping: to not be so fully alive, with all the requisite emotions and situations and sensations that living and breathing—eyes open—entailed.

When she closed the women's bathroom door behind her, she saw that Paul was standing by the bar, near a large window, staring out at the scene before him. And she knew that while his parents had left long ago, he had continued to wait. Briefly, she thought of exiting through a back door, avoiding him. But she owed him an explanation—he'd waited all this time for one, and she knew that he knew she was there.

She walked down the long hallway, past the portraits of the country club's presidents, past the bar, glancing at the clock (3:14 PM), and stopped before the same window, with a small space between them.

The buffet had been cleared in the next room; there were no families left. The man was no longer playing the piano in the corner; instead, a generic jazz-infused instrumental came from the speakers. For some reason, it smelled like burnt toast.

Without looking at him, she sensed his anger—it radiated off his body. Because she'd washed all her makeup off, she had the sensation of being naked—without protection.

The view was of the first tee of the golf course, and she watched a man in patchwork golf pants bend over to tee his ball. In her peripheral vision, she observed Paul, her skin heating with her betrayal. How long had he waited? She'd been asleep for close to two hours. It had been around noon when she'd left for the women's lounge.

Paul's hands were hidden in his pockets, and she imagined them twitching. Then she saw the evidence: The material of his slacks rippled, trembling with the movement of his pocketed fingers.

"They didn't deserve that," he said, not looking at her.

The man in the patchwork pants swung his club, and his golf ball—a speck—disappeared into the blue of the sky. The sky was clear except for a single heavy cloud—a streak of grayish white in all that blue.

"They've been through enough," he said.

She looked back to the golfers. The man's golfing companions were smiling and nodding, as if telling the man that he'd made a nice shot, and he continued to stare in the direction his ball had gone in.

"Where were you?" Paul asked, continuing to stare out the window. "Were you in the bathroom this whole time? What were you doing?"

"I'm sorry," she said. "I felt sick."

Paul said nothing.

Another man, wearing pale green pants, bent over to tee his ball.

"I thought you would have left by now," she said.

"How kind of you," he said, facing her. It was the first time she'd heard him use sarcasm, and it felt like a slap. They'd never quarreled; their relationship had been easy and relaxing—resistant to confrontations and arguments—and both were unaccustomed to the sudden burden of reality.

"Your parents scare me," she said.

He bunched his eyebrows, insulted. He gave a disgusted head shake.

"I don't know what happened."

It made him repeat his head shake. And then his eyes raked her up and down, revolted. He looked back out the window, as if he could no longer stand the sight of her.

"I'm not sure what happened," she said. She wanted the breakup to be over with, for her sake as well as for his. But for a terrifying moment, she was consumed by the loss—not of Paul, but of what Paul represented: legitimacy, stability, security, an end to financial ruin, and an end to her dependence on Grandma Eileen.

Paul stepped two paces back from the window, hands tucked

safely in his pockets. He looked all around the bar, at the tables and lights and piano, at the moving bartender and busboy, seeming to consider his situation. Then he returned his eyes hard to Esther's face and said, with an unhappy and mocking smile, "You officially and royally blew it."

13

NORA HAD INFORMATION (care of Brenda Caldwell, one of her best donors) that she knew Charlie would want, but she had decided to keep it to herself. But she couldn't hold on to it any longer, knowing that Charlie was depressed (she couldn't stand him moping around, not wanting to do anything), so she decided to call him and come clean.

Clothing for Change usually received Brenda's castoffs, but for some reason, this month there'd been no donation. Nora had called Brenda to make sure there wasn't a problem, and Brenda, along with gossiping about Esther, had invited Nora to her annual New Year's party, probably out of guilt for her lack of a donation.

"Esther and Paul aren't together," Nora heard herself say into the phone to Charlie, after a smattering of insignificant small talk. Her voice sounded remote. She imagined him leaning forward on his couch, taking in the information.

"How long have you known?" he asked.

"Three days."

"Why didn't you tell me?"

"I'm telling you now," she said, and she explained that she hadn't wanted to participate in gossip.

By his silence, she knew that he wasn't buying her excuse. She proceeded to fill him in on her phone conversation with Brenda, and as she continued to speak, she knew that his relief was overtaking any lingering anger over her not telling him sooner.

"Well," she said, "what do you think?"

He didn't answer, and she imagined him leaned back into his couch, a hand on his forehead, mouth open, as if in shock.

"I know," she said, to break the silence. "Weird."

"She left his parents?"

"I don't know all the details," she said, fighting irritation. After a pause, she added, "I think Brenda's giving Esther my hand-me-downs."

But he didn't care about her loss of inventory. "She never wanted to marry him," he said.

And as soon as she mentioned Brenda's New Year's party, she knew that he would be her date—so that he could see Esther.

They launched into a discussion regarding their plans. Even while she allowed herself to be engaged in conversation, she was questioning herself, upset at her cowardice for not confronting him. Was he even remotely aware of her feelings for him?

But he was ecstatic, his voice animated, and she conceded the reality: The mere thought of seeing Esther in a few days had helped him in a way that she could not.

14

ESTHER SAT ON the smooth leather couch, feet tucked beneath her, black satin pumps abandoned next to the marble table. In the main living room, she could see the huge riverbed boulder—displayed like a sculpture—harmonizing the house's interior with the rocky-ocean exterior (Brenda had had the boulder steam-cleaned and sealed to avoid fungal growth).

A large picture window overlooked the ocean, and the floor was made of bluish-gray slate, designed to mimic the polished and glistening surface of the sea. Brenda's guests—especially the women in their high heels—were treading carefully, hoping not to slip and fall. The caterers, wearing sensibly soled shoes, held silver trays of hors d'oeuvres and champagne and moved with discreet confidence.

Crystal vases of freshly cut flowers—rhododendrons, tiger lilies, amaryllis, and pale yellow roses—provided a sweet, clean fragrance. Beautiful surroundings usually gratified Esther's sense of well-being, but she was immune tonight, demoralized and contemplative, unable to appreciate.

Lights had been dimmed, candles lit. The fire in the fireplace near her emitted little heat; its light flickered on the walls, glinted across the silver-framed family photos on the mantel.

Worn Oriental rugs suggested an inheritance from European ancestors, although Esther knew that Brenda, at the prompting of her decorator, had purchased the threadbare rugs from the Ralph Lauren catalog.

A banner hung from the ceiling above the fireplace, a navy-blue background with Cardinal red-and-gold letters—HAPPY NEW YEAR 1995!!!—and at the borders, USC Trojan–head emblems.

More than representing a new year, the first of January signaled Esther's pressing need to pay her bills, the adjustments in her lifestyle that she needed to make. Her inability to shoulder her responsibilities, despite living rent free, was evidence of her incompetence. She could no longer summon faith that her debts would be met. Without income for small luxuries—comforts that others consumed easily, freely, without thought to consequences—life was tedious. Underneath all her emotions was the lingering bitterness that she'd been robbed of her $10,000 check.

She'd come over early to help Brenda make adjustments to the decor and to dress for the party. Brown-skinned gardeners were beautifying the front walkway. One wore a straw hat and clipped a bush, knifelike scissors *click-clack*ing, and another, with a red bandanna across his forehead, raked foliage. The house was a Spanish colonial surrounded by palm trees, with archways and thick plastered walls. Loamy foam slapped the mud-colored rocks below. Beyond was the blue expanse of ocean and sky—fat dark clouds with the sun shining between them, and patches of light on the ocean.

But then it had turned gray and dull, the water steely dark. Sean was absent, Brenda complaining, "We had a horrible fight. He needs medication for his mood swings." She handed

Esther diamond drop earrings. “We’ll have a better party without him.”

From her position on the couch, Esther couldn’t see the deck below, but she knew that Brenda’s guests mingled there among the heat lamps, enjoying the same view.

Behind a dense base of fog, the crescent moon looked like a flat smear. She imagined using her thumb to rub the moon away, the same way a wayward ant might be exterminated.

She needed another strategy. Paul Rice was no longer a possibility, thanks to her actions at the country club, and Grandma Eileen was becoming progressively more eccentric and undependable.

Her family and friends were losing their patience. They were sick and tired of her problems (her poverty). She’d been enduring their disappointment, as if they’d been arranging her marriage.

“You’re self-sabotaging,” Brenda had said, with her familiar note of detached amusement. “You wait until the last second and then mess it all up.”

“Pure Being is pure God-ing,” Mary had said, in her typical nonsensical, self-indulgent New Age speak. “All you see and want in your life partner is the outcome of your ideas about yourself. You’ve sold yourself short, honey. You need to work on your self-esteem!”

“Paul Rice is a good man, a fine man, the best of the bunch,” Grandma Eileen had said. “What the hell’s wrong with you?”

They’d gone out to dinner, Grandma Eileen upset because there was an Italian at a table near them (he didn’t even look particularly Italian), and then saddening, commenting on the death of Burt Lancaster (“One of the few men that could turn me on.”).

Later, with a direct and angry gaze, she said, “You blew

it, Esther," and lit a Pall Mall. She inhaled and smiled crazily, wickedly.

And then, as they were leaving the restaurant, "You're not getting any younger, Esther"—skin loose and puckered at her neck, hand clutched at her cane. "Think about it. You're not getting any younger."

Worst had been Paul's obligatory dry kiss on her cheek, his shaky handshake goodbye, and his look of disgusted grief: "Good luck, Esther; I wish you the best," the tone of his voice and the way his eyes wouldn't meet hers belying his message.

But no matter what, no one understood and bore the full magnitude as much as she did. Lonely, distrustful, desperate, she needed to look out for herself, before it was too late, since no one else would.

Yet she couldn't follow through, as demonstrated by her brooding alone, as if a leaden weight inside her kept her at the couch—when she should be impressing potential husbands with her sad beauty. And not far from her thoughts was her desire to get back at her family. If she could just cross the hurdle of poverty.

Her last two shifts at True Romance, even with the occasional spirit-lifting pocketing of cash from the register, she'd been unable to fake the requisite enthusiasm and approval for the women who shopped, as her manager had pointed out.

She'd had to pass Shark Island on her way to the parking lot, missing the routine of her sour apple martinis but knowing it was best to stay away, since Paul frequented the restaurant. He was proof of her failure, and she couldn't bear being near him.

The second time, she'd looked through the window to see Paul at the bar with his arm at the waist of a woman: younger than Esther by at least ten years, big-breasted, lips engorged like a duck's bill. He hadn't wasted any time (she'd assumed it would take at least a month to get over her).

On a cocktail napkin on the coffee table were Esther's three half-eaten shrimp, like small pink ears. At the center of the tabletop was a crystal obelisk, and underneath, in an accommodating nook, were two art books: *Christo: A Retrospective* and *Andrew Wyeth: A Secret Life*. Her eyes passed over a framed map of Nantucket on the wall, a glass display case of fishing lures and boating knots, and, beside the fireplace, a brass sculpture of a cowboy riding a flapping barracuda as if it were a bucking bronco, implying a jocular relationship with the ocean.

The sculpture had a moveable base, so that it could be turned to any angle. She liked the whirling sound it made when she swung the cowboy with her big toe hooked beneath the cowboy hat, her leg extended from the couch in her effort; after three spins, she tucked her feet back beneath her.

The only money Esther had received over Christmas had come from Uncle Richard, in a bribelike manner, requesting that she take Captain Ahab from the convalescent home, a payment of $1,000 as incentive. Apparently, Ahab had been harassing the other patients' pets, getting into fights and making the cats and dogs live in a "ganglike atmosphere." So the patients had met with the staff, and everyone had agreed that the only solution was for Ahab to go.

Esther didn't like the cat. He was large, old, scary, his incisors displayed outside his mouth, his head the size of her knee, his fur a yellowing white. But she needed the money and so had driven to the convalescent home.

Uncle Richard, seemingly unemotional, had written out her check—"for cat food and vet bills"—and then poked and wiggled his finger inside Ahab's cage: "Goodbye, Ahab. It's been eleven good years we've had, but it's time for you to leave."

She'd figured Ahab would become an outdoor cat, hopefully take up somewhere else. But that first night, she'd put him outside and he'd made an awful noise, like a combination moan-cry-howl.

She threw the cheerful homeless-man sculpture at the door, breaking it into three jagged pieces. "Go away!" she yelled. She picked up the chunks of clay. All the while, Ahab continued howling.

After an hour or so, when she didn't respond, he ran headfirst into her door—over and over—until she opened it and saw a snotty smear of blood below his nostril, a gash at his temple, the blood blending into his fur, making it orange.

She let him in and he kept his distance, coiled on her sofa, staring at her with his strangely masculine and oppressive gaze, mouth parted, tongue pillowed between his teeth. "I hate you," she said; she was beginning to think of Ahab as a physical manifestation of her family's abnormalities. An irrefutable and grotesque proof.

Finally, Ahab began to purr in a loud monotone hum, a trickle of drool descending from the corner of his mouth, his eyes creasing shut.

Since then, they'd come to an agreement: Ahab came inside at night and wandered outside in the day, and they left each other alone.

ESTHER LEANED BACK into the couch and watched guests milling around the entrance hallway. They were arriving in a steady stream, fashionably late. Brenda, wearing her sequined red minidress and dark sheer panty hose, had taken her position by the front door to greet, while Maria, in her maid's uniform of black dress and white apron, was passed jackets and purses.

Brenda's hand went to the forearm of a man she wanted Esther to meet. ("Jim Dunnels is fat and old, been married twice, but so what, he's loaded and likes women. Besides, you can't be so picky anymore.")

She recognized him from his photographs in the *Orange Coaster* that Brenda had showed her, celebrating his status as a "leader and innovator in real estate and business" and "his wide-ranging and generous support of local philanthropies."

Brenda was pointing Jim in her direction, whispering in his ear.

Jim was interested, but Esther turned from his gaze. When she was sure he wasn't looking, she studied him: a crease at his neck from where his fat folds pressed together. His suit was dark, he was stocky with a ruddy complexion, and he emanated a wealthy person's casual nonchalance.

Brenda and Jim laughed in unison. From her conversations with Brenda, Esther knew that Jim owned the land that Fashion Island was built on ("So, in a way, he owns Fashion Island!"). He was in the mysterious business of making more and more money, and traveled often, all over the world.

He turned his head suddenly, and their eyes met. A smile crept across his face, and she turned her gaze for the second time.

She wore Brenda's dress, embroidered with black and bronze sequins and swooped low at her back, exposing the curve at the base of her spine. The dark colors highlighted her skin tone, the shine of her hair. The communal appreciation of her beauty usually inspired her, but tonight, selfish and angry, she wanted to hoard herself from Jim Dunnels.

But she knew that he was preparing to make his way over. Brenda was prepping him, discussing intimate and provocative details about her.

In the corner of the entrance hallway, a jazz trio played softly. Women guests were dressed in sparkling apparel. Men wore suits, a sprinkling of tuxes. Pondering her future, all she could imagine was a blankness, a void. Even within the restraints of time—today, tomorrow, the next day, a week, a year—she was filled with dread, a vastness of incomprehension.

She used to have expectations: to have her share of established milestones and their corresponding emotions. Life was supposed to follow a routine, with the buffering mix of wealth—marriage, children, possibly divorce, illness, and then, finally and mercifully, death. A pattern. But her life was a confusing unknown.

Breaking into her reverie and her line of vision was a shadow, and when she turned, she saw the bulky countenance of Jim—a blur of thigh and torso—clearing into the man. He stared down at her with the confidence and merriment of a person with nothing to lose. "I suppose," he said, "there's nothing quite as lovely as a beautiful woman sulking."

Go away, she told him mentally.

"Brenda tells me you work at True Romance."

She answered him unkindly with her eyes.

"Do you enjoy your job?"

She gave him a controlled frown.

"She says your maternal clock is ticking, but that you can't find 'The One.'"

She held her silence. Her only provocation was to not speak—to not take his bait. She'd dealt with men like him, with their adversarial flirtations.

"Tick-tock, tick-tock," he said.

She turned and looked the other direction.

He gave a satisfied laugh.

For some time, they were silent. Then he said, "You're not done with me," and she heard him moving away.

Yes I am, she thought, watching his backside as he walked to the main living room; the silky cloth of his jacket creased in a triangular pattern between his shoulder blades, and the backs of his thighs pressed and bulged against his trousers.

She turned her attention back to Brenda, who was smiling and laughing and nodding. Brenda's head went back, sounding a high peal of laughter.

When her head resumed its upright position, she turned to look directly at Esther, eyes shimmering.

Esther had an impulse to slap her, kick her, hit her, scream at her, or spit in her face. Instead, she smiled while Brenda beckoned with a hand, *Come here. Come here, come here, come here!*

Esther shook her head and Brenda glowered, then shrugged, as if insisting, *Your loss, sweetheart.*

Brenda turned back to her guests, resuming her joyful aura.

Esther listened to a flirtatious conversation between a man and a woman. They were standing near the fireplace, in a corner of the room, and from her vantage point, she could see that the man's hand was cupping the woman's ass.

"You don't know what it's like!" the woman said.

"That's true," the man answered. "I don't know what it's like."

"If I were ugly and plain, no man would want me. Who would want me?"

"Not me!"

"Do you think I'm pretty?"

"Of course."

"What do you like best?"

"Hmm. That's a difficult question."

"Come on! Answer!"

Esther saw the man squeeze the woman's buttock gently in reply, and then the man and woman laughed. They moved into the main living room.

A log snapped in the fireplace, and Esther lost herself in the blueness at the center of the flames. At the base of the fire grate was a steady purple-blue hiss of gas, making the flames whip up and over the wood in a synthetically beautiful way.

As a child, she would have nightmares and would wake in a panic, make her way to her father's bedroom. He wouldn't ask her about her nightmares, knowing that she was reluctant to bring them back to life. He'd let her stay in his bedroom until she was ready to go back to hers.

"I'm here," he would tell her, stroking her hair, comforting her. "I love you." Her arms around his neck, legs looped at his waist, feet crossed at his back, as he carried her back to her bed.

She would slip into sleep, awaken—holding on, pressed against him—and slide back into sleep. Her face on his chest.

I'm here. I love you. I'm here. I love you.

She sensed the presence of someone behind the couch, disrupting her trance, a shadow against the wall.

Before she could turn, darkness enfolded her, cold palms and fingers cupped over her eyes: "Guess who?" A whispered voice.

A dark and clammy pause as she tried to figure it out. Female voice, female hands. Who could it be?

Another whisper: "Guess who?"

"I don't know," she said. "I give up. Who?"

Nora came from behind the couch, wearing a silver-fringed paper tiara and a misguided red dress, no doubt a donation to her nonprofit.

Nora tugged at the bust to readjust her small breasts at its loose-fitting and strapless front. Top hats, paper tiaras, horns, noisemakers, and blowouts had been placed throughout the house, but as far as Esther knew, Nora was the only one taking advantage.

Nora picked up a blowout from the coffee table and blew at it, cheeks puffed—it made an awful *toot* noise, paper fluttering.

When she finished, she said, "Happy New Year!"—a fierceness in her expression, an exaggerated gaiety. She wasn't wearing makeup, except for a harsh purplish-red lipstick that gave her mouth a pornographic look.

"It isn't midnight," Esther responded. She had always avoided Nora, knowing that Nora and Charlie were good friends, and that she couldn't compete (and didn't want to) with Nora's saintlike altruism.

"I've never been to a party with a fortune-teller before," Nora said. Inside the den was a fortune-teller, dangling beads at the doorway, and a small line had formed.

"Brenda has one every year," Esther said.

"You're kind of glum," Nora said, a blotch of pink crawling up her neck.

"Not really," she said.

Nora tugged again at her bust, pulling at her dress. "You could fill this out," she said.

Esther decided not to respond.

Nora placed the blowout on the table, and then clutched one hand at the wrist of her other, crossed in front at her stomach. She had bony shoulders, a skinny neck. After a long pause, she said, "Can you imagine living in a place like this?"

Esther sank back, resting her head against the couch. "I can imagine many things," she said. She didn't trust Nora's magnanimous persona or her exceeding goodwill. And Nora's surprising her had seemed antagonistic rather than playful.

"At Clothing for Change," Nora said, "we call Brenda Number Six-One-Nine. That's her address—oh, you already know that."

Esther didn't respond. As the first recipient of Brenda's handoffs, she had reduced Clothing for Change's intake, and she had the impression that Nora was alluding to this fact.

Nora gave her a long look. Her lips looked separate from her face, as if her mouth might float away.

"What?" Esther asked, losing patience.

Nora looked like she was about to say something.

"Do I have food in my teeth?" Esther asked.

"Charlie came with me."

Esther stifled an urge to look around and find proof.

"He's my date," Nora continued. "Well, not really a *date* date." And she paused before adding, "But he did come with me."

Esther was unable to come up with anything to say. She was aware that Charlie might be watching her. She wondered if Brenda's fight with Sean had to do with Charlie's coming to the party, but that was impossible: If he was Nora's date, how would they have known?

"We talk about you," Nora said.

Esther was annoyed by this implied intimacy. She was sure that Charlie's relationship with Nora was platonic, since she knew his taste (*she* was his taste), and she made no effort to hide this knowledge from her eyes.

But it backfired, because Nora said, "You could at least pretend to like me."

Esther moved so that her body was no longer sunk into the couch. The sudden turn made her attentive. Disliking people wasn't wrong unless you were called on it.

She tried to remember what Charlie had said: that she must be kind to Nora; that Nora was special; that Nora had overcome her environment. Blah, blah, blah, blah, blah, blah, blah. She had the urge to wipe the lipstick from Nora's lips and apply a more appealing color. Her face did occasionally seem gawkily beautiful.

Nora looked off into the main living room, as if to show that she didn't care if Esther had anything further to say.

Esther shifted against the couch, uncomfortable with the turn of events.

"He's out on the deck," Nora said roughly, as if the conversation had reached a hostile cutoff point. "I'd better go find my *date*."

Esther said nothing.

"Don't worry," Nora said, "I don't like you either." And then, without once looking back, she walked away.

Nora's strange and rude behavior made Esther more alert, and she watched as Nora disappeared at the stairs to the deck. To her surprise, she felt a peculiar respect for Nora, and from that perspective, Nora became more interesting. She would have liked to ponder this revelation and, furthermore, the fact of Charlie's being nearby, but then she saw Sean, unexpected, walking through the main living room—he must've come home through the back door by the kitchen.

Sean moved through the main living room, across the hallway—his eyes on her. He paused briefly in front of a caterer with her tray of drinks, each hand accepting a fluted glass of champagne, ignoring the men and women around him.

When he passed by Brenda, she stiffened and looked at Esther, panic-stricken, as if to say, *Help! Don't let him ruin my party!*

Sean sat down next to Esther with a melodramatic groan, the leather of the couch creaking with his weight. He handed her a glass, and then he swallowed the champagne from his and leaned forward to set his empty glass on the table next to her half-eaten shrimp. His shirt was thin and white, allowing a glimpse of his paunchy breasts and sausage-colored nipples, and it was unbuttoned at his throat, the thatch of hair from his chest blooming at his Adam's apple. His fist went to the center of his sternum and tapped. "Excuse me," he said, preempting the small burp that followed.

She set her glass on the table. His trousers were stretched tight across his thighs, and his hand was fisted at his kneecap, black hairs at his wrist entwined in the gold links of his Rolex watchband.

He kissed her in greeting: lips and beard against her cheek, a hand against her knee, the smell of alcohol. When his mouth left, she smiled her appreciation, although if he weren't watching, she would have wiped her face.

"God, you're beautiful," he said, far too loudly, confirming that he'd been drinking heavily. "Where have you been all my life?" It looked like he was wearing lip gloss. His eyes held a base sadness, no matter what emotion was at the forefront.

His neck lurched, as if attempting to release stress, a quick jerking motion. The movement required additional jerks, reminding her of an ambulatory chicken.

"Are you okay?" she whispered.

"Sure," he said, but then he changed his mind with a great force. "No. I'm not okay, Esther. I am not," he paused, smiling angrily, "okay." Looking at his wife, who turned from his gaze, he added, "It's a question of degrees."

He looked back at Esther with mock keen interest. "Did you know," he said, "that it actually takes three rings to get married?" His eyes widened, as if shocked by the news he'd just imparted.

"I wasn't aware," she said, even though he'd already told her this joke.

"Yes, that's right, Esther. That's right. Three rings. There's the engagement ring, of course, and there's the wedding ring—and then there's the suffer-ring."

He waited for her to laugh, and when she didn't, his head dropped. She placed her hand over his, his knuckle against her palm; and then, thinking it too risky, she removed her hand. He looked up and watched her for a long moment. "You're a sweet little thing," he said. "You shouldn't be alone."

She thought of the clothes and purses and cosmetics Brenda had given her, the lunches and dinners and nail appointments. She smiled with tenderness. "I like being alone," she said.

His smile was full of lurid implications. "I'm sure," he said, "that I would like you best alone, too—all to myself, for as long as possible, in all sorts of ways."

There was heat in her face, but she continued to smile. Before she could stop him, his arms circled her waist, pulling her close, his facial hair against her neck and shoulder. She liked Sean, always had, but he was testing her tolerance, and she struggled politely against him. He made a deep, smelling intake, as if inhaling her into his body, and then he withdrew his boozy breath, making a low-pitched, guttural noise.

"It's so nice to have an emotional connection," he said, lips wetting her earlobe. She attempted with more force to pull away, but he drew her in, the buttons on his shirt pressed against her chest. "I'm in hell," he exhaled. She caught a glimpse of Brenda—pretending not to watch.

"Stop," she said, wriggling against him. And then, more forcefully, "Stop! Stop, stop!"

All at once, he released her, leaning back against the couch with an anguished look.

"Okay, Esther," he said, his eyes eaten up with grief. "Whatever you say. Okay, Esther; okay, okay. That's right."

AFTER ASSURANCES OF Esther's affection, of her continued respect and friendship, of her sympathy and thoughtfulness and confidence, Sean—gloomy, tortured—had left for his office with its foldout sofa bed, to do what they had both agreed was the best idea: "lie down for a while."

Soon after, in a case of fortunate timing, Charlie came through the main living room. Primed by her recent experiences, his reappearance took on a spiritual quality and filled her with a sense of longing and renewal. He seemed to represent all that life had hidden from her, and all that, without his help, she could never find.

All at once, her defeats were tolerable. She felt a thrill at his proximity, an awareness that Brenda was watching, and a latent desire, for once in her life, to gain something that Brenda wanted.

He wore a dark-blue suit—the same jacket that she'd worn during their walk on the beach—and she appreciated his lanky physique and ironic expression. It was on the side of intellect and spirit that he seemed rich to her, and mysterious and deep, and he made those things more real. As she kept her focus on him, everyone and everything around her evaporated into insignificance.

Tall, hair long and not so well brushed, he paused before the river boulder and she couldn't tell what he was thinking, his hand skimming the surface. Then he appeared to be looking for something, and when his eyes found hers, he smiled. It was as if her consciousness had gone to him as straight as an arrow—they looked at each other without hesitation, a look that crossed the party and continued to vibrate, a look that seemed to say, mutually, *You! Hello, you!*

She smiled back for him with what felt like an authentic smile, her first since Christmas, setting off a type of internal sparking, and he moved directly to the couch, waving away two caterers with their trays of champagne and weaving through a pack of guests, until he finally stood before her.

"Barefoot, as usual," he said, glancing at her bare feet, indicating his intimate knowledge of her. And when he looked into her eyes, she felt an extraordinary sensation: In the time that had passed since their walk on the beach, their emotions for each other had changed; it was as if, even in each other's absence, their feelings had progressed.

She shot a quick glance at Brenda, who was sending her disapproval and anger from across the room. Esther shuddered and then sat forward, enough so that Charlie could witness the swooping curve of the dress at her back, taking her glass of champagne from the table. She swallowed, knowing that he was watching her throat. Her awareness of his desire increased her desire, and then his eyes passed over her neck and collarbone and faltered somewhere near her breasts.

She set her glass on the table and leaned back into the couch. When she did look at him again, she acknowledged with her eyes what she imagined he was thinking, and he laughed nervously.

"Jeez," he said. And then he grimaced, as if embarrassed by his inarticulate response. A pause. "I'd better keep standing," he said. Another grimace. "I mean, I'd better not sit."

She took hold of the conversation. "You make me feel"—she held his gaze—"like I can do what I want."

His eyes were serious, set on hers. She felt herself going hot, understanding the implications of what was about to happen. They let the moment hold.

"And what is it you want?" he asked. But before she could answer, he leaned over, his hands supporting him on the back of the couch, and kissed her—tenderly, quickly, in front of everyone.

He pulled away, straightened.

"I want to leave," she said, "right now, with you."

PART TWO

◈ 1 ◈

WHEN ESTHER WOKE, the first thing she remembered was that she had cried involuntarily after her orgasm, immediately in the wake of Charlie's extensive, sighing climax, and blood rose up her neck, flushing her face. She'd slept hard, no dreams, a weighty, deathlike sleep. A large wet splotch on her pillow, along with the dampness at the side of her face, proved that she'd drooled.

She looked under the covers, confirming what she already knew: She was naked. A slice of sunlight shone across the bed, striping her arm, dust motes static. She was alone, a note on Charlie's pillow: "Nothing to eat! Back soon with breakfast." And she reached up and pulled the cord, window blinds clanking shut.

A first attempt led to his closet, but the next door was to his bathroom, and she used his dull-bristled toothbrush to brush her teeth, spitting out a smeary worm of toothpaste and washing it down the drain. After she lowered the toilet seat to make use of the toilet, grateful for the last scrap of toilet paper, she lifted it back to its original, male-inspired position, trying to ignore the dried pale yellow droplets of urine decorating the rim. She washed her face with a thinned bar of soap, brownish colored and smelling of sandalwood, summoning a feeble lather by rubbing it between her hands, and dried it with the one towel available, tattered and musty. His Mason Pearson hairbrush was the only sign of luxury, and she used it to tame her hair, noticing in the small mirror above the sink that her face contained a subtle flush, a glow that came only after sex.

She watched herself, peering closer, vain and highly self-critical. The deepened shadows under her eyes heightened her beauty, accentuating the raw, sad features of her face, but the light hummed with a fluorescent, institutional tint, accentuating her flaws: a trio of newly formed pimples at her chin (probably from the rubbings of Charlie's stubble), and creases at her eyes that she hadn't noticed before—more wrinkles!

The skin on the undersides of her breasts stung. She'd used tape to hold them in Brenda's low-cut, swooping dress. She saw the curled ball of evidence, like some massive tangled spider, in the wastebasket.

Charlie hadn't been patient with the dress (she remembered a ripping noise), and then he'd looked confounded upon seeing her breasts in their taped state; in their passion, she'd allowed him to pull off the adhesive, enjoying the sensual clench of pain, the throbbing aftermath. Had she been in a more practical state, she would have used warm, soapy water to dislodge the tape.

Along with the curled ball of tape, she saw a wrinkled, translucent condom stuck to the side of the trash can like a parasite. She knew there was one more condom somewhere amid the rubbish, imagining Charlie throwing the items away before he'd left, in the hopes of her not having to consider them.

After glancing behind the faded blue plastic shower curtain, taking quick note of the inadequate showerhead, the mildewed tile, the lone corkscrew pubic hair by the rusty drain, and the

Pert Plus combination shampoo and conditioner, she decided against a shower. Checking his medicine cabinet, she found shaving equipment, Advil, an old yellowing tube of Neosporin, and an ancient box of Band-Aids. There was no lotion.

She fingered her breasts, observing the damage—pink crescent-shaped abrasions. After checking for an expiration date (3/1995), she rubbed Neosporin on the skin, experiencing instantaneous relief.

All these actions were done with a necessity and without much consideration to her situation.

But as she opened Charlie's dresser, selected a T-shirt, and pulled it on, she understood that she would pay for what had happened. Grandma Eileen believed in virginity before marriage (impossible), thereafter unvarying monogamy until death. Men were allowed to indulge in sex, but for women (unless, like Brenda, you already had unshakable power and social standing), sex was a grave affair, a sign of morality and worth.

Esther's remorse was so great that for a moment she mistook it for heartbreak over Paul. But then she remembered his shaking hands, his close examination of his fingertips after using them to rub near his ears, the pink dents at the sides of his nose when he removed his sunglasses, and his flickering, lizardlike tongue whenever they kissed.

She lay back in Charlie's bed, her head against his pillow. He was near, even in his absence—she could taste him, smell him, feel him. She closed her eyes to it, pressed her hand at her stomach.

The prelude—the touching and kissing—was within her control. But not sex. She went over what had happened:

He'd whispered something in her ear as he'd moved inside her, something that had sounded vaguely like "I want you, I want you," or "I love you, I love you," or some such combination.

"I love you, I want you, I love you, I want you . . ." and his murmurings had heightened her pleasure (as remembering was pleasuring her now, a warm wetness deepening between her legs), had caused her to make similar murmurings, their breathing and commentaries becoming oddly synchronized. But she didn't want to admit what she'd said back to him just now.

And then there was the crying. Any woman could cry, and she prided herself on not using such blatant tactics.

She was not a crier, but something had released, a space that she'd sealed off, a clean, bright pain. And like a released genie, there was no way to get it back in its bottle.

After recovering his breath, Charlie had placed his hand on her hip. She could barely see his face.

"Are you okay?" he asked.

A sense of desolation, of unending loss, tears dropping from her chin. Her body spent, empty, evaporated. She shifted, turned from him.

And what had surprised her the most: At the base—underneath everything—had been something childlike and tender.

She didn't think it appropriate to have a spiritual awakening as a result of sexual intercourse, and she was half-ashamed, half-astounded by what she'd felt. She didn't like being out of control, and she was ambivalent that Charlie had been the one to make her feel that way.

Not wanting to remember additional details (and that was just the first time; she hadn't even broached the second, maybe an hour later—tender, half-awake, rocking together), she surveyed his studio apartment.

A floor-to-ceiling bookcase dominated the room, taking a full wall. She could see the kitchen, with its medium-size refrigerator. The apartment was one big room, only his closet and bathroom separated by doors.

The furniture was selected haphazardly, as if to get it over with: bed, sofa, chair, dining table, desk. Posters of Winslow Homer seascapes—a lighthouse, a lone sailboat—in plastic frames. A triptych of photographs was above his desk, documenting the golf swing of Ben Hogan. And there was a photographic portrait in profile of an unattractive man with a spindly mustache and kinked hair (he'd told her that the man's name was Ezra Pound).

Books were stacked on the floor, against the walls—excess from the bookcase. The thought and attention he'd neglected to give to interior decoration, he had obviously spent on the acquisition of books.

He'd told her that most people read to have their ideas confirmed, that deviations unsettled and annoyed them, but that he read for all kinds of reasons. Next to the bed was a paperback of Homer's *The Odyssey.* Of course she'd heard of the book, but she'd never met anyone who had actually read it. She wondered if Charlie kept it there to impress people. But she knew that was impossible. If he wanted to impress people, he needed to get a better apartment.

She opened the book, careful not to displace the bookmark, and tried to read—but by the second sentence ("Many cities of men he saw and learned their minds . . ."), she gave up.

She'd always been fascinated by books, as if they contained a secret knowledge, but she was a painfully slow reader. And no one she knew actually read books, except for her father. But even he hadn't read that much, besides his magazines and newspapers. Grandma Eileen had said that the only book worth reading was the Bible. Even the Bible was like *The Odyssey*, written for someone else.

Aunt Lottie and Mary belonged to a reading group, but they were only trying to show off. The group met once a month, and they usually argued over what to feed the ladies. Was reading a luxury or a chore? It confused her.

Yet she believed that she might've been a reader had other things not sidetracked her: if she'd had the opportunity to stay in college, if her father hadn't gotten so sick, and if she hadn't been intimidated. She'd read some of the classics: *The Great Gatsby, Anna Karenina, The Call of the Wild*, and, well, she couldn't remember what else. In fact, she couldn't even remember what those books had been about—just a vague recollection that, at the time, they'd maintained her interest.

Beside the front door was a wooden vase with a bouquet of hideous, stiff, brown fake flowers. Worse was a pelican lamp on his bedside dresser with a yellow lampshade; the pelican was made from seashells, hardened on with paste. She saw that he had folded Brenda's dress across the back of a chair. The dress had a rip at the front, and she knew that Brenda would make her pay for it.

Esther had left in Charlie's Honda; Grandma Eileen's BMW was still parked at Brenda's.

Had he slept with Brenda in this same bed? Charlie had gained more from women than he'd lost, a perpetual bachelor. And no wonder. He knew how to please women. God—his thumb on her clitoris, his fingers inside her.

Brenda would have thought of herself as slumming, enjoying the cottage-cheese ceiling. Esther remembered Brenda's warning stare, but she'd left with Charlie anyway. It had all happened quickly: Charlie insisting that Nora would understand; they'd taken separate cars for that purpose.

"It's not a date," he'd said, echoing Nora's earlier admission, and he'd left Esther's side to let Nora know, returning with an urgency, as if Esther might have changed her mind in the interval.

On their way out the front door, Brenda had silently watched Charlie pass, stopping Esther with a hand to her shoulder.

Esther had been triumphant pulling away from Brenda's grip—a look passing between them—and she'd continued walking. (She'd relived it a number of times, for the pleasure: grip, turn, stare, release, and freedom.)

She saw from Charlie's alarm clock that it was past 10:00. Grandma Eileen had probably already used her cane to rap on Esther's bedroom door, giving her one last chance to get ready for church. Aunt Lottie, Mary, and Grandma Eileen were most likely discussing her absence. She imagined their conversation, Mary and Aunt Lottie making sure Grandma Eileen was aware that she—Esther—was letting her down:

She should know better.

And to think of all you've done for her.

She's taking advantage of your kindness.

The one thing that gave her solace was that Grandma Eileen didn't care what they thought, and made her judgments on her own.

A tapping at the front door made her sit up and wrap the sheets and blanket around her. The doorbell rang. More tapping. And then she heard the front door creaking open. "Charlie?" came a voice. "Charlie, it's not raining! Come on!"

And then Nora, wearing a nylon tracksuit, was in the doorway. Esther was used to adapting, becoming the person that the situation required her to be, but with Nora she was at a loss. A faint twinge of guilt lingered around her, as she intuited that Nora was in love with Charlie.

"We jog every Sunday," Nora said, at the same time as Esther spoke: "He's not here." And then Nora's gaze fell to the floor.

"I'll tell him you stopped by," Esther said.

"Don't bother." Nora looked past Esther, to the kitchen.

Esther was embarrassed for her, more so than for herself, because Nora couldn't even look at her. She seemed to be under a painful amount of strain, her face coloring.

And without saying anything, Nora went to the kitchen. It was obvious that she was familiar with Charlie's apartment, opening a cupboard and reaching for a glass, and then filling it with water, her thin face overloaded with her eyes, nose, and mouth—making her strangely vulnerable.

Esther wanted to say something that would appease her. She wanted to allay the barrier between them. But it didn't matter, because Nora drank her water and, without looking at her again, left.

ONE DAY PASSED, two, raining heavily, smacking against the windows, thick black clouds in the day, visible through the curtains; there were pauses of nothing, then showers of rain, sounding like fingertips tapping against the glass, and when Esther looked out the window, rainwater was streaming from the gutters, soaking the grass, running down the street.

Charlie had come home with groceries: toilet paper, a toothbrush, eggs, milk, orange juice, lotion, cold cuts, crackers, cheeses, olives—making sure they had provisions—and she'd used his shower and his Pert Plus shampoo-conditioner and it wasn't that bad, although she wouldn't want to live like that.

But what had helped change everything and convinced her to stay was when he'd pulled the can of lychees from a paper sack, and then a bag of sugar, a bottle of Cointreau, Skyy vodka, and a lemon.

"I'm going to make you a lychee martini," he said.

She watched him heat the sugar and water in a small saucepan, and then pour it into a bowl. "Who needs Shark Island?"

he said, reading from a pocket-size cocktail book; she could tell he was nervous. “I’ll show you a martini.”

Absorbed in the preparation, when his cocktail book fell to the floor, he looked up, startled, and frowned.

He shook the ingredients in two large glasses, and liquid spilled. All he had were regular glasses, and they sipped at the thick and unpleasant drink and laughed. Then he pulled off the T-shirt she was wearing. “What’s it like being a professor?” she asked, watching him watch his thumb press against her nipple.

“Mechanic, professor, president of the United States, whatever,” he said, his mouth at her neck, words hot against her skin. “We’re all the same.”

He pulled the sheets and blanket over their bodies, creating a cocoon. He showed her how to touch him, using his hand over hers. And when he came, it created a splotch on the sheet. She didn’t know how she liked to be touched, so they spent time figuring that out. She felt a shuddering orgasm, his fingers sliding back and forth inside her. He wanted to put his mouth on her and make her come again. Her face flushed, and she agreed to let him. Her head left the cocoon and she stared around the room, her body floating past the walls, dresser, and window, while he stayed underneath. Unable to stay in her skin, she asked him to stop.

Afterward, they ate potato chips and drank large glasses of milk. He asked her about Grandma Eileen. She told him about how Grandma Eileen had gotten mad at her new son-in-law, George Famous, for leaving a poop smear in a toilet after flushing one of his larger bowel movements. “Now he’s not allowed to use her toilets.” His eyes widened, and then he laughed, hand at his forehead.

She asked about his family. He reminded her that he was the youngest of three, and that, thanks to his siblings, he didn’t have as much pressure to please his parents, since the older kids had already achieved so much.

"What's your brother like?" she asked.

"Frank's older, he went to USC, played football, business major. Same with my sister, Karen—not the football, but a business major."

"What about you?"

"Yes," he said. "USC, although I wasn't a business major, didn't play football, and I wanted to go somewhere else; I just knew it would break Dad's heart. But then, I suppose I've hurt him in other ways, the way I wouldn't . . ." He didn't finish his sentence, his voice trailing off. She decided not to ask him more questions about his family.

"What about your father?" he asked.

"What do you want to know?"

"I don't know," he said, "tell me anything."

She told him about how her father used to leave her detailed notes on her pillow, complete with numerals and subtopics (*A*, *B*, *C*'s) within the numbered topics on her self-improvement, marital potential, and wardrobe, and how, although she'd pretended otherwise, it used to bother her that she needed so much constant upgrading.

"Like what?" he asked.

"God, I don't know," she said. "Everything: makeup tips, skin-cleansing diets, fashion advice, conversation starters, conversation fillers, how to be efficient with time, how to floss my teeth, avoid bad breath, avoid gas . . . um, what else?"

"That's okay," he said. "I understand."

His apartment was dark, only a light from the bathroom—door cracked open, day and night blended in the frame of the window, an overcast uniformity. It seemed permissible, given the downpour, for Esther to exit her life and responsibilities:

the overdue bills and Grandma Eileen's waiting judgment; for Charlie to call in sick to work; for Esther to call in sick to work; for them to stay inside and order in food and watch movies on his VCR that made a whining-whistling noise until Charlie smacked its side a couple of times. The rain and cold made her think about Eric, but she forced her brother from her thoughts, remembering the cash she'd given him, and the jacket.

The way Charlie looked at her made her feel like she was the only one—like he was acknowledging that he had never belonged to anyone else—but she also understood that her refuge was impermanent.

She wore his sweatpants, the waist rolled up to fit her, and his T-shirt; and he put Brenda's dress in his closet so she didn't have to look at it. The only mirror was the small one above the sink in his bathroom. She avoided it, purposely looking at the floor when she used the toilet or showered.

Their sex was frequent and tender. Those first two times had made her more cautious, and Charlie obliged her, sticking to traditional positions, nothing too wild. She felt contentment, as if in a dream. An unusual state for her, and even more poignant because of its rarity. But there were spasms of grief at the anticipated end, the fleetingness.

Not once did they speak about their future. The closest was when he said, "Women crave the illusion of security that comes from marriage, since women are treated like objects, but that's just what it is—an illusion."

And then he told her that marriage was an archaic and patriarchal institution, and that the only way a marriage could be happy was if both parties agreed not to get much happiness from it. "The minute you make love a duty," he said, "you kill the principle behind it."

"What does 'archaic' mean?" she asked. He told her.

"What does 'patriarchal' mean?"

He took his time explaining, making sure she understood, even pulling out a dictionary.

She'd always known that business, society, government, families were dominated and controlled for the most part by men—she didn't need a fancy word to tell her that men had more power than women.

But she also believed that women had power over men, if they learned how to utilize it. Was there a word for that? Some women had an extra sense of perception: They tapped into men's consciousness. She'd become so well trained that sometimes she couldn't turn off her perception—and she felt it in other women. Women were taught to see underneath. Her business was in the daily underground of events—of mingling through the unseen. Was there a word for that?

She wanted to argue with him, believing that he was simplifying marriage. But she thought of all his books.

Besides, when she asked herself what she thought, she didn't know. Did it bother her, this patriarchy? The word was thick and foreign. Did she feel that patriarchy was unjust? Was she angry about it?

It frightened her that she didn't know. All her life, she'd simply digested the opinions and thoughts of others. And no one had ever asked her to think before, to have opinions, except at True Romance, regarding wardrobe.

Nora would have all kinds of opinions, and she would know how to express them. Nora had probably read as many books as Charlie.

A flare of jealousy rose up. But it died quickly as Esther thought of Nora in her nylon tracksuit. "Nora's in love with you," she said, to reinforce her advantage.

"We have a special relationship," he said. "We're close. We love each other—but it's not like that."

She shook her head, her hair swinging about her shoulders. "I know," she said, "what's going on with her."

"You don't," he said, his face blank and innocent, and she understood that Charlie knew nothing about some things, even if he'd read ten thousand books.

2

CHARLIE AND ESTHER were in his bed with their backs propped against the headboard, watching number eighteen, *The Bridge on the River Kwai.* He'd made a list of his top twenty favorite movies, and then slowly acquired the videos. Next, he'd show her *Fanny and Alexander*, number four. Onscreen, the British prisoners were forming lines, feet stamping in the dirt as they marched and whistled. From his side vision, he watched the light from the television move on Esther's face, and when it hit just right, he could see the way her eyelashes curled. His observations had a marked penetration and profundity, as if everything around her was alive and worshipful—the pelican lamp, the blanket, the plaster wall, the light flickering across her—and it was his responsibility to notice. Her face was attentive, in tune with the movie, but even more so with his reactions. He could feel her measure his responses.

His relationship with Brenda had been purely sexual. They'd even had sex with her leaned against her dryer, the rumble providing extra stimulation. During their last argument, he'd pointed out the hypocrisy of her loveless marriage, and she'd said, "You don't get it, do you? You're just a little boy, afraid to grow up."

He believed that love created vulnerability. What he felt for Esther was sexual—but there was more to it. Already, with every moment that passed, he imagined that his own weaknesses were doing push-ups and sit-ups, gaining strength and momentum.

On the screen, William Holden, running from the guards, was shot. He fell, his tan body limp, off a cliff into the brown water of the river Kwai. Charlie wanted, in that second, to protect Esther; he wanted to protect William Holden; he even wanted to protect Brenda. He would have given his life to do so. But he felt weak, stupid, and insignificant.

And then Esther turned and smiled at him. A slow, sweet smile burrowing through him, hooking into his bowels. Her teeth glowed in the light and they looked wet. "You," she said. Impulsively, he kissed her, violent and confused, his teeth clanking against hers. She was soft, her mouth was warm, and someone made a noise like a sigh—he wasn't sure if it came from him.

He arranged himself over her, pushed against her, applying pressure to her crotch with his thigh. For a second, he lost control, he could see only black, and it was as if he were yelling with his body, screaming and crying, so he moved back.

Esther pulled off the shirt she was wearing—his shirt—and flung it aside; then she eased and slid the elastic of his sweatpants down her legs, shot them away with a foot. Even in the dark, he could see that her gaze was direct—sexually open and asking for him. He turned the TV off with the remote and then drew her down on the bed, kneeled before her, fingered and licked her, his nose burrowing into her pubic hair. He felt her body surrendering.

Excited and on the verge of discharge himself, he parted her thighs and entered her with the pleasure and beseeching he saw in her eyes. A tightening of resistance, and then he slid deeper, further.

Her eyes shone, widened and startled with his movements. Excited and amazed by her expressions, he closed his eyes, knowing if he continued to watch her face, everything might end sooner than he wanted.

The drizzle whispered against the glass of the window above them, and her breathing echoed it in whispery gasps.

"Oh, yes," she said, moving with him. "Charlie, Charlie."

He opened his eyes and saw her: rapt, eyelids half-closed, head slightly turned.

Heart thudding, he was seized momentarily with grief. Death was all around them. He'd known that death and sex were connected, but never had he felt the connection's weight. The knowledge added to his pleasure in a morbid heightening of purpose.

He fell upon her, sucked at her neck. Oh. So good.

"Oh," he said, "oh, oh."

"Oh," she responded, "oh, oh, oh."

And he was pulled and gripped inside her, a releasing and trembling within him. Distantly, he reminded himself to pull out when he came, knowing that he wasn't wearing a condom.

When it was over, she laughed happily, and so did he. He moved away, gave her room, turned on the pelican lamp. Their bodies were slick with each other. He took his T-shirt from the floor and wiped his semen from her stomach and leg.

"I love you inside me," she said, flat on her back. Her breasts lolled generously at her sides, fat and pinkened, the nipples still hard.

He was worried that he might weep: big fat grateful tears all over her. He threw the T-shirt to the side of the bed.

She moved, on her side, supported herself with an elbow, and looked directly at him, her eyes shining. The sensation of death hadn't left him, but it wasn't as forceful—he felt it as a quiet nearness.

"Afterwards," she said, "I still feel you."

"You mean it hurts?"

She laughed, kindly, and he was momentarily embarrassed: Did she think he was worried about his size? She smiled slowly, abashed. "Well, sort of," she said. "It's just, you stay with me."

Weak like a child, needy, he touched her shoulder. "Esther," he said, to fill up a scared space inside him. He wanted to say more but was afraid of belittling the immensity of what he felt. She was looking at him, and he saw with relief that he didn't have to say anything else.

"WHAT WE NEED to do," Charlie said the third night, turning from the window where he'd been watching the rain flickering in the backdrop of the streetlights, "is get away."

Esther sat on the sofa with her feet tucked beneath her.

"And I mean that metaphorically, not physically. It feels impossible, but it's possible. It has to be."

Charlie thought she looked particularly feminine. And she was beautiful, no doubt about it, even more so wearing his sweatpants and T-shirt, no makeup. A nakedness to her face—a rawness, small lines at the corners of her mouth, the beginning signs of age.

Rick had called earlier—a "family emergency," he wasn't "comfortable" disclosing any details over the phone—and he was on his way to pick Esther up. Beside her was a paper bag containing Brenda's dress, shoes, and purse.

Agitated and confused, Charlie had limited time to figure out their future—which he had avoided discussing—before the outside world intruded.

"Hmm," she said—but it sounded more like a question. She appeared visibly grave. He could barely stand to look at her. The only way to contain his panic was by talking.

"We're taught to neglect or exploit people in order to advance our own interests," he said. *What a crock of shit*, he thought. There was a giant sob collecting at his throat. *Don't leave*, he wanted to say.

"Even the ones we love," he said.

"I don't understand," she said.

He felt an unbearable tenderness—she looked so earnest.

"We're being trained to become this thing we don't want to become," he said, "and if we try to escape, we're going to be alienated and helpless."

"Remember when you asked, 'Who are you?'" she said, her fingers tracing the material of the couch.

He had to pull himself together. "I think so," he said, racking his memories—he didn't remember.

"Well, I don't even know," she said. Her fingers stopped tracing, and she looked him full in the face. "I don't know." She sounded a little shocked.

He rubbed his mouth with his hand.

"Now I think about it all the time," she said, looking away. He was relieved when she faced him again, adjusting her legs and sitting up straight.

"We have to acknowledge where we come from," he said, "but develop beyond it."

"Yes," she said.

"Not only that, but the ruthlessness of cutting ourselves off from the world, the men and women who are below us on the social ladder. We've become socialized into a form of power. To take it for granted."

Standing before her with his hands in his pockets, he could see that she was taking all he had said into consideration.

"And what I really can't stand," he said, "is when I hear people—okay, my dad—talking about how the poor have just as much opportunity. How bad affirmative action is. Excuse me, but fuck that!"

"What does he say?"

"He talks about how the poor need to pull themselves up by their bootstraps and take advantage of the opportunities afforded to every American," he said. He couldn't believe he was bringing his dad into the conversation. It was familiar territory—too easy.

"What he's doing," he said, "is blaming the poor for not being strong enough, smart enough. So they get the credit: They're rich and powerful because they're inherently better, you see, not because of social conditioning or accidental birthright. And then we can, you know, we can blame other people—others get to be blamed for turning into criminals or not fulfilling some American potential—for not being as great."

What was it about her? He couldn't decide which feature it was that made her so beautiful, one standing out beyond the others, then another and another. Or the combination.

He thought of her sitting in his bed, a towel turbaned around her head, another covering her body, back bent, reading a book. She'd been thumbing through his books—Henry Miller, Sigmund Freud, Stendhal's *The Red and the Black*, an old copy of Doris Lessing's *The Golden Notebook*, a paperback of Tolstoy's *War and Peace*. Her lips moved when she read and it saddened him; at the same time, he found it endearing, as if she were a little kid. She had a private look even when she smiled or laughed, as if she were allowing him to see into her. He felt a pain where his heart was.

"Let's take the women at Clothing for Change," he said. He would give her a solid example. He and Nora had spoken extensively about her clients.

But even as he spoke, he had the sensation that his liberal views were a luxury. If Nora were here, she would call him on it. *You have to live your radical views*, she would say. *Otherwise, they're just entertainment.* He expunged Nora from his thoughts, but sadness continued to gnaw at his heart.

"The women at Clothing for Change," he said, "have to be grateful for our handouts. They become a part of the agreement to hide the reality—that having access or benefiting in any way from those in power means having to hide these inequalities and incongruities. The women are asked to be passively grateful, and to hide the loose ends of how they got to where they were in positions of need."

She nodded, prompting him to continue.

"The wealthy have a horror, you see, of being exposed to the sights and smells and realities of disadvantage—to the people—to these people's being the same, essentially." With a small shock, he realized that he was repeating Nora, verbatim.

"Because then," he said, "they would have to acknowledge their dependence on those beneath them to continue the illusion, and, even worse, their own proximity to an accidental life of servitude."

"Sounds like my life," she said.

He walked to the sofa and sat, facing her. Her family life was like one of those appalling *Vanity Fair* articles, a self-righteous and voyeuristic entrée, explicitly chronicling the moral cowardice of wealthy families.

Comparatively, his family was placid, accepting. It would be easier not to get involved in her problems, but he was elated and tense. Being with Esther was a wonderful and crazy thing.

As if reading his thoughts, she said, "Being with you, it's like I'm coming out of a long sleep." An unbearable sadness seemed to come over her, and he wanted to look away because it frightened him.

"I remember," she said, "when the nurses would make my father rate his pain on a scale of one to ten, he would always say eleven. No matter what, he'd say eleven."

"Why?"

"Because that way," she said, "they might actually do something about it." He had the sense that he was mistakenly giving her the impression that he understood what she was trying to tell him.

She paused, her forehead wrinkling. "I'm ready to separate: from my family, from Newport."

The air was electric, like a slap on the face.

"When I told my dad," he said, "that I wasn't interested in his business, I was scared, of course. I couldn't put my heart and soul into it. And when I told him, I was doing what I needed to do. The whole family was mad. They were all disappointed. My dad tried to talk me out of it for months. But I was firm. And you know what? The whole time, I was afraid. I was afraid but I was alive."

"I feel that way now," she said.

Without looking away from her face, he took her hand. He was surprised to see a miniscule booger at the hole of her nostril, latched at the end of a hair, and he watched it flicker with her breath.

In order not to look at it anymore, he kissed her, and she opened her mouth, drew his tongue into her. His tongue wavered inside her, in the shapeless wet space, and when he pulled back, he missed the lost feeling. He went back for more.

The next time he pulled away, to regain his composure and breathing, her face looked blurred, her mouth a gash, and there was a visible sadness—an aura—that continued to surround her. He was drawn back again, preferring to be lost.

He glided the back of his hand across the slope of her left

breast, pausing at the imprint of her nipple against his shirt, then down the right. He felt the appreciation in her body, a release of pressure inside her, and he realized that this was what he should continue doing: keep touching her, keep kissing her. *Don't stop.*

3

RICK'S BANGS WERE angled at his forehead, his expression foreboding, lips slightly pursed. His sweatshirt had blue cursive lettering at the front: LOOK BETTER NAKED. Esther wondered what it meant, but this wasn't the time to ask. Grandma Eileen's Mercedes' windows were fogging, and he turned the key to start the engine, pressed a button to defrost the windows. Drizzle sparkled across the windshield, wipers swiping it, and sparkled again.

"Oh, sister," he said, shaking his head. "I don't know about this." He looked down at her bare feet and the paper bag with Brenda's things and shook his head some more.

Esther numbed her way back to reality, estimating how much damage she could possibly have incurred from her two-day, three-night absence. Disappointment and resignation fought for priority, but she had Charlie with her—he was in her pores. The rain made steady taps against the Mercedes, and there were halos of fog and sprinkles around the streetlights. Her feet were cold and wet, and she realized what she must look like, wearing Charlie's sweatpants and T-shirt, no bra.

Rick didn't speak as he pulled the Mercedes away from the curb outside Charlie's apartment, the headlights glowing in the light rain, the wipers whirring in the background. He made an abrupt turn, taking them in the direction of Santa Ana. He drove past the bus stop near Winchell's, where she saw her brother's figure sleeping underneath a clear plastic tarp.

Rick didn't say anything, but she understood that he'd brought Eric the tarp. She pressed her cheek against the cold glass of her window. Streets, buildings, and lights rolled past, glistening and wet, and she floated through the passing scenery, separate, belonging to no one.

Her breath clouded the glass, muffling her view. They drove for twenty minutes or more, and she wanted the drive to continue, but Rick pulled up next to the curb, with a view of the ocean, and stopped the engine. He kept the key turned for heat. The ocean and sky were black, lights blinking from the bell buoys and boats, the windshield speckling with rain. Beyond the hum of the heater, she could just barely hear the murmur of waves.

"You'd better thank your lucky stars," Rick said, rubbing his hands across his thighs, as if wiping perspiration, "that Grandma Eileen didn't die."

Panic and exhilaration rolled through her. She couldn't help but be excited by the idea.

"Captain Ahab," he said, shaking his head. "I've been feeding him; she told me to stop, but I kept feeding him."

She'd purposely forgotten about the cat; his name caused all her worries and responsibilities, all the waiting bills, to resurface, colliding in one worrisome thrust at her chest.

Rick duplicated Grandma Eileen's throaty voice: "'Don't take care of him. Let him starve.'" He coughed into his fist. "She was already mad," he said, "because Brenda had her BMW towed, and we got the phone call from Harbor Towing. Brenda must really hate you, to have the BMW towed."

Dread coiled inside her, but she tried to remain calm.

"Oh," he said, "and Grandma Eileen found her Christmas gift to you"—he stared at her accusingly—"in the trash."

"How?" Esther asked. She'd put the broken pieces in the trash can by the side of the house.

"'Go get the car,'" he said, adopting Grandma Eileen's voice again. "'Esther needs to pay that fine.'" He paused, staring at her dramatically. "She must've been looking for Ahab at about three or four this morning," he said, and his lips tightened. "By the way," he said, "Nora's the one who finally told me where you were. That Brenda wasn't helpful *at all.*" His eyes gleamed mischievously.

"Tell me what happened," she said.

"What an awful cat," he said. "A monster, so big and ugly. He's like a dog—so big. And that first night you were gone, he kept banging his head into the front door, even though I put food by your door, like he knew you weren't there. *Bang! Bang! Bang!* And his *meow*, what a noise—and I couldn't get him to shut up. I threw golf balls at him and he looked at me with those yellow eyes, telling me to fuck off."

"God," she said, imagining Ahab's gruesome stare.

"I know," he said, and then the story came rolling out of him, breathlessly: "I thought I'd taken care of Ahab, but he must've come back at about three or four this morning, I'm guessing, and that's when Grandma Eileen went after him, with that old pellet gun of Gurney's; she said he used to shoot the seagulls with it. And I'm guessing here—this is purely conjecture—but she must have fallen over the speed bump, the one close to her house, what with all the Heinekens she'd been drinking, and the way she was carrying the gun and her cane, and the rain.

"I came over at seven in the morning, like I always do, and I found her asleep in her bed, wearing her flannel nightgown, with blood everywhere. I found the pellet gun outside, propped against the garbage cans."

He leaned over and found a pack of Grandma Eileen's Pall Malls in the glove compartment. He tapped the pack against his palm. One cigarette surfaced, and he pulled it out and lit it with the car lighter.

"Bless her little heart," he said, waving smoke with his hand. "That must've been when she found the sculpture in the trash, when she was out there in the rain."

"Is she okay?"

"Oh, yes." Smoke coursed from his nostrils and drifted, disappearing out the cracked window. "A broken nose," he said. "You'll see. Ahab got away, but she said she got a good clean shot, right at his head; she was loaded, so who knows."

"Shit," she said.

"But that's not the worst part," he said. He paused, stared out his window. "That's not why I finally came and got you." He stared back at her with a terrible anticipation.

"What?"

"Richard—Uncle Richard—I don't know how to tell you." He offered her the cigarette, and she shook her head. "Pills," he said, stubbing the cigarette in the car ashtray. "Peaceful, really." He wiped his hands against his pants. "He'd been storing sleeping pills in a sock, where the attendants didn't look. No note, but his roommate said that he was just waiting to know that Ahab was taken care of, that once he'd found Ahab a home, there was no reason not to."

She didn't know what to say, and for a long moment they watched each other silently. She wasn't that surprised by the news, and her lack of an emotional response worried her. Was she becoming as insensitive and uncaring as Grandma Eileen?

She went over her last encounter with Uncle Richard, trying to remember if there had been signs of his impending plan: Uncle Richard sitting at the side of his bed, lonely and ghostly, his cashmere socks matching his V-neck sweater, poking his finger inside Ahab's cage ("Goodbye, Ahab. It's been eleven good years we've had, but it's time for you to leave.").

He'd tricked her into taking the cat. And then she remembered how he'd watched her put Ahab in his cage in the backseat of Grandma Eileen's BMW, fumbling until she fit it in. The memory took on a profound weight, as if she'd seen a glimpse of the future but hadn't known it at the time.

After shutting the back door, she'd turned to see Uncle Richard standing by the window of his room; he was holding back the curtain with a hand, staring out at the parking lot, forlorn and bewildered. When he saw that she'd seen him, his face drained of expression—it went blank and empty—and he let go of the curtain and disappeared behind it. But even with the curtain closed, his expression lingered, as if he were still staring at her.

Rick was watching her closely. Something crossed his face, as if ignited by whatever he saw in hers, and he wiped his nose with the back of his hand. His features seemed to hold all the grief and shock and disappointment that she should be feeling. He was trying to contain it, but his face crumpled, and, in the horror of his expression, she realized that his emotions were uncontrollable. He choked on a sob and his hands covered his mouth. He hunched forward and made a groaning sound.

"I'm sorry," he said, speaking into his hands. "I don't know what's wrong with me. I didn't even *know* the guy. It's just so *sad*."

A heaviness came to her own throat. For some reason, she remembered walking to the parking lot of Coco's restaurant with Uncle Richard when she was a kid. It was drizzling and Uncle Richard said, "Hurry, run to the car," and she said, "It feels good," and he said, "Not on my bald spot, it doesn't," and he leaned over so that she could touch the soft skin of his bald patch with her fingertips.

BLACK LIGHTS SHAPED like coach lanterns were on either side of the door to Esther's living quarters, and perched above the door—to scare the seagulls—was an owl made of aluminum but painted to mimic hand-carved wood. The owl seemed like an omen, and as Esther opened the door, she wondered how she could get rid of it without Grandma Eileen's noticing.

"He was the scariest cat I ever saw," Rick said, picking up Ahab's food dish—hardened with cat food—and following Esther inside.

He set the dish by her kitchen sink. "I'll bet he goes away into the hills to die, the way the Indians used to do."

She longed to take a shower and be alone, but vacillated about whether to ask Rick to leave. Once she was alone, the reality of her situation might tackle her, leaving her breathless.

She knew she wouldn't be able to sleep without medicinal help—the conversation with Rick had stirred up all her problems again, forcing her to survey her predicament from the far less romantic vantage of Grandma Eileen's house and influence. And she didn't even want to finger the implications of Uncle Richard's suicide, as she knew that all tributaries of sorrow led to one large, unending grief.

Her answering machine blinked with messages. She hesitated, but there wasn't much she could hide from Rick anymore, so she pressed play.

"Esther," came a man's voice, and there was a labored sigh. "This is Sean. Sean Caldwell." Pause, strenuous breathing. "Of course you know this is me. I don't know why I said my last name. What an idiot. How many Seans do you know? God"—a shuffling noise. "What's wrong with me? I'm sorry. Jesus. Sorry, Esther. Listen. I got your phone number from Brenda's address book. I just want to hear your voice. It'll make me feel better."

Esther looked at Rick, and he swiped one forefinger over another, indicating that she'd been a naughty girl.

"Anyway," Sean continued, "I've been thinking about you—thinking a lot about you, really. I need you to call me. Please call, Esther. On my private line; my number is . . ." Esther pressed the button to stop the machine.

"Now I know why Brenda hates you," Rick said.

"You're wrong," she said. "If I had an affair with her husband, it'd give her more freedom."

Rick set his mouth in an embellished, disapproving grimace.

"Oh, God," he said, after a silence, rolling his eyes, "you know who really hates you? Aunt Lottie and Mary, they hate you!"

"They were waiting for a good reason." After a long, serious pause, she said, "I wanted to know what it was like."

"What *what* was like?"

She wanted to explain, to say something, maybe: *I wanted to know what it was like to be with Charlie. To be with a man because I want to be with him, not for any other reason.* And she was trying to decide how to word it and, beyond that, how much to disclose, but Rick must have seen it in her eyes, because he said, "Oh, honey. Was it worth it?"

THE NEXT MORNING, at Rick's suggestion, Esther tried to confront Grandma Eileen, finding her promisingly alone at the terrace deck, staring out at the metallic shimmer of sunlight on the ocean—glittering *xxxxx*'s across the surface.

Half-inch-thick glass set into the terrace wall protected the space from the cutting wind. Beside Grandma Eileen was a mesquite door table with an oxen-yoke base, and on the table were her Heineken bottle and a large plastic ashtray with CARPE DIEM and its translation—SEIZE THE DAY—written across the base, a flowering of cigarette butts surrounding the words.

Esther stood near the Jacuzzi paved with green slate. She wouldn't grovel, she decided—she wasn't ready for that—but she would be patient, reasonable, practical, appropriately repentant, and tactful. Potted geraniums dotted the terrace, and there was an oily, metallic sea smell.

The violent look of Grandma Eileen's broken nose shocked Esther, made her remorseful. And it further lent a disturbing fortitude to Grandma Eileen's features, as if she were a boxer finished with one fight and ready to take on another. "Goddamn cat," she said, her face becoming defiant and disgusted and evasive all at once. The gout had returned in the big toe of her right foot, and she sat in a recliner, her stout leg cushioned and elevated between pillows.

"Rick says no funeral," Esther said. "He says that you've already had Uncle Richard cremated."

"I killed that cat," Grandma Eileen said. Bruised wedges were beneath her eyes, and her nose was taped, nostrils flared.

"I'm sorry about the BMW getting towed," Esther said. "I'm going to pay you back." The apology was a formality. She wanted to defuse the incident. And she hoped Grandma Eileen would still let her use the car.

"I killed that cat," Grandma Eileen said, seemingly obsessed with the topic. A strand of pearls roped around her neck held back her throat, and underneath the pearls was a large diamond hanging from a gold chain. Mottled, sun-damaged skin was exposed at the *V* of her sweater, and her breasts were flattened at her sides.

"Shot him, right in the head."

"Maybe he's alive," Esther said.

"Dead," Grandma Eileen said. She gave a massive head shake. "Making all that noise."

"Did Uncle Richard want to be cremated?" Esther asked.

A silence hung between them. The air seemed moist and stagnant, so much so that Esther wished the thick glass barrier wasn't there to hold back the wind.

Grandma Eileen took a sip of her Heineken, closing her eyes, as if in deep concentration. The diamond at her throat winked as she swallowed, and calm spread across her face. When she finished swallowing, her eyes opened. She set the bottle on the table; it thumped against the wood. Her eyes were bloodshot and leaky, and she swatted at an escaping blob with the back of her hand. "I don't like Communists and I don't like losers," she said, and Esther knew that she was speaking of Charlie. "He's a loser. He screws married women." She paused, heaving with emotion. "You're like the rest," she said. "You let me down."

Esther felt her stomach go cold. She wanted to defend Charlie because she wanted to defend herself—all condemnations of him were directly connected to her. She opened her mouth to speak, but nothing happened. Her hands became clammy and she just stood there, stupid with shame.

A seagull passed. Her sense of desolation increased. She looked out to the coastline, to where it flattened at the horizon, and she had to squint. The ocean and sky glared back at her, bright and clear after all that rain. *Who let you down?* she wanted to ask. *Who am I like? My dad? Eric? What are you talking about? I've always loved you. I've always been here for you.* She concentrated her attention fully on Grandma Eileen, willing her to speak, but Grandma Eileen closed her eyes, as if taking a nap.

But Esther knew she was awake. Her bosom rose and fell with her long breaths and her lips quivered every now and then, as if she were mumbling secrets to herself. The elastic of her peach-colored polyester slacks had come down a little at her stomach, where her sweater didn't cover; the ridged pink indentation of the elastic's former grip marked her skin. Despite everything, Esther experienced a surge of miserable affection for her grandmother. For a long time, she stood before her, purposely ignored, but finally Grandma Eileen turned and opened her eyes.

"Leave me alone," she said, and Esther granted the request.

4

THAT NIGHT GRANDMA Eileen was in bed, woozy after all the Heinekens and pain pills, her vodka martini, half an Ambien. The only light came from the television, vaporous and flickering, the eleven o'clock news: a housewife lynched and killed in Ghana by an angry mob, the body dragged. Savages. Plans being made for the Million Man March in Washington. No one would show up anyway. Always, the O. J. Simpson trial. Fucking stupid incompetent Judge Ito. Japanese. A segment on Jay Leno's "Dancing Itos." How could they call that news? Weather and sports next.

Not really wanting to, during the commercials Grandma Eileen went over everything that had happened when she'd stalked Captain Ahab. She kept reliving it. Stumbling on the crack in the road, falling and smacking her nose, the palms of her hands on the grainy street. Blood dripping on her flannel nightgown, seeing Ahab's shadow. Drizzly rain. She remembered the grip of Gurney's pellet gun in her fingers, and the thrill as she pulled the trigger. A sense of having hit Ahab, and then he'd disappeared behind a bush. Had she really shot him in the head? She couldn't be sure. But she wanted to believe that he was dead. She'd felt, when she shot him, a relief, like she'd destroyed and vanquished everything that was against her. She could blot them out forever. If only she could be sure.

She smiled a little in the darkness, thinking about what Mary and the others were saying about her, shooting a cat. She tried to wiggle her toes, but her body was a fat blank of deadness, including the gout-ridden big toe—the drugs doing their work, moving sluggishly through her veins.

Mary and Lottie would think she was crazy, that she was a crazy, mean old woman. And of course they'd be right. She loathed them all, but she loved them, sometimes. Her smile flourished for a second, then disintegrated back into a frown as she watched the laxative commercial, knowing that she hadn't had a decent bowel movement in three days, despite all the Metamucil Rick forced her to drink. She imagined him waiting for her to drink the grainy water in its glass, little flickers of what looked like dust, tasting like wood and grass. If she didn't have a crap by tomorrow, he'd bring her two pink pills.

Rick would come in soon to turn off her television and say his final goodnight. For the last month, she'd been trying to talk him into sleeping with her overnight. She hated when he left. She'd have to wait until 7:00 in the morning to see him again.

She felt close to Rick and had shared with him some of her tragedies: the supposed death of her mother and father when she was four. Her aunt had told her that her parents had died in a car accident, but she knew that wasn't true, because it didn't make sense. She'd grown up believing that her parents were still alive, that they'd taken a long trip, and wondering when they might return; finally, after waiting years and years, she'd let herself think of them as dead.

"What did happen?" Rick had asked, his hand at his cheek. When she hadn't answered, he had said, "How did they die?"

"I don't know," she had answered, a mass of ugliness twisting her heart. Dad had left first, and then Mom had abandoned her. Sent her to preschool with a note in her knapsack, directing the school officials to call her aunt.

Grandma Eileen had even alluded to Gurney's many affairs. The whore he said he loved. How once he'd come home with his woman's scent all over him, and when she'd asked him to shower, he'd refused and gripped the back of her neck, pulling her head into him, into his smell. ("Men," Rick had said, letting his lips press together.) And the time when Gurney had come home drunk, insisting that she wasn't his wife, and that he didn't really live here, and that these weren't really his kids.

When she'd shot Ahab, it had felt like she was killing Gurney's betrayal of her, destroying him—even if Jesus Christ had already sent a brain aneurism years ago to punish him. But she loved Gurney, always had; she'd worn his clothes for months and months after his death. And she'd been as cruel to him as he was to her, refusing a divorce and celebrating his anguish.

Her bedroom door opened slowly, and Rick began walking to her bedside, smiling, pausing only to turn off the television on his way. He turned on her bedside lamp and she squinted, adjusting to the light.

"Why were you so grumpy with Esther?" he said, and his mouth did his usual downward pout.

"I was not," she said, cheeks burning, nostril stretched across her face from the tape.

"I think so," he said admonishingly, tucking the blanket and comforter under her chin. "Do you need a final potty visit?"

She didn't know how to respond, because he talked to her like she was a child, and because she wanted to say yes, just to have him be closer to her—to have him touching her. Her reliance on him confused her.

"Esther lied," she said, to change the subject.

His head was above her, and he shook it, continuing to pout. He was her moon and stars. She wanted him to stay. Once, he'd climbed into bed with her, snuggled his body against her back.

"Sleep with me," she said.

He continued to smile.

"I want you to," she said—but it came out like a croak.

"I don't think you should be mean to Esther," he said. "She made mistakes, but she wants to apologize."

"Drop it," she said, anger spiking, causing a sharp flash of pain in her chest. A black void of grief lurked, having to do with Esther and Richard and the cat and her dead parents who weren't really dead and the whore whom Gurney said he loved and on and on, and she let Rick see it in her eyes.

"Okay," he said. "Dropped."

She saw that he was about to make his way to the door, that hesitation he gave when he was through with her. "No," she said. She felt her face go small and weak. "Stay. Please."

"Now, now," he said. But he came back, sat beside her, and stroked her cheek. "Poor little nose," he said, barely tapping a finger against the tip. "All broken." And she knew that he'd stay there until she fell asleep, which wouldn't take long, God bless the Ambien.

"You're a mean old bird," he said affectionately, smoothing hair from her face.

She was a little girl. Her eyes were closed; it made his presence more glorious.

"Meany-beany," he said.

"I know, I know," she said, her words blending together so that they came out as "Agnowagnow." And then she felt his fingertips on her forehead, against her cheek. He was touching her all over her face.

5

CHARLIE MURPHY HAD earned a reputation at Orange County Community College, not among his colleagues, but among his students (particularly the young women), who encouraged each other to take his sociology courses to fulfill those irritating humanities/social science requirements. It wasn't that his classes were easy (because they weren't), but that Charlie was entertaining, handsome, and tall.

His dark, slightly curly hair was a little too long for a man, and when he was nervous, he used his hand to flip it from his eyes. But he was masculine, his thighs and stomach and arms defined and muscular. His eyes were a pretty brownish-hazel color—serious and sad, as if he suffered a special burden. His students could tell that he experienced life deeply. Yet he made an effort to be light and breezy, and they were appreciative. They wondered about his personal life, and unimaginative rumors spread: He's gay; he's straight; he's bisexual; he's married; he's divorced; he lives alone; he has a girlfriend in another country. And they often felt as if they were making a complicit agreement, in a strange way, *to help him.*

He said things like, "I'm not telling you when to do your

homework—you're adults and don't need a babysitter—but I'm telling you when to have it done. It's pretty straightforward, right? I really like attendance, and when you're not here, I miss you: It's as if we made a date and you didn't even show up."

But what really impressed them was when he said, "If you come out of this class and do your work, I personally guarantee that you will become *not only* better educated, but *also a better person*." They doodled in the margins of their notebook paper, and then scribbled over their doodles. They leaned over and whispered to each other:

"He's so cute!"

"I love his corduroy jacket."

"How old do you think he is?"

CHARLIE WAS AN adjunct professor, and a movement was gaining momentum to raise his position. His most-talked-about course, Social Class & Inequality, had been canceled due to its controversial subject matter, only adding to its buzz. Brought back by popular student demand, enrollment had tripled, requiring the largest auditorium at Orange County Community College.

A letter was being passed among his students, initiated by a core group of female supporters, to nominate Charlie for an award for most influential professor. If he won, it would be the first time in the history of OCCC that an adjunct had received the honor, which included a monetary stipend of $2,000.

The letter was a blend of admiration, sincerity, bluster, and juvenility:

> Dear fellow students,
>
> Charlie Murphy would never ask us to nominate him for anything—he's too modest. But we know that many of our

faculty aren't as shy or modest (we've been asked to do this kind of shit more than once!), and this kind of stuff really looks good on their files or whatever (which is great for Charlie when he gets to be a full professor—ha! ha!). The other profs are jealous and he hasn't gotten the recognition he deserves, but it's time for that to change! And we can be the ones to change it, because that's the only way it will happen.

Which is why we think we should all really sit ourselves down for more than ten minutes and write him the best fucking letter of rec. we've ever written any prof, because, at least in our opinion, he truly dedicates his time and effort and makes us *think*. So let's sharpen our pencils and blow the dean away, shall we?

◈ 6 ◈

ESTHER HAD NEVER taken her job at True Romance that seriously, but now it was purely out of routine that she showed up to work. And when she walked past Shark Island, glancing at the singles mingling at the bar, along with the familiar pull of disappointment, she felt a sense of invulnerability.

Esther wasn't even that jealous when she heard that Paul Rice had proposed to the woman with the duck lips at Shark Island. The most expedient courting ever. Right at the bar, where they'd met. A ten-carat, radiant-cut diamond ring, rumor had it, hooped around a red-striped straw, and pierced through a pineapple slice garnishing Duck Lips' piña colada.

Esther's confidence was connected to Charlie. She wore a type of armor—what she came to think of as Charlie Armor—against Grandma Eileen's silent treatment and disapproval, against Brenda, Aunt Lottie, and Mary, possible only because she saw Charlie almost every day, and when they weren't with each other, they talked by phone.

None of her difficulties had changed. Her problems had not been solved. In fact, in the course of recent events, more problems had emerged to attach to the old ones. But now it was easier to pretend that they didn't matter.

Grandma Eileen hadn't handed her back the keys to the BMW, so Esther was forced to borrow Rick's Grand Marquis, with its coughing-stuttering engine, its tilting to the left, while Rick was allowed his choice of Grandma Eileen's four vehicles.

Rick's relationship with Grandma Eileen was perverse. For example, just last week, after her personal massage, meant to alleviate her arthritis and increase her blood flow, Grandma Eileen had come staggering through her bedroom door, slick with body oil, hair wild and robe loosened, hand gripping her cane.

"How do you feel?" Rick asked, with his customary cheerfulness.

"I feel," Grandma Eileen answered, a demonic look coming to her eyes, "like I could throw you down on the floor and fuck your brains out right now."

"Now, now," Rick said, blushing.

"Does she say that kind of stuff to you all the time?" Esther asked later. "She acted like I wasn't even in the room."

"She doesn't mean it," Rick said, his fondness for Grandma Eileen displayed openly on his face. "She just really, really, really likes her massages."

Does she know you're gay? she wanted to ask. *Does she know that you're Jewish?*

"Oh, please," he said, as if reading her thoughts, "like I even care what she thinks."

A new female companion was accompanying Brenda on her errands, dining with her, shopping and going to the nail salon, and they were spreading malicious rumors, blaming Esther publicly for being a "homewrecker."

And to make matters worse, Sean continued to call Esther, leaving messages, sometimes alluding to his proclivity to ponder the benefits of suicide, claiming that she was the key to his salvation. He was also sending tulips, fueling rumors.

Once, she'd answered the phone accidentally (she had a code with Charlie: two rings, hang up, and then call back), and as soon as she heard the heavy breathing, she knew that it was Sean.

"Esther," he said, "I need you. I can't go on like this."

"Stop calling," she said. What bothered her the most was that he wasn't interested in her—he was interested in how she benefited him. "Where are you?" she asked, hearing a roar of applause.

"What?"

"Where are you?"

"I'm on my cell phone."

"No," she said. "Where are you?"

"At the high school football game—we're ahead, second half."

She imagined him sitting in the stands, teenagers around him, the brilliance of the field's lights. He'd been a football star in high school.

"I'm no good without you. I miss you. I don't have anyone to talk to."

"I'm seeing someone," she said.

She heard another roar from the crowd.

"Touchdown," he said.

Despite everything, she missed her friendship with Brenda, and it soured her that she could be replaced so easily.

"Don't hang up," he said, and she did.

Rick assuaged her loneliness at home. She confided in him to a degree, insisting he swear himself to secrecy. And she trusted him, especially after he confessed that he'd been stealing ("a little here, a little there") from Grandma Eileen. (He felt "awful" but now had accumulated enough money for a vacation.)

Esther had trouble imagining her future, but Charlie had a vision, connecting her to him, though not in the matrimonial sense, and including options such as living in Spain or France; and when he was visibly and audibly present—in his words, with his assurances—she believed in such possibilities.

Charlie made her understand that she was a woman and not an object, with complexities and flaws. Listening to him, she would sometimes close her eyes, and no matter what he said, the sound of his voice soothed her. But they didn't even have to talk. Silence could gather for long intervals, and it was as if they were communicating without words.

Charlie believed in her, and that was the only thing that mattered. By surrendering to her feelings, she was able to overcome her doubts. She abandoned herself to a love that would not make her rich.

Every night before she went to sleep, Charlie entered her mind and fell asleep with her. There existed for her a greater worth, beyond her looks, beyond her family, and she floated on hope, far away, where all those materialistic people and their trivial expectations didn't matter.

There began a time of relief: Wearing Charlie Armor, she was no longer as anxious about how to apportion her measure of wealth. Her constant failure to do the socially appropriate thing, her designation by Mary as an "enigma," all of it was thwarted by her ability to see through the hypocrisies, to acknowledge her allotted role as only a sham in a larger sham.

The fact that she was considered a failure didn't press on her with the same devastating weight. Instead of falling into the void of despair that constituted her grief, she avoided thinking about her father. And Uncle Richard.

All her previous worries—bills with their red FINAL NOTICES, Eric, her stunted educational background and lack of professional skills, Grandma Eileen's declining affection—were muffled and blurred by a sweeping euphoria.

She had led, for as long as she could remember, a superficial life, with no idea of what she might truly want.

She still didn't know, but now she might figure it out. Uneducated and ignorant about many things, she was open and aware and willing to learn. And she was reading books that Charlie gave her. She'd finished *The Old Man and the Sea*, by Ernest Hemingway (eh), and now she was reading *The Scarlet Letter*, by Nathaniel Hawthorne (zzzzz . . .), and *Why I Am Not a Christian*, by Bertrand Russell (fun!). All her thoughts and feelings were connected to Charlie, as if his wisdom and strength might pass into her. She was lit up with him.

Who am I? she wondered. *Who am I, really?* Instead of the usual vacuous pit of fear, these queries excited her.

Even if she continued to play her part, to walk and talk and dress like Esther, she was consciously estranging herself from Grandma Eileen and from everything safely familiar. There had been instants, gleams of hope, before, but never an extended amount of time like what she now had with Charlie.

She would think back on the last few weeks as having lived in a haze of carelessness, a fitful optimism—and the day that would come into sharp focus was the one when Jim Dunnels visited her at work, because she would think of it as the first chink in her Charlie Armor.

She was late to work that day, and as she rode the escalator, she watched the Catalina Express in the distance, slicing through the ocean, creating a *V*-like wake of foam. It wasn't until she was with Charlie that she was truly alive, and she went through her days in pleasant anticipation. Then came the heady discussions, the intensity of a love affair in bloom. Everything around her was more profound: Her desire had given rise to deeper yearnings and an aching, boundless curiosity.

How artificial and small-minded the other women looked, riding the escalator. In an hour or so, they'd be sitting at the outdoor tables of restaurants, pecking at low-calorie salads, avoiding starches, and discussing their small dramas under the immense dome of an indifferent sky.

Then it occurred to her that these women had sorrows and confusions, just as she had, but she let the realization slide because it cut through her epiphany, left her less energized.

They were everywhere, hurrying through Fashion Island, buying more and more, acting out their dumb roles, living to impress, constantly upgrading their appearances to compete with each other. It was as if they had all made an agreement to live in a state of selfish and self-centered vanity.

All of it—the superficiality, the materialism, the desperation to stay young and attractive—she wanted to excise from her life like a cancerous tumor. And the only way to rid the ingrained reality would be all at once, in some violent, irreversible manner—like death. The drama of her observations made her keenly awake.

She walked swiftly past Shark Island, allowing a sidelong glance through the window—a glimmer of her reflection, her houndstooth miniskirt and platform pumps: the gamine look, like a young Julie Christie or Jean Seberg.

And past her reflection, she saw the singles at the bar, and a television screen showing waves rolling on a white shore.

She almost ran into an older, squat Mexican woman (or was she Dominican, Guatemalan, Puerto Rican? Esther had never really thought about these things before), inconspicuous in her dun-colored vested uniform with red trim, pushing a cart with her cleaning products, a broom poking out at the side.

"Sorry," Esther said.

"Is okay," the woman answered.

Esther made a point to say, "How are you?"

And the woman was so polite and grandmotherly, with her broken English and strangely bulging eyes—"*Bien, gracias.* Very good, thank you"—that Esther wanted to hold her hand and speak to her longer.

And she knew that Charlie would be pleased when she told him about it later. ("She's so sweet and kind, and everyone just ignores her while she sweeps up their trash. I wonder how she came here—what her story is. Maybe she sends money back to her family, maybe she's illegal, maybe she has three jobs.")

For the first time, she was paying attention to people on the sidelines of wealth. ("The defects of a ruthless society," Charlie had told her, "will always be shown clearly in the plight of those who are disempowered. Much can be learned by observing those who live at its margins.")

The love that had exploded in her soul had made her more generous. She was magnanimous, ignoring physical flaws (the fat people waiting at bus stops, even Nora, with her beaky face). The dimness of their existence would normally frighten her, as if their dour-seeming lives were contagious, but she was open to another perspective now.

Esther was connected because she was different. And when she thought about it, weren't we all connected in a great cosmic sense? How had she not recognized this before? And these people were everywhere—how could she have ignored them?

Underneath was a benevolent gratitude for her higher status. Whatever she'd been doing year after year, she could hardly say that her life was tougher than theirs. They couldn't afford the price of admission to her lifestyle.

By the time she arrived at True Romance, even when her manager, Debbie, pointed out that it was the third time this week that she'd been late, Esther didn't get upset.

In her midforties, Debbie was the slightly haggard single mom of two teenagers. A masculine-looking woman, she was also a Lauren Bacall impersonator, paid to attend corporate events and flirt and entertain the businessmen, but her age was beginning to catch up with her. Debbie was a warning of what Esther might end up like at forty, if she wasn't careful.

True Romance was decorated preemptively for Valentine's Day with blinking red hearts strung along the ceiling and across the shelves, scented candles, and hanging cutout paper Cupids.

A crystal vase of snow-white tulips was near the cash register. Esther pretended to read the card while Debbie watched. She knew that Debbie was too proud to ask whom the tulips were from, and that she pined for flowers of her own.

Unfortunately, they were from Sean ("Give me the word, I'm yours"). When Debbie wasn't looking, Esther ripped up the card, imagining what could have been written had the tulips been from Charlie: *I want to take care of you. Forever. I love you. Always. Love, love, love. You are my love.*

Debbie was walking up the aisle of dresses, moving toward a customer—a good candidate, with her stocky figure and shoulder-padded business suit. She small-talked the woman, setting her up for her sales pitch: "First, I'll visit your house and evaluate your wardrobe, establish an understanding of your personal style and the image you'd like to project. Next, I'll edit your current clothing strategy and introduce new pieces. This will revitalize your look and bring you up to date."

"I'll think about it," the customer said, and she left the store, proving that Debbie had spooked her and that she would do her best not to think about it.

"I'm going to sort through inventory," Debbie said to Esther, not without hostility, and she left for the back room.

Leaning against the register table, Esther looked at the list of debts she'd scribbled on a notepad: "1. Brenda's dress $300 + 2. Towing bill to Grandma Eileen $150 + 3. Visa $14,672." This was enough to discourage her, and she turned the notepad over.

She watched the only customer: an older woman, hair parted down the center of her scalp and fastened in a bun at the back of her head, indifferently fingering a dress. She'd worked long enough at True Romance to recognize that customers were essentially the same: the same insecurities, the same wants, the same hesitations; they were all the same. She felt a belligerence, knowing she might quit whenever she wanted. Anything was possible, as long as she was with Charlie. If the woman asked for help, she could say no. *Does this look good? No, no, no. Go find someone else. I don't want to talk to you.*

And so it was that the door chimed and Esther saw Jim Dunnels, fat crease at his neck. The older woman was leaving, Jim holding the door open for her. He wore a dark suit—probably for its slimming properties—and when he came toward her, she straightened.

"Can I help you?" she asked.

He laughed, the flesh on his neck wobbling.

"Can I help you?" she repeated.

He stood before her with his hands behind his back and his legs a little apart. And then he inclined toward her, as if rising on his toes, and then back down. "Oh," he nodded his head gravely. A line appeared on his forehead. "Hmm. Yes. I think so. I think you can help me."

He stepped close and she took a step back, but she couldn't help considering: *When you close your eyes and kiss a man—even let him enter you—with your eyes closed, it could be any man. Why does it matter? Why not pick Jim and then close my eyes?* ("So, in a way, he owns Fashion Island!")

She turned away toward the cash register and he moved

behind her. She felt his stomach and then, as he pressed into her, the outline of his penis, like a roll of coins against the back of her thigh.

Then he moved away. It was over so quickly, she was already pretending it hadn't happened.

"I'm seeing someone," she said, facing the cash register.

"That's okay."

Her face burned and she turned to him. When she met his eyes, she knew that the shame that showed in her face was exciting him sexually.

Debbie came from the back room, aiming her usual disgruntled expression at Esther, but her mouth morphed into a smile when she saw Jim. And then Esther could see Debbie connecting the dots incorrectly, a slight glance in the direction of the tulips and back to Jim—a clenching in her jaw.

THAT SAME EVENING, instead of going over to Charlie's, Esther had a sudden urge to confront Grandma Eileen. Something about her meeting with Jim Dunnels had set her off track. A terrible pall of futility had settled over her. How hard it was to escape from certain feelings. Her earlier rejoicing over her physical and spiritual communion with Charlie and with the larger world was overshadowed by the supremacy of her financial situation. A future of servitude loomed over her, no matter which way she looked. She needed an assurance of a future that did not include destitution. She couldn't trust Charlie, even though she wanted to.

She was startled to find Captain Ahab's dead body on the sidewalk, near the steps to her door, and she couldn't help but interpret it as a symbol of something, but what?

Ahab was nestled peacefully, so that at first she thought he might be napping in the hazy sunlight. But then, as she came closer, she saw that the hair around his head was mottled with red-black blood, and that near his ear was a tiny black hole, probably where Grandma Eileen had shot him with the pellet gun.

His hindquarters were bent inward, misshapen, like a corkscrew. Had a car hit him? Had he lived on, for weeks, with a pellet in his head, only to come back to her doorstep to finally die?

His back end was soiled, either from dirt or from his own excrement, and flies were buzzing there. His tail was gone, but then she saw that he was lying on it. There was a fly on his lip and another fly at his eyeball, which was open and staring vacantly up at her.

She went inside and called the Humane Society, and as she spoke into the phone, she felt the tears collecting at her lids. One slid down her cheek, pooled at her upper lip, and she took it with her tongue.

For some reason, she felt a welling of tenderness for Ahab. And guilt pressed at her, knowing that Uncle Richard had envisaged a long life for Ahab, and that she had let him down.

She remembered her father's telling her how Uncle Richard had tried to work for his brother Gurney: He'd drive into the parking lot of Gurney's offices, park his car, and just sit there with his head bent over the steering wheel.

"Would he come inside?" she'd asked.

"No."

"What would he do?"

"He'd stay in his car, sometimes for hours, with his head hanging. Finally, he'd drive away."

Why had he loved Ahab so much? *Where's the bar in this place?* she heard him say. *I've been looking all over for the bar.*

She put a white kitchen garbage bag over Ahab's carcass and

waited for the Animal Control people to come and dispose of his body.

To her surprise, she found she wanted to pray for him, to say a few words on his behalf. She fought the impulse but finally gave in, knowing that no one was there to judge her.

"I'm sorry," she said, staring at the lumpy white garbage bag. "You were a good cat. You just wanted to be loved. You were scary. You can be with Uncle Richard now." The tears were moving freely, and she felt foolish but relieved.

The smell bothered her—she was sure now that it was excrement and not just dirt at his back end—but she knew that she had to deal with it only temporarily.

"I don't understand anything," she continued. "I don't know." Her grief was turning self-indulgent, so she stopped.

When the small white Animal Control truck appeared, she waved for them and went back inside. She didn't want to watch them scoop Ahab away. Besides, there was nothing she could do for him now. But she decided not to tell anyone. Partially, she was ashamed, implicated, and she didn't want others to know.

But the main reason was that she didn't want Grandma Eileen to know that Ahab was dead. She had a defiant sense of vindication imagining Grandma Eileen imagining Ahab continuing to live, or, at the very least, Grandma Eileen questioning Ahab's existence, never knowing for sure whether he lived or had died. She was sure that this was what Uncle Richard would have wanted, and she owed it to him.

For a long time, she stood at her balcony and watched the ocean. It began to rain. Big drops fell on her shoulders; the part in her hair became damp. She watched the rain pucker the ocean until it became steady, and then she went back inside. She called Charlie and told him that she had a headache and wouldn't be coming over.

"Look, Esther," he said. "If I thought there was anything I could do, if you want me to come over right now and talk to your crazy grandma—"

"No. Well, maybe. Well, no. There isn't anything you can do."

"Have you ever seen *Planet of the Apes*?"

"Yes," she said.

"It's like they're all apes and you're the only human."

She smiled, knowing that he was pleased on the other line, envisioning her smile. She wished to halt time and then backpedal to the past, and then stay there with Charlie, forever, believing that the present and the future promised grief. Jim Dunnels and Captain Ahab had thrown a bright spotlight on her circumstances. She knew that what she felt for Charlie was love and that it held all sorts of consequences. Over the phone, there was the reality of their not being able to touch, and it lessened her confidence.

"I had lunch with the dean today," he said.

"How was it?"

"Fine; I'll tell you about it when you're feeling better. Listen: The important thing is that you stay strong."

"All right," she said. "I will."

She sat on her bed for the longest time and went over what she would say to Grandma Eileen. ("You see, I never meant to disappoint you. I need you to believe in me.") Most of the time, she ended up giving in to Grandma Eileen—the most convenient way to live—becoming the version of herself that met with her grandmother's approval. But it was becoming more and more difficult to bend herself to Grandma Eileen's will.

Her hopes and dreams revolved around her—she felt she could touch them with her fingers. She thought about how Charlie liked to tilt her head back, feeling for the curve of her throat below her ear, tracing with his fingertips and then kissing her there.

The memory strengthened her, and she began to form in her mind exactly what she needed to say to Grandma Eileen. Surely she could reason with her grandmother. She decided to take notes; she could look at her list to help. She kept it short and to the point:

1. I'm sorry about what happened with Captain Ahab.
2. It was wrong of me to leave the cat.
3. I'm sorry that your BMW was towed.
4. I don't want to disappoint you.
5. Please understand.
6. I need to make sure that you don't cut me out of your will.
7. I need your blessing.
8. I'm sorry I threw away the sculpture—I know it was a gift.

She crossed out the references to Captain Ahab, and then rewrote the list without mention of the cat.

When she knocked on Grandma Eileen's bedroom door, it was Rick who answered. With exquisite control, Rick managed to send Esther a welcoming and affectionate signal without jeopardizing his allegiance to her grandmother. The room was cast in a bluish light from the television. They were watching a show called *I Should Be Dead* that, through dramatized reenactments, chronicled near-death experiences.

Grandma Eileen was lying at the side of her bed with her back to the headboard, and her gout foot was elevated and propped on pillows. The bruised wedges beneath her eyes had settled to a faded yellow-green, and her nose was no longer taped. She ignored Esther, and when Rick asked, she refused to turn the volume down with her remote.

The male voice-over was loud and distracting: "The will to survive despite insurmountable obstacles . . . Don't panic . . .

Flying off the handle can be a death sentence." Esther wondered if Rick had been lying in bed beside Grandma Eileen before he'd answered the door, as the arrangement of pillows and bedspread suggested.

In only a few seconds, she was able to determine as she watched the television that a man had crashed his plane in the African bush and had shattered his legs. His ankles felt like they were going to explode inside his laced boots, and the voice-over informed viewers that if he didn't get his boots off, the swelling would make self-amputation his only option. A close-up showed what appeared to be ferocious red ants making their way toward the man, who was keeled over and screaming in anguish. The camera angled in on the impossibility of undoing the elaborately laced boots.

"I think it's almost over," Rick said.

The man began dragging himself to a thorny tree, ants crawling on his arms, eating him, and he finally reached the tree, leaving a dusty trail in the dirt; he was attempting to push himself up and balance, when the screen, with a last twinkling glimmer, went black. Grandma Eileen held the remote, and for the first time in days, she spoke to Esther: "What do you want?"

"I need to talk to you."

Rick stole a glance at Esther, and she saw that he was afraid that Grandma Eileen might detect signs of his divided loyalty. Without saying anything, he left the bedroom, shutting the door quietly behind him.

"Well," said Grandma Eileen, "hurry up."

The blood rushed to Esther's heart and she was afraid. Instead of speaking, she tried to hand Grandma Eileen her notes, but Grandma Eileen wouldn't take the list, so she just set the paper in her lap.

"It explains," she said.

"So what."

"It explains."

"Who cares," Grandma Eileen said, staring at the black television screen; the tip of her tongue peeked between her lips like a pink wet finger.

"I need to talk to you," Esther said, trying to summon Charlie into the half-darkness of the room. To feel him in every sound, in herself—to be strong. But in his physical absence, a thousand doubts seemed to overtake her. She remembered the fly at Ahab's eyeball, the empty stare, and her heart gave a wild jerk.

"I don't care," Grandma Eileen said, turning the television back on with her remote, "what's in your goddamn letter." Her cheek was blended into her neck, and her neck swelled over the collar of her flannel nightgown. She rested the remote on her belly, swatting away the paper so that it landed on the floor.

Esther saw the credits for *I Should Be Dead* rolling across the screen, set to a bombastic soundtrack of horn instruments. Sweat collected at her armpits and her guts tightened as the problem became clear: She wasn't ruthless enough to get what she felt she deserved, and, no matter how illogical or unfair, power would always be on the side of money.

She leaned over, picked up her paper. Her interactions with Grandma Eileen had the effect of casting down her courage. When she stood back up, she was surprised to discover that she was dizzy. For a second, everything was blurred, but then her focus came back.

"Horseshit," Grandma Eileen said. She said something else, but Esther couldn't hear over the volume of the television. But then Grandma Eileen repeated her statement, as if to make sure its meaning was understood: "You don't matter and it doesn't matter."

7

"I'LL TELL YOU what, Charles: We've never received so many letters from students," said J. D. Galbraith, dean of Orange County Community College, crouching to sit in a corner booth at Shark Island. He smiled and scooted over to make room for Charlie, who had won the award for most influential professor by a landslide. A medium-size wiry man in his early sixties, Mr. Galbraith had thin hair the color of pale sand, and his face had the wrinkled, perpetual tan of a dedicated golfer's. He wore a dark blue suit, no tie. "These students really pulled for you, and I didn't think they cared about anything besides watching their MTV. It's quite a thing."

Charlie sat in the booth, his slacks gliding against the faux leather. The restaurant was bustling with the lunch crowd. Servers rushed from table to table, carrying trays with plates, frosted glasses, milk shakes, and wicker baskets lined with waxy paper and filled with french fries. The entire staff, including the busboys, wore Hawaiian-print shirts, Bermuda-style shorts, and high-top tennis shoes.

Charlie took a sip of his ice water in a plastic glass large enough for a giant and considered the coincidence that he was at Shark

Island. When Mr. Galbraith had invited him to lunch, of course he'd said yes, and in the air-conditioned cool of Mr. Galbraith's Mercedes, he'd deferred the decision of where to dine.

Their table faced the bar window, and Charlie thought about what he might tell Esther tonight. (*I was facing that same window where I first looked in and saw you, and I had to listen to this pompous-ass go on and on, when all I really wanted to do was think about you.*) Although his own voice in his ears sounded smug, he tried to look directly into Mr. Galbraith's eyes to convey his sincerity.

"Students appreciate when someone treats them like adults, and that's all I do. I treat them with respect and give them the consideration they deserve. It makes them want to step up to the plate and be adults. It's pretty simple."

Mr. Galbraith wagged his head, indicating his amazement. He had an excited look about him and an unnerving tendency to stare. A drooping and broken palm frond bobbed at his shoulder.

"Well, I appreciate what you're saying, Charles, I really do, but you're being modest. How do you manage to keep their gnatlike attention in this day and age? I have two teenage daughters, and all they want is to be entertained and go shopping." He flapped out his napkin and placed it in his lap. "I can't get them to read a book."

"I don't have teenagers, Mr. Galbraith, but my experience has been that my students are competent when given the opportunity."

"Call me J. D." Mr. Galbraith's eyes flashed around the restaurant. He made eye contact with a waitress and summoned her by lifting a hand, snapping his fingers, and waving.

("I mean, what could I say?" Charlie would tell Esther. "That Shark Island is a pretentious, mediocre restaurant that caters to idiocy? He looks like the Channel Two weathermen, with that leathery tan and the way he dresses—like he's going to start telling me about high-pressure fronts. And he kept going on about kids and MTV. He probably hasn't read a book besides Tom Clancy or Dean Koontz, but he's dean of a college! I mean, come on.")

Their waitress, an anorexic blond with a red plastic name tag pinned to her chest—HEATHER—seemed beleaguered, despite her dutifully cheerful presentation of the specials. Mr. Galbraith was condescending ("Hello, Heather. You want a good tip, sweetheart? Ignore all your other tables and take care of us"), and Charlie could see that he would be the type of customer who thought his joking was in good fun, but in reality demanded that everyone present acknowledge his power.

Charlie tried to compensate by smiling sympathetically, and Heather smiled back, her eyes locked into his for an invigorating, sexually charged instant.

Mr. Galbraith ordered a masculine Heineken, and Charlie's one open act of defiance was to order what Esther would—a sour apple martini, at which Mr. Galbraith chuckled tolerantly.

As Heather walked away, they watched her bony backside in her shorts, a plum-size gap between her thighs.

"She's a skinny little thing," Mr. Galbraith mused, and Charlie shifted uncomfortably. Anorexic women made him squeamish: sexy even though they shouldn't be—like gawky girls on the cusp of adolescence, disturbingly breakable.

"So I hear you're a golfing man," Mr. Galbraith said, pouring his beer into a chilled plastic mug, a smile beaming from his face. His eyes were an empty pale blue. He set the bottle on the table and wrapped both hands around his mug. "When you hit that ball in the right place and drive it down the fairway"—his hand left his mug and made a sweeping motion over the table;

he made a noise like a soft whistle, the tip of his tongue near his front teeth—"there's nothing like it in this world."

Charlie was relieved that they had a common interest, and for several moments they spoke about the elusive nature of golf, and how, in many respects, golf was a metaphor for life.

"It's three percent mechanics and ninety-seven percent psychological," Charlie said.

Mr. Galbraith nodded. "I understand what you're saying, Charles, but I just wish I could lower my handicap."

"Now, this is only my experience, J. D., and I don't mean to imply that I know what's best, but for me it's all about coming to understand my place and learning to transcend tensions."

Mr. Galbraith nodded his head approvingly.

"Again, this is just my experience. The main lesson is that I should live for the moment and not let the bad shots bother me. Think about it: You're trying to put a tiny ball in a tiny hole on an expansive course, set with sand traps and bodies of water; you can't take that seriously. There's a tremendous amount of humor."

"I suppose you're right, Charles. I've never thought about it that way."

"And really, golf encourages Eastern thought to go with our Judeo-Christian tradition."

"I'm not sure I follow," Mr. Galbraith said.

"Well, let's see. It's a happy medium. Think about the golf swing itself: We're all trying to hit a straight shot with a circular swing."

Mr. Galbraith's bottom lip jutted out in thought.

"The more I analyze my shots," Charlie said, "my techniques, the further away I can get from their true essence. Besides, no matter how much you practice, no two shots are ever alike."

"I see what you're saying, Charles."

"Life is all about paradox, and golf teaches you to live with absurdity."

Mr. Galbraith laughed good-naturedly. "I'll tell you what, Charles: I appreciate what you're saying, I really do, but if I could make it through a round without blowing my top, that would be a spiritual thing."

Charlie laughed. Mr. Galbraith reminded him of his father—a certain appealing affability, a permissive acceptance.

"I'll tell you what's spiritual," Charlie said. "Think about the quiet on Pelican Hill, maybe a few sprinklers going, making it smell like wet grass, late afternoon, five-ish, with those incredible shadows, those shades of green, the ocean as a backdrop, sky overhead, and there you are, walking along the fairway, a few clubs in your bag."

"That's nice, Charles. That's very nice."

They were quiet, appreciating their shared love. Charlie's martini was tart, and before he was halfway done, Mr. Galbraith was snapping his fingers and ordering another round.

With the flush from his second sour apple martini and Mr. Galbraith's appreciative reception, he was enjoying himself. (*It wasn't so bad*, he imagined himself telling Esther. *I mean, the guy's just human, when you think about it. Trying to make his way, like the rest of us. And he's charming, in this everyman kind of way, which is fascinating. I'm sure he's spent a lifetime cultivating that persona. It's how he got to be where he is.*)

The sounds of the restaurant and Mr. Galbraith's loud voice resonated into one excited drone, and Charlie's vision was a colorful blend of attractive people and palm trees and surfers riding waves on television screens.

Mr. Galbraith's recounting of his recent hole in one on the fourth hole of Pelican Hill had a staged quality. His anecdote about golfing with Billy Graham was long and rambling ("I'll never forget how Billy wanted to walk instead of using a golf cart, saying he preferred 'a good constitutional' where he could observe nature firsthand") and held great personal significance, because his eyes misted.

And then, in the reflection of the window, Charlie was distracted by a mirror image of Jennifer Platt's back, the *V* of her silky dress plunging at her spine. Jennifer was sitting at the same barstool where he'd first seen Esther.

A resurgence of humiliation came over him as he remembered his fumbling attempts at seduction, the feel of her nipple between his fingertips, the underwire of her bra pressing into his hand; but then he remembered that Jennifer harbored no ill feelings, and besides, it had happened a few months ago.

Jennifer's barstool turned so that he could see a leg crossed over the other and the side of her face—she was smiling rapturously.

Her arm extended, and a cluster of women congregated around her hand. Even from the booth, he could hear the women disguising their envy ("Oh my God! Jennifer! It's just so gorgeous") in what appeared to be exaggerated vocal admiration of an enormous diamond engagement ring.

"Now, that's a happy girl," Mr. Galbraith said, leaning back into the booth. In a singsong voice, he added, "Somebody's getting married."

"She's a former student. Plans on studying sports medicine."

"By the size of her ring, looks like she won't be studying much besides the inside of a Neiman Marcus."

And then Jennifer, as if in extrasensory perception, turned her head and aimed a brilliant smile in their direction. She rose a few inches from her barstool, hand raised, flashing her engagement ring and pointing at it.

I'm engaged, she mouthed. *Can you believe it?*

Charlie smiled back his congratulations and she waved. He

raised his martini glass in a toast and she followed suit. Then she was swept back into the fawning admiration of the women.

"What a cutie," Mr. Galbraith said. "Good for her. I can't wait for the time when my daughters bring home some good news. Of course, their weddings will cost a fortune—they'll make sure of that—but after they're married . . . phew!"

Charlie laughed in pleasant commiseration.

Mr. Galbraith bent his head over his clasped hands, as if in thought. When he looked up, he was smiling, but there was a glint in his eyes. "Now tell me about this class"—he made his voice authoritative—"Discrimination in Society."

"Well, J. D., the class is actually called Social Class & Inequality."

Mr. Galbraith ducked his head, as if to conceal his expression. "Okay then, Charles, tell me about Social Class & Inequality."

Charlie wondered if he had imagined the note of sarcasm.

"Well, J. D., as a matter of fact, what I'm trying to do is get these kids to think about their privilege, probably for the first time in their lives. I'm attempting to show the larger context."

Mr. Galbraith met this information with skeptical silence.

"I'm teaching these students about what it means to be living in an environment that doesn't acknowledge these things."

Mr. Galbraith pensively buttered a thick slice of bread.

"You see, I think it's important to confront students, make them think about their objectives. It's good for them to have their ideas challenged."

Mr. Galbraith nodded and chewed on his crust.

"And my greatest hope is that when they finish my class—and I know this sounds idealistic—they'll be more empathetic."

Mr. Galbraith nodded while he continued to chew. After a pause, he said, "That's a noble objective, Charles, but in some respects—excuse me for saying this—shouldn't we enjoy what we have and not feel guilty? After all, life is short! Some of us have worked damn hard. And it's not our fault. It doesn't make us bad people!"

"I understand what you're saying, J. D., I really do. But most of my students will end up with a stunted maturity."

Mr. Galbraith was unconvinced, his mouth set in a grimace. "I don't mean to be disrespectful, Charles," he said, "but it sounds to me like you're promoting socialism. And we know how that worked out for those Russians, East Germans, Chinese—oh, and let's not forget those North Koreans. To paraphrase Winston Churchill: The only way for all of us to be equal is for us all to be equally poor."

"That's not what I'm talking about," Charlie said.

Mr. Galbraith smiled, and Charlie had the sensation that he was deciding how to change the subject. But Charlie didn't want to be dismissed. He was contemplating what to say next when he saw Paul Rice enter the bar. Paul walked to Jennifer, and one of his shaky hands lodged itself at the bare skin of her back. He put his other hand on her shoulder, and then he leaned in for a prolonged public kiss.

"The lucky groom," Mr. Galbraith said, taking on the voice of an announcer. He leaned in and, in a tone of sober responsibility, added, "Paul's father is one of our most generous supporters; I'd better offer my congratulations." He rose from the booth and walked to the bar.

Charlie watched as Mr. Galbraith shook hands with Paul, kissed Jennifer on the cheek, and, after a moment of smiling conversation, gestured toward Charlie.

All heads turned in his direction.

And, just as Charlie had feared, Mr. Galbraith led Paul and Jennifer to their booth. When Charlie rose to meet them, his napkin fell to the floor. Halfway down to pick it up, he saw that

Paul had extended one of his unsteady hands. He decided to leave his napkin, lifting to a full stand and partaking in a sweaty-palmed, aggressive handshake.

They stood near the corner booth in the direct path of the servers and busboys, forced to navigate around them. Mr. Galbraith made the introductions. Jennifer's silky dress was knotted at the small of her back, a slit at the side, ending at her thigh. She pretended not to be that familiar with Charlie.

"What can I tell you?" she said, explaining the speed of her engagement. "Love at first sight. We were both nursing broken hearts, and then we found each other. I thank God every night. It's so true, you know: When one door closes, another door opens." She faced Paul, took his hand in hers. "Isn't that right, honey?" Her tone carried a hint of urgency.

There were pink notches at the sides of Paul's nose, markings from his sunglasses, which were propped on his head. "That's right," he said, but when he looked at Charlie's sour apple martini, his face took on an afflicted expression. His eyes lifted, taking in Charlie.

"Honey?" Jennifer said.

Paul continued to stare at Charlie, sending him a clear message: *I know who you are and I know that you're with Esther—that woman broke my heart, chewed it up, and spat it out, and she can do the same to you.*

Charlie dreaded uncomfortable situations. He did his best to disguise his anxiety with a smile. Despite everything, he felt an allegiance to Paul because of Paul's distress.

Jennifer had become visibly grave, holding Paul's hand. But then Paul shook his hand from her grip, tucked his fingers in his pocket, and moved half an inch away from her, enough for everyone to understand that whatever he was suffering from, he wanted to be alone with it.

Jennifer's eyes brimmed with tears, but she was maintaining (*Do you know what I mean?* Charlie could hear her saying. *Do you know what I mean? Know what I mean?*). Paul continued to stare at Charlie, and Charlie experienced a weighty ambivalence: With Esther's complicated past and complicated present, she guaranteed him complications.

Sensing the uncomfortable nature of the meeting and perhaps wishing he hadn't orchestrated it, Mr. Galbraith at once launched into a distracting joke: "I was golfing the other day with my friend Chuck. I got home late and my wife asked, 'What took you so long?' 'That was the worst game of golf ever,' I said. 'Chuck hit a hole in one on the first tee and immediately keeled over dead from a heart attack.' 'That's awful!' she said. 'I know,' I said, 'it was hit the ball, drag Chuck, hit the ball, drag Chuck, hit the ball, drag Chuck.'"

Charlie laughed along with Jennifer, and he noticed how Paul barely smiled. But the joke had fulfilled its purpose as a conduit to a smooth exit, and when Paul and Jennifer walked back to their positions at the bar, Charlie was relieved.

Her thin wrists quivering, Heather delivered their king size–proportioned plates—steaming cheeseburger and fish tacos—and her appearance seemed perfectly timed. They ordered another round of drinks, and a natural silence developed as they began to eat.

With each bite of his fish tacos, Charlie felt the sobering effects of food. He was grateful to Mr. Galbraith: He hadn't asked Charlie to explain the earlier tension with Paul and Jennifer.

He decided that Mr. Galbraith, in some respects, was a class act. But he reminded himself not to succumb to Mr. Galbraith, knowing that their worldviews were fundamentally at odds.

Mr. Galbraith used his knife to slice his cheeseburger into quarters. He concentrated on his meal; between bites and chews, he wiped his napkin over his mouth, icy blue eyes revealing nothing. The silence wasn't uncomfortable, and Charlie was certain that Mr. Galbraith had more to say, that he'd brought him to lunch for a specific reason, but there was no rush.

And then, with a fork balanced over his plate, shredded cabbage and carrot from the coleslaw caught in the prongs, Mr. Galbraith said, "Let me tell you something, Charles. Between you and me, you understand—this doesn't leave the table. My job is basically that of a salesman, and it's not that different from yours." He nodded as if in agreement with what he'd already stated. Then he set his fork on his plate, indicating that what he had to say was far more important than eating.

Charlie chewed lettuce and tortilla and a piece of tomato, keeping his eyes on Mr. Galbraith.

After wiping his mouth with his napkin, Mr. Galbraith continued, "Last year, we were able to redo our basketball courts and the swimming pool. Did you know that? All because I golfed five times with a certain somebody who will remain unnamed but who willingly made a sizable donation." His head made an unmistakable nod in the direction of Paul. "All for the students. And that's where we're the same. Because what you're doing, Charles, is also expanding students' worlds. And what I'm here to tell you, Charles, is that that is no small feat."

Charlie took a sip of his ice water to wash down his food. He ran his napkin across his mouth. "I appreciate that, J. D. I really do."

Mr. Galbraith crossed his fork and knife over his plate in an *X*, and then pushed his plate a few inches away from him on the table.

"Well, I'm sure you do, Charles. I'm sure you do. But it feels like you've been hiding. How could we have missed you all these years?"

"Now, J. D." Charlie was shaking his head. It was unconscionable for Mr. Galbraith to take any kind of blame. "It's not your fault. I mean, as an adjunct, I had time to figure out some things on my own."

Charlie knew that Mr. Galbraith was about to offer him a promotion—it felt like cosmic timing. Charlie's father had called him this morning, letting him know that a "large check" was on its way (he hadn't indicated the amount) to help Charlie "settle down, buy a home, and start thinking more seriously about your future."

"I mean it, J. D., there's no hard feelings." While he certainly didn't disparage the pay increase and respect that came with a promotion, a rise in position at a second-rate community college wasn't his ideal. But he could feel his ego pawing at the idea anyway.

Mr. Galbraith was in sober contemplation, his mouth set. "Well, Charles, it's about time your accomplishments were recognized."

"Well, thank you, J. D. I don't know what to say, except that I'm very honored and I feel that I'm ready for the responsibility."

"I'm sure you are, Charles."

Mr. Galbraith smiled, a triumphant, we're-together-on-this smile. His arm came across the table, over the basket of french fries, freckled age spots merged on the back of his hand, and Charlie gripped it in his own; they shook on it.

Charlie kept his grip firm, the way his father had taught him, and despite how he had struggled to separate from his family, it was his father he thought about, imagining what it would be like to have his wholehearted approval, finally, after all these years.

◈ 8 ◈

ERIC GRIPPED THE sand with his toes, the sea sucking against his feet, retreating and bubbling, a strand of seaweed catching at his ankle and then slipping away. The motion of the tide drawing back over the sand sounded like water sliding over pebbles. His jeans were soaked and heavy, rolled to his calves. The sun was a bright yellow monster, chewing at his head, neck, shoulders, so he kept his gaze down.

He saw the sand crabs burrowing into the slick surface, a clicking noise, invisible except for the tiny dark dents they pressed into the shoreline. He leaned over, scooped wetness, and watched a translucent, iridescent quarter-size shape dig up through the sand in his palm.

He and Esther used to collect sand crabs in a red bucket and then release them back to the sand. The sand crab in his hand looked like a little piece of cloud. In its shape and color, he saw the domed skylight above his father's bed: the color of lead when it was overcast or foggy, dividing into squiggles with rain, and, when it was sunny, sending a shimmering square of sunlight swaying onto the bedspread, or the wall, or the curtain.

And for a moment, he was a kid again, lying in the big bed

with Esther, underneath the skylight. He saw the round perfection of Esther's shoulder, loving her so much, loving their mom. The smallest memory sending tremors, toppling his heart: his mom wearing her blue nightgown (she was under the covers, he couldn't see her nightgown, but he knew she was wearing it), her shoulder the only thing visible above the bedspread. But it was Esther's shoulder, with its cluster of freckles. She was the one who had found their mom dead from an overdose, but that was only because he knew already—he knew, he knew—and he wouldn't go near her bed.

But he'd called 911, like on television when something awful happens, and he was in her closet when the police arrived, and then the paramedics, and even a fire truck; and for a long time, no one could find him. Her shoes, her smell, her clothes rustling the top of his head. Most of the clothes had plastic bags over them.

He tried to ignore the noises, but he knew that the men were taking his mom away on some kind of trolley with wheels. He could hear Esther crying, and he shut his eyes, forced it away. When they found him and made him come out, the sunlight was pale and gray, and it was already morning.

Their mom had loved him (he remembered everything, even though he wasn't supposed to), but she'd abandoned him anyway, abandoned Esther, even though she hadn't meant to. Esther didn't remember. He had decided long ago to leave the memories inside, where they couldn't cause more harm. And they were his memories, no one else's. Maybe he was hoarding them, feeding off them. The psychologists and psychiatrists, his father, all of them trying to find out what he knew, what he remembered, and he wouldn't tell them.

He and Esther had been taken to Grandma Eileen's house. And then, finally, to her son's house ("I'm your dad," he told them, and then he adopted them to prove it). All through their childhood, the bay had been their playground: hunting for crabs in the crevices of the rocks, clusters of them, with their shiny backs—when they moved, it was sideways, with their pincers raised; poking their fingers in the soft, fleshy centers of the sea anemones, tucked in the rocks—purple, gray, green, red—so that they closed up like the petals of a flower, but quickly, like mouths sucking at their fingers; at low tide, walking through the clearish-green bay water, up to their thighs, heads down, in search of starfish and sand dollars—when Esther walked ahead of him, he stepped in her dissolving footprints.

They'd see the shadows of sand sharks moving over the sand, disappearing behind rocks or bunches of flowering seaweed. He loved the spiky-skinned starfish—yellow, orange, red, pink—with rows of tube feet on their undersides, growing back missing limbs, mouths and stomachs caving inward at their centers. The dead ones were dry and brittle, arms curling upward, colors faded (they collected them, set them on Grandma Eileen's deck—until she threw them away because they smelled).

Sometimes they'd spot a stingray, its outline against the sand, the same color, half-buried, and they'd throw a rock or a shell, watch it rise like a space ship and swoop away, tail flicking a pattern in the sand.

One time, Esther stepped over a stingray but Eric's foot landed on it—like stepping on a giant lip. The tail kicked up, stung him in the heel. It felt like a bite and then it stabbed all the way up his leg, into his chest. The stingray lunged away like a ghost, leaving a cloud of sand. He ran back to Grandma Eileen's house, Esther following. His feet didn't feel like they were touching the ground, an electric current of pain running through him, making him powerful.

When they got to the house, Grandma Eileen thought it was

Esther who had been stung. ("Why are you crying?" she asked her, when she saw that Eric was the one who was hurt.) He soaked in a bathtub with baking powder; he passed out for a little while. When he came to, he was on Grandma Eileen's bed, on a thick terry towel, another towel covering his "private area," and his foot and leg throbbed. She let him drink as many Cokes as he wanted, and he and Esther watched a marathon of *The Twilight Zone* on the big-screen TV for hours, while he burped from the carbonation, until eventually the pain subsided.

The memory moved through Eric, and then he saw the pale green wallpaper of their mom's bedroom, and their mom in bed, fixed there, at the edge, close to the bedside table, lying on her side with her knees crooked inward, her shoulder above the bedspread (Esther's shoulder), and her hip creating a small mountain under the covers.

Before she overdosed, she took a hot shower, the steam thick, and when she opened the bathroom door, it crawled out. He sat cross-legged on the floor and watched her towel off; then she rubbed lotion all over her body, everywhere, so that her skin glistened. The mirror was coated with steam and she wiped at it with her palm, created a circle of visibility, but it clouded up again. Her hair hung in wet curls between her shoulder blades. She slipped on her blue nightgown—a sheer material—a dark patch between her legs, and the circle of her nipples still moist with lotion.

Little man, their mom used to call him: "Come here, little man." She was always in her bed.

"Get out of bed, Mommy! Get up! Please!"

He spooned Chef Boyardee ravioli from a can when Esther had no teeth, because there wasn't any milk (babies drank milk) and he didn't know what to give her; he knew enough to smush the ravioli into a mush with the base of the spoon, but when she started choking, her face turning purple, he thought he might have accidentally killed her—*Oh, God!, Please breathe.* But then a fingertip-size piece of ravioli catapulted from her mouth, landing on his chest.

"Hand me my cigarettes, little man. I love you, little man."

"Mommy. I love you, Mommy. I'll take care of you, Mommy. I love you."

"You're my little man."

She let him sleep with her; he breathed her in and became her. Her chest and legs and stomach pressed against him and he could smell her: nicotine and a coppery smell, reminding him of blood. She whispered, told him stories. With gleaming eyes, she murmured things and he pretended to understand. Sometimes she looked serious—angry—and he was frightened.

"He thinks he can pay me off," she said. "One kind of loneliness," she said. "I traded one kind of loneliness for another." She said that she was nothing. They were nothing. They were nothing to him except trouble. Her brown eyes filled with sorrow and pain, and he felt it beating into him. Pounding into him.

Yet she loved him with her sorrow, and her love had a power and rhythm—it was unstoppable.

No one could see it or take it away. He wanted to yell: *Her love is unstoppable!* But he let the waves and sky yell for him. And the words flew up and over him, carried everywhere.

He pressed the tip of his finger to the sand crab's covering, gently, and it felt like he was touching the tip of his own nose.

He looked up—the tide was creeping in, and the ocean seemed to curve around him, ready to overtake him. It was as if the ocean were holding back, gaining strength. He could feel it breathing, surging.

Whenever his mom fell asleep beside him or pressed her lips

onto his face or rubbed his back, he felt her history being passed into his body. And once, she showed him a photograph of a man: "I am a secret," she said, holding the photo, "and you and your sister are secrets"—letting him see for only a second—"and secrets are invisible, we do not exist."; then she ripped it up, let the pieces fall on the bedspread.

But he had already memorized it: The man wore a blue and green–striped tie; he sat behind a desk, his big hands folded somberly before him; his head was tilted to the left; he was squinting; he wasn't smiling.

The same squint, the same hands, and the same tie of the man in the photograph on Grandma Eileen's bedside table.

Eric met him only once: Gurney's fat fingers sliding through his hair, an empty stare. And then, a few years after that, they were at a funeral: Grandpa Gurney had died from an explosion in his head.

ERIC FELT A tickling on his palm, the sand crab sidling to the edge of his hand. *Careful, little man*, he said or thought or thought and said, said and thought—at the same time—he wasn't sure. Regardless, the words surrounded them, benevolent and sad.

He kneeled over, let the sand crab crawl off his skin, and he watched it burrow, deep, deeper, until the crab and its hole blotted themselves out.

Gone. Sorrow climbed up through his lungs, reached for his throat. *Where'd you go, little man?* But he let his grief be smothered by a numb euphoria, like a damp towel spread over a flame.

He stood and watched the water in the distance, where there was only openness, stretching out and out and out. The water looked as solid as steel, and he shuddered at the thought that a propeller could cut through it, like a scalpel through skin. He touched the scar on his abdomen, under his shirt, the thickness against his fingertips, remembering Scott and his father standing near the doorway of his hospital room. Scott's shiny blond hair, slick and combed over his head. Scott had let him try pot, and then cocaine and Ecstasy. His father had blamed Scott; it had given them something more to fight over. But it wasn't Scott's fault: the opiates were what soothed Eric, finally brought him home.

A LARGE WAVE pushed itself upward, smashed down, crashed and heaved, and it came to Eric, slapped against his thighs, wisps of spray all over. He steadied himself, his toes gripped the sand, but he could feel his body waving like a tree limb in the wind.

When he had regained his balance, he licked the salt at his lip, tasted it all the way inside him, and the water thundered in his ears, a rushing noise. Sunlight reflected and broke against the surface all around him, multiplying everywhere, like looking through a diamond.

He closed his eyes to it—it was too much—and sounds rushed through him: seagulls and waves slapping against each other, and a kid yelling happily, and then another kid (or the same kid?) laughing.

All over his skin, even inside him, burning through him, was the blissful and terrifying mix of heroin and ocean, smoothing his memories, taking away all of his humiliations, his thousands and thousands of failures—all of it whirling free, like the clouds of spray sliding away in the wind. *Little man, little man, little man.* The best part was the kid's laugh—it continued to echo through him, and when he opened his eyes, a wave was wide and soaring, the blue at its center caving inward, and then it stretched and yawned into foam.

He wanted to curl up like a seashell and dream and not think not think not think not think. Already he was aware that his high would not last. And he might get dragged out with the tide, sucked away. He thought of the seaweed and the shells, pulled back to the ocean, deep down, where it was dark and cool.

The sunlight was naked and ugly, and it made him feel unprotected and exposed; he wanted to take his hand and shove the sun away.

Above the shore on the beach was his shaded space, underneath the lifeguard stand. He turned, saw the jacket Esther had given him, waiting in the sprawl of shade. The fur collar looked like a squirrel staring back at him.

There was no lifeguard because it was still winter, and he felt the relief of not having to worry about a lifeguard telling him to leave. Seagulls were swooping, flashes of white, toward the trash bin, where he'd vomited pizza and beer.

A pizza box was next to the jacket, half-buried in the sand, and he knew that inside the box were the cash and his drugs and his lighter and his spoon and his needle. He didn't want to remember the bank teller's face, because not only had he hurt her, but it reminded him of the other girl's face, the one he'd given his last $20 to; that was why he'd robbed the bank (although he knew it wasn't that simple, but that was what he needed to believe).

She was with another girl, they were smoking cigarettes—so young!—and they'd come up to him, and immediately she'd handed her friend her cigarette and then put her hands all over him, and he knew that all she wanted was his money, that she'd say she'd give him a blow job or lick him or fuck him if he gave her some money. And he wanted to tell her, *Take it, take my money. You're beautiful. What are you doing? Why are you doing this?* Her friend stepped back, smiling. He knew that he smelled and that he was disgusting, that he had bad teeth, bad feet, bad fingernails, bad etc., etc., etc. He could see it in the girl's friend's eyes, and he looked away, concentrated instead on the white-pink part in the young girl's hair. And when her face tilted up, he met all the sorrow that waited for him in her eyes. He fell inside her, and she let him.

Her fingers were in his jeans pocket, and when she found the $20 bill, her hand hesitated for a second, and then her fingers dug into his thigh. He hardened, wanting her fingers to reach him, to wrap around him. Just a sad-eyed girl, a little creature, so young, and he wanted her to kiss his mouth, to feel her tongue. He wanted to grab her and shake her and tell her not to rot away.

She and her friend left with his $20, laughing and talking, ignoring him, and he didn't get a blow job or a kiss or a lick or a fuck, so he lay beneath the bus stop and jacked off, hand down his pants, eyes squeezed shut. Just to make her absence bearable. *Thump thump thump*, his hand hitting his jeans, on and on and on (it took so long because he kept going soft), until, finally, the warmth released and spread across his thigh; and now his jeans were wet from the ocean, but before that place on his thigh had been stiff when he walked, a reminder of her.

He was moving toward the shade of the lifeguard stand, carefully, crouched like an animal, and the memory of the girl's face made him feel like he was watching the bank teller again, his finger in the jacket pocket, sweat tickling down his rib cage, passing her the deposit slip: "I have a gun, give me all your cash."

And then he went back in time, saw himself walk into the bank, wearing Esther's jacket, its fur collar tickling his chin, his hand sweating in the pocket, ready to become a gun.

He wanted to tell the bank teller not to cry—*It's going to be okay, you'll see; it's not really a gun*—but he was unable to stop anything, frozen and helpless. Three tears slid down her cheek—one after the other after the other—from the same eye, as if following each other, leaving a wet, smeary trail in her makeup, but she was quiet and passed him the money. And with the memory of the girl with his $20 bill and her friend who had looked at him and let him know that he had bad everything and the bank teller girl and himself all at the same time, all of them together, he fell asleep in the shade, the jacket tucked between his legs.

A BUS WAS idling on and on; it wouldn't leave—the engine heaved and heaved. Eric tried to huddle deeper beneath the bench. He waited for the bus to take off: a clenching noise as the brakes released, the bus door shutting with a *swoosh*, a squeezing of air. But it seemed to idle forever, unlocking him from a dream in which he was dumb and innocent.

The sound crawled into him, threaded through him, and woke him. It was the ocean. His mouth and nostrils were filled with sand—*thpppt, thpppt*, he spat it out and opened his eyes to gnatlike bugs. When he swatted, they disappeared, as if evaporating—there were more of them hovering over a thick patch of dried seaweed.

He rolled to his right, pushed himself up, and spat out more sand. His head ached and his mouth was dry and the sun was spreading orange, hitting him in the thigh and arm and torso.

He scooted into the shade, wiped his face with the jacket, and tried to remember who he was, where he was, and what he'd done.

The sky was the color of the inside of an abalone shell, and the waves were beating against the shore endlessly. He'd woken alone, but now they came to him: the young girl and her friend and the bank teller. He needed to endure his pain and what he'd done, and there must be a way to blot out the sky and ocean without dying. Everything around him—including himself—was unbearable, and he cradled his head in his hands.

9

NORA WAS LEANED over, sorting through the third of four large black garbage bags, placing clothing in three piles, based on cachet—all from Number Seventy-two, a woman who lived at 72 Bayside Terrace and spent her winters in Taos, New Mexico: a size 4, with a disposition toward dark mauves and deep greens, silky cottons and cropped jackets—when she heard the phone ring. She wasn't sure what time it was, but Clothing for Change had been closed for hours, and the window by the phone showed that the sky was black except for a misty cone-shaped shaft of orange light from the street lamp, and the street was quiet except for the occasional car passing, tires slick on the rain-wet road.

Nora had decorated Clothing for Change with old furnishings, intrinsically unglamorous, hoping to give it a homey atmosphere. A donated Steinway grand piano—wood scratched, tuned imperfectly—was in the corner by the three dressing rooms, each partitioned by a dark-blue curtain. A three-way mirror allowed for a visual of back, side, front, and beside the mirror was Nora's video camera, set up on a tripod.

She had lost track of time, imagining the dinner where

Seventy-two had worn the black Chanel cocktail dress, the charity function where the pantsuit had made an appearance, and the Caribbean vacation where the two-piece swimsuit and beaded cover-up had been used. Sometimes Seventy-two's clothes had small stains—a fleck of maroon-colored lipstick, a tawny foundation smear, speckles of wine—but tonight the majority had arrived with tags, never worn, and Nora knew that Seventy-two had fought with her husband again and, in an irrational fit of revenge, a European shopping spree had ensued. In the cold light of rationality, a month or so after the fight, the clothes had been dismissed as too flamboyant, not her style, and some not even her size, but instead an optimistic size 2.

While Clothing for Change would benefit from the marital dispute, the only good thing for Seventy-two's husband would be the tax write-off. Simply by the look Seventy-two's live-in maid had given while handing the bags over, Nora had known she had a jackpot. Now, if only she had more parolee clients who were size 2's and 4's and 6's . . . instead, she would sell the clothes at a discounted bulk rate to Moving Up!, a secondhand store off Pacific Coast Highway that sold to women who aspired to be Seventy-two by at least looking like Seventy-two, and she would use the proceeds to buy size 10's and 12's and 14's.

"Coming," she said to the shrill ring, walking past the wall adorned with framed awards attesting to the moral goodness of Clothing for Change. She leaned over to pick up a *People* magazine from the floor, the cast of *Friends* smiling from the cover, and placed it on the side table. Next to the side table was a stuffed sofa where clients sometimes fell asleep. Nora saw it as a compliment, indicating that the women felt safe. A hand-knitted afghan from her deceased paternal great-grandmother was folded on the arm of the sofa, and she let her fingers pass over it. Nora had attached a personal mythology to Nana

(Nana had never married, had had a wooden leg, and had lived and died in Nebraska) and, by proxy, to the blanket, which had traveled with Nora through childhood, college, and the Peace Corps.

Nora's relationship with Charlie had become strained, but she found herself hoping that it was Charlie calling anyway. She didn't get to see him alone, much less talk to him anymore. He was the same, but because she had to watch him deliver himself to Esther, she wasn't. And the handful of times she'd been invited for dinner, Esther had been condescendingly generous ("Red really looks good on you, Nora. You should wear it more often"), as if the sharp, awe-inspiring Esther she'd hatefully respected had been swallowed by a love-riddled, empty-headed, falsely gracious woman.

She would tell Charlie—if it was Charlie—that she was busy and find a way to hang up.

"Nora," Charlie said when she answered, and then, "I tried you at home first but figured you'd still be working." His voice made her involuntarily want to regain their closeness; he was speaking in a low, urgent tone, almost whispering, and even though it implied instant intimacy, it made her uneasy.

"I got in a valuable delivery," she said, glancing at the Hefty garbage bags. "Actually, I'm kind of excited about it."

"Listen," he said, "something horrible has happened."

She felt a clutching at her chest, imagining death, seeing it as a black color for an instant.

"It's Eric, Esther's brother. Remember her brother?"

She'd seen Eric two days earlier. Usually she slipped him dollar bills, but she had not wanted to get out of her car and had driven past him. She heard a jingle, signaling a door opening and closing—a late-night customer at the liquor store. Clothing for Change was located in a mini-mall; Donut King,

H&R Block, and Fiesta Tacos were closed, but High Time Liquor stayed open all night.

"I know who he is," she said.

"God," Charlie said, and she imagined him sitting on his couch, wearing his jeans that were softly faded at his knees. "He's in big trouble, Nora. And Esther won't even talk about it. I can't believe this, but it looks like he tried to rob the Bank of Newport over by the beach—you know the one, off of Marguerite. I guess he did rob it, in a way. They've got him on videotape and everything, and it's just so sad because he did it with his finger. He was wearing this jacket—I guess Esther gave him the jacket—and he put his hand in one of the pockets with his forefinger sticking out, and he handed this teller a note that he'd scribbled on the back of a deposit slip, and it said he had a gun and to give him cash. And I guess it looked like a gun, just his finger, pointed, hidden."

"God," she said.

"I know," Charlie said. "Here's the thing, though: He took the cash—it wasn't even that much, around $400—and he went and bought heroin. They found all the paraphernalia under a lifeguard stand, according to the police report. And he ordered a pizza and a couple of Coronas. Then he got sick, maybe from the heroin—I don't now—most of it in one of those blue trash bins. Scared a mom and her kid; she reported him."

The phone receiver was cradled between her neck and shoulder; she was looking distractedly at her own forefinger, pointed in the pocket of her sweat jacket, a skinny gun. "That's awful," she said.

"Yeah. And then he must've felt bad, probably because the teller was so young and he'd made her cry, because he walked all the way over to the police station and turned himself in. He'd used only about $60, and he handed over the rest of the cash.

That's the only thing he's got going for him, the fact that he turned himself in, but it doesn't look like it's going to make a difference."

"I'm sorry."

"I know. Me, too. He's in big trouble. We're talking federal offense, ten to fifteen years. That is, if they don't get him on Prop 184—you know, three strikes. Apparently he's had some minor scrapes with the law: one possession, back when he was seventeen or something, and a shoplifting a few years back. But everyone's so gung-ho right now."

She was well acquainted with Proposition 184; her parolee clients had mourned its recent passing, an unmistakable majority: 72 percent in favor.

"God," she said. "How's Esther?"

"She won't talk to me. She's here. Well, she's in my bed. That's why I'm calling. It's like she's a mannequin or something. She's just so cold, Nora. She won't leave my bed. Even her body, it's cold, like she just got out of a really cold shower. I think maybe she's having a nervous breakdown or something. I don't know what to do."

BEFORE NORA LEFT for Charlie's, she unfolded and read the first page of two pieces of yellow lined paper that she'd tucked safely in a side pocket of her purse, on which she'd written, as honestly as possible, in a stream-of-consciousness burst, her feelings about Charlie.

> We were very close. We are very close. I feel like he manipulates me. But I let myself be manipulated! I swear he flirts with me, etc., and then denies it. He says things, how much he admires me, etc., etc., all the time. But he makes me feel insecure, the

> way he looks at me. He's definitely not attracted to me. I mean, really. I can tell. Oftentimes, I feel really bad about myself, as if my insides don't matter at all. I think I fell for him a little bit and I think he fell for me a little bit? I try to control him. I hate him. No I don't. That's not true. I love him, that's the whole problem. He's an idiot. Then he started dating Esther. Stupid and pretty. All about his ego. Ego-boosting. He invites me to dinner just to show her off. To brag about her. Is he trying to make me jealous? I know she's pretty. Does he want to rub it in? He stopped calling. We don't jog anymore. He's always with Esther. When he needs something, he calls. I feel like he uses me. He's a kiss-ass. He's there for me only when convenient. But it's my fault for having all my emotions tied up in him. I relied on him. I fell for him. I told him too much, probably. I let him know too much about me. But I didn't tell him the most important things. And now I'm glad. If I had, it would only be worse. I don't stand up for myself. I let him say things. I'm selfish. I want him to myself. Now I'm jealous of his girlfriend. And it hurts me that he's with her because she's pretty and not that smart. She's not equal with him. He can't be with me because I'm as smart as he is—and equal or better than him (better, honestly).

She knew that it was more of the same on the next piece of paper, so she ripped up the sheets and threw the remains in the wastebasket. Then she got down on her knees, eyes closed, hands holding on to the rim of her sofa. "Oh my God" was all she could come up with.

"Oh my God, oh my God."

She was out of practice, years since she'd tried earnestly to communicate with God, but she hoped her confusion was an authentic prayer. And something about offering herself up, with all her ugliness, was the closest she could come to an honest entreaty.

She prayed because she didn't want to experience a perverse pleasure from Esther's misfortune, and her heart was leaning and expanding in that direction; she prayed because her resentment and jealousy weren't as intense, and even this was somehow disingenuous; she prayed because she preferred Esther as a failure; she prayed because crisis made her come alive in a way that was voyeuristic and opportunistic; she prayed because she knew that Charlie would probably not be up to the challenge that Esther presented, and this satisfied her.

But it was useless; the idea of a vengeful, Armageddon-obsessed deity continually interrupted her thoughts.

WHEN NORA ARRIVED at Charlie's, she knocked on his door, and it was like he was standing right next to it, waiting, because he opened it immediately. "Thanks for coming," he said, his face rubbery with emotion. "I don't know what to do."

They went inside, and the corners of his mouth thickened as he looked at Esther, slumped in his bed. When his attention returned to Nora—his eyes dark and serious—she felt as if he were thinking about something he couldn't share. And then he told her that he needed "to get some fresh air, maybe take a walk" and he looked so agonized that Nora was glad when he left.

By the time she was looking at Esther in his bed, she was unexpectedly calm, knowing that she would place Nana's afghan, which she'd brought with her, over Esther's sleeping body.

Then she came closer and saw that Esther's eyes were open, and her body recoiled because Esther appeared to be concentrating, but in a vaguely detached manner, on the blistery plaster of the wall. Her mouth was also open, but just barely, and her knees were tucked in so that her arms were clasped around them, as if forced into a fetal position by a lock her arms made. She wore a navy-colored halter dress, a braided tie at the front, and the jerseylike material was gathered between her knees so that her calves were visible. She was barefoot, and, sadly, her toenails were painted an optimistic sherbet color. The bedside pelican lamp was on, and the light shone full on her hair and face. Despite everything, she looked beautiful, and Nora experienced a familiar tug of jealousy.

Beside the lamp were a glass of water and two Valiums that Charlie had procured from a sympathetic neighbor.

Nora spread the afghan over Esther, and for a long moment, nothing happened. But then Esther sat up from the bed, using her hands to balance, with caution and timidity, and the afghan slipped off her lap, falling to the floor. She seemed to be attempting to make sense, but taking in Nora's presence only partly. She blinked, as if she'd been asleep with her eyes open and was blinking awake. Her skin was very pale, and she sat motionless, hands linked together in her lap, a strand of hair caught in the saliva at her lips.

"Esther," Nora said. A few minutes passed, and she tried again. "Esther."

For a long time, Esther stared, as if unable to come to. Then finally she mumbled something, but Nora could hear only the words "him" and "money." But then she spoke loudly, looking at the wall: "I didn't bring him money." She swiped the hair from her mouth. "I was too busy, too happy. It's my fault." Anguish broke over her face, and she turned and stared at Nora. Her expression terrified Nora, made her woozy.

"It's not your fault," Nora said. "He's a drug addict."

Esther stared at her.

"He's a drug addict," Nora repeated, making her voice rational and authoritative. She reached for the Valiums and the glass of water, and then handed the pills to Esther.

Mechanically, Esther drank the water, swallowed the pills, and handed the glass back; then she lay in the bed, turning away from Nora. Nora would have taken this as an indication that her presence was not wanted, had the movement not been accompanied by a faint but distinct "Please stay."

When Nora was certain that Esther was asleep, breath rhythmic, she lay in the bed next to Esther and went over the situation in the mental privacy that Esther's slumber provided.

After much contemplation, a consensus welled up inside her. She understood that none of what had happened and what was happening and what would happen had anything to do with her; it was as if she had glimpsed a space or a void, a vastness in relation to her insignificance, and whatever power she had imagined she had, even in her emotions, didn't matter; like the ocean, the space didn't care, and it would continue existing in a forceful way nonetheless.

Her sense of self obliterated, in a way that was neither comfortable nor uncomfortable but left her vapory, aware of a deeper nobody-self. And, most surprising, she wasn't disappointed, settling into the relief of her nothingness.

10

"THAT'S TWO HUNDRED dollars and forty-two cents," Esther said, removing the tags from a silk-and-wool tuxedo dress, folding it inside pale silver tissue paper and closing the tissue with a heart-shaped sticker. She placed the tissue bundle gently in a gold-and-black True Romance bag. (Debbie was at one of her frequent and mysterious gynecological appointments and wouldn't be back until well after lunch.) A vase of pink tulips and mini–calla lilies was at the corner of the counter—she'd read the card earlier:

I am a warm cotton towel
When you are soaked to the bone
To be wrapped around you
And give you warmth.

And then she'd ripped it up, knowing that it was from Sean.

Two nights before, Esther had woken to find Nora sleeping with her in Charlie's bed. She'd tried to seal off her grief, but then, for a long time, the weeping wouldn't stop, as if by being permissive, her grief had acquired a supernatural force. All snot and trembling and heaves. *Allow yourself to let go*, she had thought, *and see what happens.* It was as if she had been witnessing her emotional pain reflected in Nora's compassion. And she'd felt insane for a brief period, possibly an hour, repeating things, whimpering—"I don't need anybody" and "I'll go away" and the slightly varied "I'll go far away."

Nora, to her credit, had waited her out; there had been a nightmare, and more comforting, but when she'd awakened, she'd found that she was alone in the bed—a dingy old blanket wound between her legs.

This morning, she'd showered and readied for work, wearing her halter dress (although she kept makeup at Charlie's, she hadn't brought any clothes). Her eyes were puffy from crying. Determined to get Eric out of jail but not knowing how, she believed that the first step was to show up to her job. Charlie had slept on the couch, and when he'd told her, propped at his elbow, wary and pale, that she should call in sick to work, she'd wanted to tell him that by following her routine, she was clinging to the periphery of normalcy; that if she let this part of her go, all that held her together, the fabric of her, might fall away, and there'd be nothing left.

She'd been taught to put on a formidable front, having grown accustomed to the sight and smell and reality of misfortune. She soothed her swollen eyes with a hand towel soaked with cold water, the way her father had taught her. Again. And again. Left eye, right eye. And as she did so, she remembered his doing the same for her.

She'd been pushed from behind on the school playground, second grade, her arms flailed out—no way to stop the fall. She'd scraped her palms. In the nurse's station, even after her hands had been bandaged, she had been unable to stop crying, and her father had been called.

As soon as he arrived, the tears gained momentum. He sat on the cot next to her, waited. He wet a paper towel with cold water from the sink, and when she was done crying, he pressed it gently against each of her eyes. Again. And again. Left eye, right eye. He told her to take deep breaths. He took the breaths with her. "You're lucky," he said. "You're young; your face snaps back." He showed her how to pinch her cheeks—"Now it looks like you've been running."

Esther hadn't rung the sale in, and the woman glanced at the blank digital window of the cash register for the amount. She steadied her large, nautical white-leather purse on the register stand, opening it and fishing for its matching wallet. "I'm sorry," she said. "How much? I didn't hear you." She wore silver pants of a metallic material and a sailor-collared blouse. On the cusp of middle age, she had a centimeter of silvery roots at her part. In keeping with the nautical theme, she wore diamond-encrusted earrings designed as anchors.

"Cash or credit?" Esther asked, pretending to recalculate on a solar-paneled calculator.

"Cash," the woman said, wallet parted. Despite her showy appearance, her eyes carried an apologetic note. Briefly, Esther imagined holding the woman, the way Nora had held her two nights before.

"Two hundred and forty dollars and forty-two cents," she said, concentrating on a space between the woman's cheek and her anchor earring. She felt pinpricks at her forehead; her palms went damp.

The woman gave her the exact amount, in cash and coins, and Esther opened the register and placed the money in the correct slots. Two twenties: hers. A small, comforting certainty.

Her hands were a little shaky as she passed the woman the shopping bag. "It's a lovely dress," she said, but the woman only frowned.

She waited before ringing the correct amount of the tuxedo dress into the cash register—2-0-0.4-2. The drawer opened with a ring, but she didn't take the cash—just knowing the twenties were waiting for her was good enough.

She waited until two customers—both idlers and possible shoplifters themselves—left the store. Once, she imagined she saw Debbie lurking near the entrance, and she waited some more. The music had stopped a while ago, but she hadn't gone to the back room to start the CD player. Debbie was on a Counting Crows kick—the only CD in the player was *August and Everything After.*

A crystal heart decorating the window created a freckle of rainbow sunlight on the oyster-colored carpet, and she watched it shimmying there. Then she closed her eyes, leaned into the counter. And she was walking on the pier with Eric—it wasn't raining, but there was a weightless drizzle, like moving through a cloud. Her father wasn't there in her memory, but she knew that he must have been, since they were kids and he wouldn't have let them go alone.

Below the pier were the surfers in their dark wetsuits, reminding her of seals, their heads turned in the same direction, vying for the next wave, moving up and down with the swells.

Near them on the pier, a man with no arms was reeling a fish from the ocean with his toes, spinning the line, pulling the fish out, even unhooking it.

"What should I do?" the man asked, enjoying their attention. The fish flapped on the wood next to his bucket. "Throw it back!" Eric said. She joined: "Throw it back! Throw it back!"

The man took the fish between his bare feet and flipped it

over the pier, tossing it like a ball. They ran to the edge, watched the black fleck fall. Once it hit the water, it turned silver, and then it slipped away, disappeared.

She opened her eyes, wondering what it was like—freedom—imagining it as oblivion. A deadening exhaustion coursed through her, and she wanted to curl up on the floor, right next to the freckles of sunlight, and sleep.

On impulse, she rang the drawer open and fingered her twenties, pulling them from their slot; she closed the register and knelt down to get her wallet from her purse underneath the counter.

She heard the jingle of a customer entering through the door, and when she lifted herself to a standing position, she was light-headed, steadying her hands on the counter, her right hand still clutching the twenties.

She saw that it was grim-faced Debbie; behind her was the nautical woman. The door jingled again, and in walked a stern policeman, his weighted belt saddled with a gun and handcuffs, and with him, an undercover security guard she knew as Ray, a man she was able to flirt with guilt-free because he was happily married with kids. Sickness whirled up inside her, her body liquid with disbelief, as though what was happening was an extension of what had happened to Eric.

As they moved toward her, the twenties slipped from her fingers and fell near the waste basket. Her legs went jittery, and she steadied herself against the ledge of the countertop.

Debbie came behind the register, brushed up against her, and opened it; she extracted the money tray with a loud *clang*.

"That's it," she said, handing the tray over the counter to the policeman. She leaned over, noticing the twenties on the carpet.

The nautical woman's face was resigned: "We've got you on videotape."

"I'm sorry," Debbie said unapologetically, kneeling to retrieve the money. Her words came from underneath the register in a dutifully burdened tone: "I knew something was going on. I had to do something."

Esther's heart beat in an angry panic. She wanted to tell the others that this had nothing to do with her. This was about Debbie's being divorced and having to work long hours; this had to do with Debbie's wanting someone to give her flowers, day after day; this had to do with Debbie's ungrateful teenagers, with Debbie's having to dress and talk and act like Lauren Bacall for perverted old men at business conventions.

"Did you know that in most states, including California," Debbie said, standing, the twenties between her fingers for everyone to see, "an employee who steals can be charged with shoplifting *and* embezzlement?"

Humiliation swept over Esther—it seemed to spread and expand inside her. She wanted—needed—to lie down.

Ray stepped forward—"Excuse me"—removing her purse from underneath the register counter, genuinely sad.

"Ray," she said, but she couldn't finish the sentence, not knowing what to say.

He gazed gloomily at her, but then he looked away. "Is that really necessary?" he said in a beleaguered tone, and she followed his gaze and saw that he was referring to the policeman, whose palm was at the ready, placed on his handcuffs.

HANDCUFFS WEREN'T NECESSARY, but Esther did have to walk between the policeman and Ray, each with a hand on her elbow. Debbie and the nautical woman followed close behind, Debbie diligently holding the register's money tray. Esther kept her head down, her hair swept over her face, but she knew that she would be recognized. Her insides were hollow, a postponement of shame.

All was bright around her, the sun hot on her scalp, and she knew that the sky was cloudless and clear. She thought of Charlie kissing her goodbye that morning, his lips dry—the kiss had felt chaste, as if he were a child—and it bothered her all at once, made her indignant, although she didn't know why.

They passed Shark Island, and she heard a shriek of laughter rise above the music. She glanced through her hair to her right and saw distinctly, in the small crowd of people that had formed, Paul and his fat-lipped fiancée paused at the entrance to the restaurant, watching with a look of disbelief.

She redirected her gaze downward, and for the first time, she acknowledged her similarity in physical appearance to Paul's fiancée's: He'd upgraded to a younger version of her. It occurred to her that all women were disposable, and all at once, searing grief coursed through her, caused her to suck in the air with a strange wheeze-suck noise, in a sudden, certain recognition of her own fate.

Ray's grip at her elbow tightened, not in reprimand but in concern; she felt him staring at her, willing her to hold it together, pulling her to a full stand, so that she understood her knees had buckled a little. Then he leaned in and whispered, "C'mon, baby. Not much farther. Almost there."

They passed by the fountain, and she heard the water splashing and the children playing. She kept her head down, watching her feet move over the tiles. She imagined the children watching her, despite their parents trying to distract them. "What'd she do?" she heard a child ask. "Mommy, is she bad?"

Individual tiles had been drawn and colored by children—sunsets and clowns and puppies, with their names and ages beneath: Susan, age five; Mathew, age seven; Leslie, age eleven—

and as she stepped on their names, she imagined what the kids might look like, hunched over, painting their pictures.

Everywhere—in the fingers at her elbows, in the stores surrounding them, in the people watching, in the palm trees and tiles, in the cloudless sky—shame waited to overtake her.

Ray hadn't lied—it wasn't much farther. Soon they took a service elevator down to the basement, the only sound coming from the policeman's handheld radio, a scratchy noise and a sharp female voice, until he silenced it with a thumb; and then they were walking through the dark bowels beneath a parking structure, away from all the watching eyes.

Several long hallways later, they reached a metal door. Ray opened the lock with a key and swung the door open to reveal a room that she hadn't known existed, even though she'd suspected it did. Ray led her to a swivel chair in front of a wide oak desk, empty except for a stack of official-looking papers and a phone.

She sat and he moved away, seeming to understand that his kindness might make her cry. If she cried, she might not be able to stop, and she didn't want Debbie and the others to feel gratified. But, surprisingly, she was able to contain her emotions, because lurking beneath her shame and grief was an unexpected relief. Nothing more could happen to her; she'd collapsed inside—there was nothing left of her, and nothing left to hide. It was almost as if she were dead.

Debbie was making a phone call. Ray, the policeman, and the nautical woman were in a low-voiced discussion, now and then casting glances at her, confirming that she was the subject of their discourse. She saw that the screens of the televisions on the side of the room were set to different sections of Fashion Island, in fuzzy black and white, people moving in delayed stretches.

She watched the slow-motion jerking of a woman fingering a long scarf, letting it go, and then walking from one sales counter—zoom—to the next, and she was incredulous that she'd been so stupid as to steal without an expectation of getting caught.

PART THREE

◈ 1 ◈

MORE THAN ONCE, Charlie had told Esther that in the worst kind of environments, where women were kept supplicant and subordinate to men, where their worth was dependent on men, they sometimes preyed on each other as a misguided revenge and out of sheer desperation and fear: destroying reputations, ambushing opportunities, stealing husbands and male admirers—all to procure or retain status and financial security. And the greatest paradox was that women were often condemned for their mercenary, relentlessly ruthless, and narcissistic values, while at the very same time, society encouraged and nourished women in these directions.

"So essentially," she said, "what you're saying is that everyone thinks I'm a failure because I'm not exploiting people well enough. Because I'm not vapid enough. Not selfish enough."

"Not exactly," he said. "It's not that simple. But yes, I would agree that what is most beautiful and moral about you, these are the things that are holding you back. For instance, how many times have you been proposed to? Two, three times? Well, it doesn't matter. I don't really want to know. The thing is, you haven't married, because of love—you want love. Normally, this would be considered a good character trait."

These grave and deep thoughts, and how they applied directly to her, as well as those of lesser significance (*My fingernail polish is chipped, but I can't really afford a manicure, and really, what's the point—it'll just chip again*), preoccupied Esther as she sat in a dark corner booth of The Quiet Woman, waiting for Brenda's presence.

Brenda had called her and, in a neutral tone, had requested the meeting. Esther had agreed, with the specific goal of calling a truce, raising the white flag, before Brenda dragged her over the coals any further. Her cachet had been reduced to such devastating proportions that she felt the slight promise of Brenda's relenting in pity. Not only was Esther broke, unemployable, shunned by Grandma Eileen, and therefore on the verge of homelessness, but she had also acquired the reputation that went along with being arrested for stealing. And the malicious spreading of rumors, heralded by Brenda and Debbie (and anyone who had witnessed her walk of shame through Fashion Island), had helped to saddle her with the heavy and burdensome "slut," "easy," "cheap," "thief" labels, which she knew (on account of her father's history) to be nearly impossible to erase.

People, family, everyone (Charlie!)—she felt them distancing themselves, afraid that her misfortune might rub off on them. Lonely! Lonely! She found herself confronted for the first time with the fear that the very same man who had awakened her from a long and ignorant slumber might possibly want to shelter himself away and slumber in peace.

She'd given herself to Charlie so freely, in a fit of wanton expenditure, without thought of benefit, and had found it strangely liberating. She'd discovered that the act of loving was more fertile outside the profit system, and she knew that from here on out, she would seek it not for its material consequences.

Ironically, she blamed her father, for having loved her and loved her well, and she was angry with him, even more so because he was dead; he'd created a desire in her to experience love, and that was in conflict with fulfilling his goal for her. Marrying a man for wealth and power had been her priority, so important that it had overshadowed everything else, like constantly wearing a girdle that restricted her movements and breathing. But everything had changed. She'd been turned inside out.

When had she changed? It wasn't clear, but it was tangled up in Charlie: his back arching over her during sex, the flash of pleasure and awe in his face. How sometimes when she came, she felt something—her essence, her personhood. A confirmation of her intrinsic worth, with or without money. A feeling of belonging—of protection. She imagined it might feel like that to suckle at a mother's breast.

"Would you like another cocktail?" her waiter asked. He was handsome, but when he smiled, she saw a gap between his front teeth. She contemplated the price of another apple martini ($3.75, her second), knowing that she could no longer depend on Brenda to pay the bill, but answered, "Yes," thinking of the alcohol spreading through her veins, quelling her nerves.

Lately, she felt as if she was going through the motions of living: shaving her underarms, dressing, applying makeup, smiling and talking. In the stress and upheaval that were her life, her physical appearance had suffered. Since her arrest, she had had trouble summoning the enthusiasm to care. It had taken all her effort to shower (the first time in a week) and dress for Brenda. (She'd overheard Charlie on the phone—"The way you can tell a cat is really sick is if that cat's dirty because it isn't cleaning itself"—and wondered who he was talking to, knowing that she was the cat he was worried about.)

The more her circumstances deteriorated, the more she relied on Rick. And she often thought of Nora. Nora had witnessed the exposure of her soul "that night," and vice versa—they both knew it and were shy and uncomfortable with each other. That measure of intimacy should be reserved for lovers. They had recently settled for mutual avoidance as a convenient solution, but nothing could change the fact that a forging had occurred: She felt a constant closeness, an inbred, ongoing connection of consciousness, even in physical absence.

Brenda was already over half an hour late, and there was the chance that she might not show, although Esther suspected that she was merely making a statement with her tardiness.

Near Esther was a small curtained window, and she pulled back the curtain to a dark sky, a yellow moon riding the hump of a palm frond. Small and insignificant, she let herself dissolve, but then she was pulled back into her body, hearing the woman in the next booth say to her male companion, "Fuck you. I'm not going to think about you now. I'm tired of thinking about you. Go away."

The man spoke in a hushed, somber tone, his hand stroking her arm, and whatever he said was effective, as the woman calmed down, wiping the tears from her eyes with her cloth napkin.

Immersed in her thoughts and in the couple's exchange, Esther was startled when Brenda slid into the booth with a rustle of silk and a gust of perfume (Giorgio Armani?).

"I heard about everything," Brenda said, bright-eyed. "About the arrest and Jim and your brother. He's in rehab? Right?"

Before she answered, Brenda continued, "Looks like someone needs a hug," sliding even closer, and, to Esther's surprise, she was quickly squeezed in a stiff-armed embrace.

Esther would have been relieved at this instantaneous lack of hostility had her heart not clutched in anxiety at the mention of Jim Dunnels. How had Brenda known? The clutching at her chest transformed into a general nauseous feeling, as if she were in Jim's Ferrari once again, parked in an alleyway, explaining her dilemma and asking for his assistance, the overhead light casting a yellow-white hue. She dug her fingernails into her palms, just as she had when Jim had reclined his seat, his pants unzipped and pulled down to his thighs, his penis unlocked from his boxers, resting in the layers of his fat in a creamy pink knuckle.

On principle, she had not been able to take it in her hand or mouth, as Jim had proposed; and when, despite her best efforts, tears had squirmed from her eyes, dropping and sliding down to her chin, he'd laughed, saying, "C'mon, Esther. It's not that bad." And then she'd looked out her window, to a tear-streaked view of a cement wall, trying to ignore the slapping sounds and grunts coming from his direction, until, minutes later, he leaned over her to retrieve a small hand towel from the glove compartment.

Dropping her off at Grandma Eileen's, he hadn't said anything, and neither had she, feeling his eyes hot on her back as she walked to her doorway, her face wet and her nose clogged with snot.

But then, days later, her shoplifting charges had been miraculously dropped, her court date wiped away ("So, in a way, he owns Fashion Island!"); and then, four days after that, her brother's trial had been dismissed, the judge sentencing him to a drug diversion program instead; and then, soon after that, Eric had been transferred from Central Men's Jail in Santa Ana to Seaside Sober Living in Newport Beach (the fee for his unlimited stay at an oceanfront recovery home had been paid by an anonymous benefactor, Esther had been told), where he was drug tested weekly, and where, as proof of his success, she'd recently witnessed him acquire a light blue thirty-day chip. (He'd given her the chip, his eyes sad and sincere. "Don't worry," he'd said with his tragic smile, "I have at least ten of them already.")

She did her best not to think about Jim's motivations, to not think about Jim at all, but when her thoughts slid in that direction, she suspected that her humiliation had been an erotic stimulus, and that she had serviced him without touch.

She unclenched her fists, pink dents at her palms, and for a few seconds, gratitude mixed with her anxiety and shame as she thought of the chip (this time he might stay sober!) tucked in her wallet.

Brenda was resting her head against the back of the booth and looking at her with a directness that also seemed lazy and indifferent—an expression of superiority.

Esther tried her best to keep her expression blank and hospitable, though her thoughts were still consumed with the implications of Brenda's knowing about Jim, mostly because it meant other people knew, which meant even more people knew, which meant Charlie.

Even though nothing had happened, besides the exposure of Jim's member and the auditory proof of his pleasuring himself, she had willingly sought him out and met with him, in the hopes of soliciting his help, and was guilty. And besides, she knew it wasn't so much what had happened, but what people said had happened, that mattered.

She tried anyway: "Nothing happened with Jim."

"Uh-huh," Brenda said, smiling grimly. She still had her head against the cushion of the booth, and she placed both hands on her stomach.

The waiter came for their order, and Brenda sat up, glanced

quickly over the menu, ran her fingernail down it, and stopped on her selection, tapping it, choosing not to speak.

"French onion soup?" he asked.

She gave him a noncommittal half nod, and he looked at Esther for help. Esther let him know with her eyes that yes, Brenda wanted the soup, and then she ordered the same thing, since it wasn't expensive.

When the waiter left, she fiddled with her cocktail napkin, smoothed its edges against the table. The glow of shame that had settled over her would not leave, and instead of looking at Brenda, she pretended to examine the cuticle of her right forefinger, her chipped polish.

"Listen," Brenda said, "let's let the past go. Pastor Ken says that I need to forgive you."

Esther wasn't sure whether Brenda was serious, because when she met Brenda's eyes, she saw mischief. She also sensed judgment—not necessarily regarding her character, but about her appearance. In order to buoy her spirits, she decided that she would find a way for Brenda to pay the bill.

"I mean it," Brenda said. She coughed into her hand, and Esther thought she saw her smiling, but couldn't be sure.

"I'm not kidding," Brenda said, and this time she smiled openly. Esther reached for her glass of ice water.

"I've been meeting with Pastor Ken," Brenda said, smoothing the napkin on her lap. "We're working on a program of healing. We're on forgiveness."

Esther took a drink of water, and an ice cube knocked against her front tooth. Water dribbled from the side of her mouth, and she wiped it away with her napkin.

"I don't want to be friends again," Brenda explained. "I just want to get this forgiveness thing over with."

Restless and agitated, Esther noticed that her right hand was trembling slightly at the table and that the water had created dark splotches on her blouse. She smiled, at the edge of an abyss. *If the world had its way*, she thought, *I would be cowering somewhere in a pit, accepting my fate.*

"Sean's on medication finally," Brenda said, reaching for the breadbasket. Her manner was detached, but then she looked fierce. "Why do I have to do all the work to get better, and all he has to do is take a pill?" She frowned. "I want a pill!" She stamped her fist on the table; the breadbasket and bread plates wobbled, the water glasses and martini glasses shook. "Give me a pill!"

"I thought you *were* on medication," Esther said.

Brenda met the statement with a blank stare. "I've been thinking a lot about the Virgin Mary lately," she said. "Have you ever really thought about it? Imagine getting pregnant when you're still a virgin." She broke open her roll, put a small piece in her mouth. "Poor Mary," she said, barely audible, chewing. "When you think about it, really think about it, she got the short end of the stick."

"I didn't do anything wrong," Esther said.

Brenda seemed to acknowledge her, as if she was tired. Her hands went to her stomach and she leaned her head back against the booth, in a philosophical posture. "You broke the unwritten rule."

Esther wanted to point out that the rule of never dating a friend's ex (Charlie) might not apply to married people, but she kept her silence.

Brenda sat up a little from the booth. "We're meeting with Pastor Ken," she said. "Sean won't do the healing program, but he's agreed to the meetings."

Esther was relieved, knowing that the rumors might stop. Sean hadn't been concerned with her problems, only with how she could alleviate his suffering. The phone calls had stopped, the flowers had stopped—all around the same time as her arrest.

Brenda seemed to be studying her. "I forgive you," she said, in an ingratiating tone. "I know that you've been suffering," she said, and her head went down. She shook it a little, as if in empathy. "Pastor Ken," she said, directing her attention to Esther again, "once told me that we're lucky to suffer, because suffering is a tremendous opportunity for spiritual growth. Jesus Christ suffered more than anyone, and he's the son of God." Her smile was serene. She looked beautiful. She was imperturbable, enigmatic, hidden.

Bitterness rose in Esther's throat, and she wanted badly to bestow her forgiveness as well, but she knew that it would only bring more trouble.

I forgive you, she said to herself anyway, in a tight and mean voice. *I forgive you, Brenda*. And even though she didn't say it out loud, she knew that it showed in her eyes.

2

ESTHER'S BREATHING WAS steady beside Charlie, her body turned from his, on her side. She smelled like honey, but underneath was a womanly smell—more like vinegar. The Valiums she'd taken earlier, in combination with the cocktails she'd no doubt consumed, had put her out quickly, into a heavy sleep. Whatever had happened at her dinner engagement had left her in a foul mood, and Charlie had been relieved when, rather than examining the source of her displeasure, she'd destroyed any possibility of discussion through medicinal measures.

A hazy bar of light had escaped through a dent in the blinds, reflected from the neighbor's motion-sensitive porch light. A little too sensitive, going on and off at random. Psychotic light. Once, he'd taken out the bulb. If it didn't stop, he'd do it again, leave the bulb on his neighbor's welcome mat.

Not one for drug consumption himself but anticipating a long, sleepless night, Charlie had taken half a Valium, the only noticeable result being a sporadic cottony sensation in his toes and fingers, pulsing, recurring, like the stupid porch light. He lay still, held his breath. He put his fingers next to Esther's thigh, felt the warmth of her, and let his breath come out. Then he held his hand above his face, studied its black silhouette. He waggled his fingers and, in frustration at his insomnia, flipped himself off.

The problem: He was very alive. He didn't want to blame Esther, but she did make him feel more alive, with her shoplifting arrest and her problems and her constant presence. So alive that death was right there, willing and waiting. Death could swallow him. Without his wanting them to, possibilities scurried through him, a cinema of morbid visuals: choking on a salad crouton; tripping on a curb, hitting his forehead on the street; fainting on the toilet, head slamming into the porcelain lip of his bathtub; a brain aneurysm, like a firework going off, and then black; falling asleep at the wheel, his Honda veering, veering, veering right, slamming into a truck; a drunk driver going the wrong way, a black dark night, headlights blinding him, and crash; diseased, right now, right this second, unaware—cancer cells streaming through his blood, or some other lurking silent ailment. No sense of security, feeling this alive. None.

His body was heavy on the mattress, and he had begun to sweat. Moistness crept over his skin; he was aware of every sensation: adrenaline rippling in his veins, wrenching him.

He turned so that he lay on his side, facing away from Esther. At least his neighbor's motion-sensitive light had gone off.

He'd experienced the beginnings of a panic attack before, but had always been able to climb his way back by imagining good things, just like his parents had taught him to do when he was a kid, interrupting their lives with his nightmares and fears. ("Just think about all that's good in the world; concentrate on being happy.")

He used to think of his golden Labrador (Buttercup!), visualize her panting, squinty-eyed, happy dog face and dog breath. Or how his father used to tuck him into bed, making the blankets tight and firm over him. His dad used to say that the blankets were "an armor against bad things."

Charlie was the youngest of three—a surprising but welcome "whoops!" long after his parents had ceased thinking of themselves as reproductive agents. He had gotten the best of them, been indulged by their love and attention.

His mom used to sing songs she'd created especially for him. His favorite, set to a perky tune, was an endless list of all the folks (and animals and deities) who loved him: "Momma loves Charlie; Daddy loves Charlie; Buttercup loves Charlie; Gangy loves Charlie; Pop Pop loves Charlie; Auntie loves Charlie . . . ," going on and on, and usually ending with God and Jesus loving him, so that he'd feel himself surrounded and consumed (and slightly suffocated) by a safety net of love.

He heard his mom's voice singing. And he saw himself swinging his golf club, driving a ball into an endless blue sky. His legs bent, arms back, and the swing—*phoosh*—as graceful as flying, his club, arms, legs, torso as one.

Over and over, like counting sheep.

But these visualizations and good thoughts seemed immature and futile, and he searched for adult thoughts to comfort him.

Immediately, he came up with women. All the women he knew. How much he appreciated them. He saw their skin, a blending of them. And then he focused on Brenda's endless legs, the curve of her calves, her slim ankles. The small cleft—like a tiny thumbprint—in Jennifer's upper lip, her bottom lip as plump and soft as a marshmallow. The smooth flesh of Esther's neck, below her ear and at her throat. And an endless array of young, beautiful women, sitting at their desks, watching him in class: crossing their legs, leaning forward, smiling at him—adoring him.

He traveled further back, all the way to high school, remembering Angie's thin waist, her lanky frame. Nipples as small as quarters. She had been a cheerleader; he used to love to watch her high kicks for the thrill of her awkward clumsiness, in the midst of all her perfection.

She'd been his first and he'd been hers, in her father's Buick, parked in a weedy shelter near the Back Bay, rain pattering on the roof and windows. They'd had trouble getting the car seat to lower, and then it had thumped down all at once, making them laugh.

Angie was married now, three kids. The last time he had seen her was at Vons, navigating the cereal aisle, one kid sitting in the grocery cart, the other two holding on to it. Middle-aged and bravely unwilling to dye her dull gray hair, she'd smiled sullenly and he'd kissed her on the cheek chastely, remembering the way she used to ride him—how skilled they'd gotten at the gymnastics of sex in a Buick.

He hoped that Angie would slide him back to sleep—not the old Angie, but the young one. His fingers grazed his penis, desiring the distraction of lust, but it was warm and soft, sluglike, unresponsive.

And he slipped back to death. His nerves wouldn't allow him to sink into safety. Panic whirled inside him. He listened to Esther's even breathing, moist and oblivious. He thought of waking her, making her share his turmoil. But she would only add to it with her wide-eyed and troubled stare. She was wrapped in the sheets, peaceful.

Horribly alive, Charlie tried to pray: *Dear God*, he thought. What was he doing? Composing a letter?

Nothing more came to him. Because there was no God. There was only a void of death, an ending.

As a child, he'd felt something: *Our Father, who art in heaven, please, please. God bless Mommy and Daddy*. Dismal, small life, no relief. What did it mean? His heart thudded—like it might come out of his chest. He was wet with sweat.

Certain that he was having a heart attack, he leapt from the bed with a plaintive squeak of the mattress, took off his T-shirt and boxers, and lay naked on the cool wood floor.

He saw a mouse under the bed, and his heart and head clenched at the same time, in a sort of panic-awe, until his eyes adjusted to the dark and he saw that it was his sock, scrunched in a ball.

From his peak of fear, his life became as small as a speck, and as useless. Panic continued to course through him, moving freely, without hesitation, but along with it came shame. He'd been afraid of his own sock!

He took long, deep breaths. His heart continued to thud, but he no longer thought it was a heart attack.

Feeling that his thoughts had led him into this nonsense, he went tense with anger, snapped back a little, his stomach churning. His breathing slowed, his heart calmed.

And he had inadvertently led himself to a solution, making the seeming futility of life bearable again: an exhausted reticence that, one way or another, he had no control over whether he lived or died, and he was too tired, too overwhelmed, to fight it.

He didn't care. But lurking closely was a cowardly awareness that he might not be a great man. That perhaps he'd been fooling himself with all his books and ideas and rebellions. Perhaps the key to life was to be comfortable—to seek comforts to ward off the void.

An overwhelming desire for a glass of milk took hold of him. White, pure milk, gorgeous in a glass—a solid something.

He got up from the floor, went to the kitchen, and opened the refrigerator. The light illuminated all the food products and beverages, humming with certainty, and as he reached for the carton of milk, appreciating the feel of cold air circulating around him, he made a decision: *I need to protect myself. I cannot live like this.*

◈ 3 ◈

THERE WAS A familiar weight in Eileen's bladder; she refused to wear adult diapers, no matter what Rick said. *I have to go to the bathroom*, she thought. *Then I'd like to smoke a cigarette, drink a Heineken.*

Her cane was beside her bed, leaned against her nightstand, and she paused and stared at her left foot. Gnarled toenails, veins popping at her ankle. One purplish vein looked like it might explode right out of her skin. There was a scab on her big toe because of Rick. She'd sat in her chair, watching the movie *Red River*, while Rick clipped her toenails; watched John Wayne tackle an Indian in the river, plunge a knife into him—once, twice, three times—the water splashing. And then Rick had cut too close and she'd yelped. "Sorry," Rick had said, plucking tissue from a box, wrapping it around her big toe, blood soaking through. "The least of my problems," she told him. And it had been worth it, the smile he gave her.

All that effort, just to stand. "Up and at 'em," Rick would say if he were here, holding on to her.

Aaargh! Uuugh!

"Here we go," she heard Rick say. "You got it."

And then she was standing, both hands clutching her cane. Alone. No Rick.

She waited for the dizziness to fade; then she waited for the swarm of flies to leave her head before she moved.

She saw her image in her three sliding closet mirrors as she used the cane to get to her bathroom. *Hello, asshole*, she thought. *Fuck you. Asshole, asshole*, walking slowly, slowly, bare feet shuffling on carpet, back hunched in her flannel nightgown, vision blurred—the work of the sleeping pills and the Heinekens, mixed with Prozac. Dr. Franklin had called it a sexy antidepressant. *Sexy. Sexy. Asshole. Asshole.* And then she was out of sight of the mirrors.

The doorway to the bathroom was open, the light kept on. She made a turn, a tug on her feet, a mix-up—why was the carpet swollen in one place and sunk in another? An instant, a flash—many falls before—an exiting, a letting go, a giving of time, space, person. An acceptance: She gasped and braced for impact.

And her head hit the door frame, cane flung to the side. Her head—her neck—took the brunt. Other times, a leg, an arm, her torso, her ass, helping conclude, buffer, but this time—this one time—her head against a door frame.

She was curled on the carpet, making sense of her surroundings, ashamed, in pain. She imagined stars swirling around her head. The skin was peeled back on her forehead, and when she touched two fingers against the warm place and drew them back, she saw that they were dark with blood. The alarm from her alert bracelet had sounded and the phone was ringing and she was lying in the doorway between her closet and the bathroom and the toilet was making a noise like a gurgling stream.

"EILEEN. JESUS, EILEEN. Are you okay?"

Even as her son-in-law lifted her, helped her to the bathroom, pulled her flannel nightgown up beyond her thighs, held her steady while her urine dribbled into the bowl of water, toilet making its gurgling noise, her mind would not quiet.

Thief, she thought. *Of course I'm not okay. Leave me alone.*

She was helped back to bed, Lottie on one side, George on the other; they tucked her in, covers at her chin, set her cane by her nightstand.

"It looks like a scrape," she heard Lottie say. "Like a scraped knee, but on her head. It doesn't need stitches."

The silhouette of her daughter and son-in-law staring down at her—concern, pity—and she wanted them gone.

She wanted to make sense in private.

"How does your head feel?" Lottie asked.

"Leave me alone," she said, thinking, *It hurts like hell*, and she shut her eyes to them; she was already leaving them, dismissing them.

Mr. Nobody. She hadn't thought about that in a long time. When she'd sent her gay son to a psychologist, she'd sat in for five minutes of his first (and last) session—he must have been ten or eleven, right before puberty hit.

"I wish I wasn't a boy," he'd said, "and I wish I wasn't becoming a man."

"Is that so?" Stupid psychologist—long eyelashes, probably a gay. One gay helping another gay.

"Yes. And I wouldn't want to be a girl, either." Panic had rolled through her, but looking back, she recognized that he was clever—her clever faggot son.

"Then who or what would you like to be?"

"I wouldn't like to be anyone; I'd like to be Mr. Nobody."

"But if you were Mr. Nobody, you'd still be somebody."

"I wouldn't like that; I'd like to be just nothing."

Mr. Nobody. Mr. Nobody. She had the sensation that she was like fog: here and not here at the same time. And then she was asleep.

WHEN SHE WOKE in the morning, she opened her mouth, but there was only a garbled sound. She leaned on her elbow, in such a position that she saw her expression in the dresser mirror: Her eyes were loose with fear, like in a horror movie before the character lets out a scream.

She looked away.

Her head floated and then crashed with pain; floated, crashed with pain. She made her way to the bathroom with her cane and then abandoned it near the toilet, descended to her hands and knees near the specks of blood on her white carpet, a streak of blood along the door frame. The urine ran down her thigh, and she tugged a towel from its rack and swiped herself.

Crawling to her closet, she saw that Rick had laid out her sweat suit on the orange chair, but it was too tricky. A cream-colored sweat suit, two blue stripes down the sides; the zipper jacket had pockets and a hood. She'd changed into it at Christmas after she'd peed her pants. Her family had sat around the pinewood table, drinking wine, picking at their meals, and only Rick had noticed the dark stain down her pant leg.

She opened the sliding, mirrored closet door, looked up at Gurney's polo shirts in various hues, his selection of cashmere sweaters, a camel-hair jacket that he used to wear to funerals, and his Lands' End slacks with their elastic waistbands. She'd kept his clothes all these years, even when Lottie had insisted that she throw them out. She pulled on one of the polo shirts, and the hangers rattled.

Lying on the floor, she hooked her flannel nightgown over her head, right arm, then left, and pulled it off. There was a sparkling of light and a stabbing in her neck as it went over her head. She found underwear from her dirty-clothes hamper: left leg, then right. She jerked the peach-colored polo shirt on, light sparkling again, stabbing neck pain. The shirt was inside out, backward, the collar rubbing on her chin. It was small on her, tight, but there was no way to get it off now.

She crawled to her chair. It took twenty-three minutes, inch by inch—she watched the minutes glowing on her electronic clock. She held on to the chair and rose, the room spun, and she vomited. It looked like melted chocolate, all down her chest. And then she realized that it was blood.

She slumped into the chair and waited for Rick. It was almost seven, and he was never late.

Mr. Nobody. Mr. Nobody—everywhere in the room, and in every sound, the tears rolling down her cheeks; she tasted salt and blood—bloody salt.

When she saw Rick, she was relieved and she tried to talk to him, but she couldn't get her mouth to work. A noise came from her; it sounded like a whimper. *I love you*, she wanted to tell him. She could see by his eyes that he was terrified. "Eileen, it's me," he told her. "It's Rick. You stay here, Eileen. You're cold. I'm going to get you a blanket."

Her head beat as if someone were hitting it with a fist. Rick moved across the room, did things she couldn't see, and returned with a blanket. A drop of wet clung and trembled at her nostril, heaving in and out with her breaths. She tried to send a signal to her hand to wipe it, but her hand wouldn't move.

Again, she opened her mouth to speak, but nothing came out. Rick's mouth was stretched in tension as he placed the blanket gently over her body.

As his face came closer, he became more out of focus. "Here," he said, and he was wiping her nose with a tissue. The small pressure made a sharp pain grip her neck, and then it slowly and horribly filled her body.

Everything went out of focus again, and then into a fuzzy glare. She moved her eyes to the window, looked at the stretch of dark blue and lighter blue sky.

As she watched, a sailboat crept into her sight, and then another. Their sails leaned to the side, white and puffed with wind, and the people moving on the boats were as small as ants.

Jesus Christ, she thought. *I'm going to die.* And then the boats moved past the frame of her window where her eyes could not follow.

"When this is over," Rick said, gripping her hand, "we'll watch *The Searchers.* How does that sound? Huh? How about that?"

HER HEAD FLOATED; she was lying in a hospital bed, her wrists tied with restraints. Then panic, stab in her neck, crash in her head. Rick's voice, trying to comfort her: "I'm here, Eileen. I'm here."

Bang! Bang! Bang! No way to express the pain, the stab at her neck, the explosion in her head, her language gone.

Her eyes did not settle until she was in a coma.

AND SHE FOUGHT. Even in a coma, the next day, surprising the nurses and doctors. Brain stem injury, C1 cervical fracture. Fall with head trauma, gastrointestinal bleeding. A broken neck.

Rick remained with her through the following morning and

into the afternoon, and then Esther joined him; the others did not come. Despite everything, she lingered.

EARLY EVENING, RICK and Esther left for the cafeteria, to get coffee; while they were gone, her vital signs dipped, as if on impulse, and she slipped away all at once.

4

IN THEIR AUTUMNAL years, Charlie's father and mother had been doing "some serious soul searching," and whatever they'd discovered in their soul quest had impelled his father to write their last-born son a check for $200,000, with the request that Charlie finally "settle down and buy a home."

Charlie was able to greet the check with news of his promotion at Orange County Community College, further recommending himself as a worthy recipient. He'd been more than satisfied by this generous figure and was quietly enjoying its implications, when, with the liquidation of a building or two or three or four in his father's business, and a rearrangement of his father's trust (he wasn't sure of the specifics; he preferred to be in the dark), Charlie learned that the "soul searching" was in continuance, and that as a result, he and his siblings—in a month or two, "when the ink dried"—would be worth close to $3 million each.

With sudden riches came certain responsibilities: He needed to acquire a lawyer, a financial advisor, and a real estate agent. As soon as possible. An aura of importance settled over him, followed closely by a sense of immediacy, knowing that his person was backed by such a large sum.

He told no one of his impending wealth, especially not Esther, as that would have only further complicated their relationship—she had enough to think about. He was protecting her—or was he? He couldn't think about her right now. Their relationship was too confusing; come to think of it, she had always confused him: Falling for her seemed evidence that he was entrenched in the culture he criticized openly. She was becoming increasingly unstable, as her arrest demonstrated.

Thinking about her—about them—was like being lost in an unending maze. He was done thinking about the relationship, for now. She was impossible to understand. If he waited the situation out, he might gain clarity, like golfing in the early morning fog until it dissipated with the sun's light.

Charlie walked a little straighter; he purchased new underwear and socks and set up an appointment with a "personal shopper" to update his wardrobe; he got a haircut at an expensive salon (short and masculine, his mother would love it) and purchased the suggested hair care products, regardless of cost. He thought more before speaking, feeling that his words carried a certain weight ("Say what you mean and mean what you say," his father had often told him), and he became impregnated with the idea that his future held great possibilities, that he could no longer be a spectator to his own fate, but must participate actively in its grand arrival. It was his birthright.

He could do a great many things as a rich man that he had not been able to consider before, and the love of knowledge that so occupied him could be cultivated with travel—he was already planning a trip around the world! Maybe two trips around the world! Indonesia, China, Africa. Why not? He could go back to school, get his PhD. "Doctor Charles Murphy" had a good ring to it.

Why not take advantage of the money? It was his birthright. He wouldn't squander it on stupid material possessions—he was different from the majority of wealthy people. He appreciated money for what it was: a means to an end. He didn't need *things*. Well, maybe a few things, just because.

A nice car—God, any car he wanted. Sweet Jesus. He could buy a Porsche if he wanted. Three million dollars! Not that he'd ever buy a Porsche. He could buy his own membership to the country club—he wouldn't have to use his parents' every time he wanted to golf.

But he'd draw the line: He'd make sure to use the money for worthwhile purposes. Maybe he'd even donate a generous figure to Clothing for Change. Yes, he would. Anonymously, of course.

Although he had always appreciated his parents, any lingering resentments were wiped clean, and now when he thought of them, it was only with gratitude and love. His siblings had conformed in all the ways he hadn't, pleasing his parents, and he'd secretly harbored animosity, jealous not of their accomplishments, necessarily, but more of how their accomplishments suited their parents. But this, too, evaporated in a golden shimmer of goodwill.

Whereas before he'd attended family events and dinners and meetings with an amiable resignation (the unconventional outsider, beloved nonetheless), now he found himself looking forward to the company of his blood kin.

And it was with giddy anticipation that he walked to the driving range of Pelican Hill, where his brother, Frank, stood waiting. Frank had arranged the meeting, and Charlie had been honored and surprised that his brother wanted to spend time with him, as that was not ordinarily the case.

Charlie carried a bucket of golf balls, his driver and a few other clubs tucked under an armpit, and as he neared, Frank's arms spread open in an expansive welcome.

"Charlie, my brother," Frank said.

"Hey there, brother," Charlie said, setting his bucket and clubs on the grass. And then he was embraced in a masculine hug with the requisite back slaps—a hug that had been passed down from father to sons.

Although their greetings were marked by an affectionate familiarity, Charlie thought of his brother more as an authority figure (Frank was nine years older) than as a genetic equal, and had developed during childhood and all the years that followed a commingling respect and distaste for him.

It was hard to shake: Around his brother, he often had the perverse sensation of having just been pulled over by a policeman for a traffic violation.

He'd always been more comfortable with his sister, Karen (five years older). She was amused but not threatened by his liberal politics. She'd nicknamed him The Family Weirdo, but when he'd asked her to stop calling him that, she had (except during phone greetings—"Hey, Weirdo!").

Having married a well-known businessman (Tom Tefflinger, or Double-T, as he was often called) and produced three children in quick succession, Karen was responsible mainly for the upkeep of their home and children, as well as for alternating visits to the gym and the tennis court to keep her figure trim. Aside from a brief scare with breast cancer (the tumor had been removed, her breast remained intact), she led what she termed "a charmed life."

Frank held an MBA from Stanford, but rather than spread his business acumen in Charlie's direction, he liked to tease him ("Hey, I'm curious, Charlie: Does that liberal arts background help with the stock market?").

Charlie trusted their father to arrange his will so that Frank couldn't strip Charlie of his share of the family fortune, because, if given the opportunity, Frank would leave him in the dust. But Charlie didn't blame his brother or hate his brother—he figured it must have been what they taught at Stanford business school.

"What a day, huh?" Frank observed, his gloved hand taking a swipe at the emerald-colored grass. The fountain near them gurgled like a happy baby, a bubble of water in the center. Beyond the driving range, the ocean and sky stretched in blue agreement.

"Beautiful," Charlie concurred.

Frank's attention was on him. "I like it," he said, nodding his approval of the recent haircut. "Nice."

"Mom's going to love it," Charlie said, his face flushing at the thought.

"So will Sheila," Frank said, bending over to tee his ball. "She's been asking me for years, 'Why won't Charlie cut his hair and shave?' 'I don't know, honey,' I tell her. 'Charlie's always been a little different.'"

Frank had been married for over twenty years to Sheila ("I am my kids' mom," she said, when asked her occupation), and a whole wall of their parents' house was devoted to photographs of the three progeny this contented union had produced (the opposite wall was devoted to Karen and Double-T's offspring).

Frank stepped back, taking in the driving range with a happy squint.

Sheila had never liked Charlie, he had never liked Sheila, but he felt his grooming habits should be left out of the equation. "I shave every day," he said.

Frank shrugged.

"I'm not kidding," he said. "I shave every day."

Frank crooked his elbows inward so that his arms made a *V* from his torso, his golf club like a baton.

Charlie decided to let it go, but he could hear Sheila's voice, the note of self-righteousness: *It's simple. I don't care how smart you are. You can be a professor of everything, for all I care. You need a wife. Just imagine what a good woman could do for you. A good woman would make you* accountable *for your actions. I'm tired of standing back and saying nothing and watching you go from one bad choice to the next. Your picker is broken. Don't laugh! Admit it, Charlie. Your picker is broken. Big boobs and blue eyes—those are your requirements! That's it, it's settled: I'm going to set you up on a date!*

Frank leaned over his golf ball, crooked his knees.

Charlie set up a tee beside him. The sounds of balls being struck reverberated around him, and he went into the motion of his swing. In his experience, the driving range was a productive way to clear his head, and his head needed clearing.

He'd taken literally and with no small amount of relief Esther's declaration that morning to "leave me alone," the dark beam of her eyes drilling through him. Earlier that morning, he'd been telling her about a theory he'd read recently that sex had evolved as a form of cannibalism—one primitive organism eating another and, in the process, exchanging DNA. He was talking—"Did you know that in some organisms, sexual reproduction has been shown to enhance the spread of parasitic genetic elements, like yeast and fungi? We need these things. The most honest sexual interactions have a component of destruction"—when she'd interrupted him, saying, "Oh, please, Charlie, be quiet. I haven't had breakfast." She watched his reaction and then added, "Maybe you're just afraid of commitment."

"This isn't about commitment," he said. "It's about looking at sex through the clear eyes of science; it's about the possibility of a better understanding, an understanding that is not crippled by sentimentality."

"Okay," she said, but it was obvious that she was agreeing so that he would stop talking.

And they'd gotten in a fight the night before, and all because he'd told her that a friend of his had said that she looked like a model.

"Is that why you're with me?" she said. "So that your friends can tell you that your woman looks like some stupid model?"

"You don't know that models are stupid," he said, for some reason feeling the need to defend them. "You don't know that for a fact." He'd meant the statement as a compliment and was hurt by her reaction.

She was silent, and her look seemed to reduce him to a man who was interested in her for her beauty—and not at all interested in her as a person, which seemed unfair. He tried to explain this, and she interrupted, saying, "It's the way you said it."

"What do you mean?"

"Your voice," she said. "You sounded so *proud*."

"Now you're mad at me for the way my voice sounded," he said. "Think about how unreasonable that is."

"You never ask me what I think," she said.

"Sure I do."

"No," she said, "not really."

"About what?" he asked. "What do you want me to ask?" He could feel social forces, pressures, stereotypes, and misconceptions collecting, waiting to ambush them, to overtake them.

"Anything," she said, turning her face from him. "You never ask me what I think about things."

This, he felt, was one of those trick conversations. But in a strange way, he knew she was right.

He put his hand on her shoulder, and she faced him. They looked at each other expectantly, but there was nothing to say.

He understood that she was under a great deal of stress, but even so. She'd flinched that morning when he'd touched her arm. And the look she kept giving him—it was as if she were accusing him of something he didn't understand.

There was a word for the way she was behaving, but he couldn't think of it. What was the word? It was on the tip of his tongue. Whether her desire to be left alone was in earnest, it was easier to comply with than to question. She'd been sitting on the bed, with her head cradled in her hands, and he was having trouble getting that image of her out of his mind.

Morbid. That was the word. She was morbid.

During his other relationships—even during his affair with Brenda—he'd lived carefully: making sure to sleep at least eight hours each night; reading novels and inspirational books, along with his academic pursuits; exercising three times a week; eating fiber; and evacuating his bowels each morning. But with Esther, he experienced a loss of control, a loss of routine, a loss of order.

Morbid. She moped around his apartment, she spent the night without asking, she'd basically been living there for the past month. She wasn't taking care of herself, wasn't showering or wearing makeup, and he had to remind her some mornings to change her clothes. She looked older, sadder.

Sometimes he'd look at her and see a middle-aged, severe Esther. Not as bad-looking as Sheila, with her thick waist and broad shoulders and that flap of skin under her chin that signaled the beginnings of a double chin, but still.

It was like Esther had stopped caring.

"I'm tired of trying," she'd explained one night (all in response to his simply reminding her to brush her teeth). "I shave my armpits and then they just grow more hair and I have to shave them again. I brush my hair and then it gets messy and I have to brush it again. It goes on and on and on. I'm just so tired of it all! I'm tired, Charlie. Don't you see?" And then she flagged her hands in front of him, wiggled her fingers. "Look, see? My polish is chipped; the nails are breaking. What's the point? I'm tired; tired, tired, tired."

This is as beautiful as you'll ever be, he'd wanted to tell her. *You'll never be as pretty as you are right now, and you're wasting it.*

She was always staring at him, studying him. That awful, condemning stare. She was stony and cold—remote.

But she perked up when she went to visit her drug-addled brother at his recovery home. He watched her come alive. Sometimes she went with Rick—he honked the horn for her, one long beep. ("Why doesn't he just come inside?" "Because he thinks you don't like him." And again, she'd given him that stare.)

Charlie hit a quick succession of golf balls—he'd set three in a row—*clack, clack, clack*. The sound of his club making contact satisfied him, echoing through his body with a mysterious warmth. His balls landed within yards of each other, like a constellation of stars leading toward the flagged hole.

The sun had come out of a cloud, making everything look new and dramatic, and what was left of the morning fog melted and disappeared. He watched Frank squatting, his shirt dislodging from his khakis.

"You know what?" Frank said, standing. He settled himself over his golf ball, hips swaying. "I'm gonna hit this one all the way"—and he swung, smacked his ball—"to the moon."

5

ESTHER WAS DRAGGED through the final dregs of a nap-dream: she and Charlie on the beach. A sailboat floated across the surface of the ocean. And then suddenly Charlie ran and leapt into a wave, his toes visible—then he was gone, swallowed. When she woke, she stretched and widened into the cool spaces of his bed, feeling a fatalistic despair.

She got up and sat at Charlie's desk, scribbling him a note. It didn't take long. She finished and moved to collect her clothes from his closet, placing them in paper bags. She thought of his measured stare, his sweet and musty body odor, his pouting mouth.

She was hastening the process, trying to take away some of the sting. In the bathroom, before collecting her toothbrush and things, she sat for a moment on the toilet, and then she let her head fall between her knees. Her breasts pinched together; she smelled the stink of her armpits. *Swing for the fences*, she heard Eric say. *Swing for the fences, Esther. Keep your eye on the ball. Head up, chin up.*

Blood rushed to her face and she stood quickly, all at once, and screamed. Everything around her was enveloped in light, floating over the surface of things, so that she couldn't see. She waited for the mental fireworks to evaporate. And when they did, she was so hopeless, so sad, that she had to lean against the wall to keep from falling.

6

CHARLIE BEGAN TO suspect that Frank's meeting him at the driving range had another purpose, beyond that of brotherly bonding, and his suspicion was confirmed three Coronas each later, at the clubhouse, when Frank admitted, "We're worried, Charlie. Dad, Mom, Karen, Double-T, Sheila, me. We're all worried."

"Jesus," Charlie said, "you called a family meeting without me?"

Frank grimaced.

"They appointed you talking head?"

"Can you blame us?" Frank asked, palming cocktail peanuts.

"I don't understand."

"We're hearing things all over town, Charlie."

"What things?"

"Just last week, Mrs. Logan—you know, Mom's doubles partner from way back—told her that Esther had been with Jim Dunnels. Jim Dunnels, Charlie! That guy owns Fashion Island! Why else do you think she'd go after him?"

"I don't believe it," Charlie said, gut sinking. He shook his head, his eyes concentrating for a moment on the hairs at his wrist. When he looked up again, he was dizzy, as if he'd stood up too quickly in bright sunlight.

A long pause followed. Frank chewed his peanuts, swallowed. They both drank from their Corona bottles in an uncanny unison, watching each other warily.

"And Sheila," Frank said, wiping the side of his mouth with a cocktail napkin. "Marlene told her about a month ago that Esther had something going on with Sean. Sean Caldwell, Charlie. I didn't want to tell you, but Sheila says I have to."

"Not true."

"Marlene's daughter works at Newport Floral, and she said that Sean sent Esther tulips, two, three, four times a week!"

When Charlie didn't respond, he added, "She has the receipts, Charlie."

"Not true," Charlie said, more angrily than he had meant to.

"Okay, okay. Easy there now, compadre. I'm on your side, remember?"

"No. Not Sean."

"Okay. Maybe. Maybe not. But Jim Dunnels?"

"Wrong," Charlie said.

"How'd she get off those theft charges?" Frank asked.

"Nope," Charlie said.

"Her brother's out of jail, Charlie. How'd he get out of jail?"

"No," Charlie said, shaking his head, "nope, nope, nope, nope, nope."

"C'mon, man."

"Nope, nope, nope."

"Look, we're worried. That's all. Does she know? Did you tell her about the money?"

"You don't even know her."

"Look, Charlie, you gotta be careful now. Women will go

after you for money—you know that. It happens all the time. And she's gone after these other guys, Charlie, and something tells me it's not because of their good looks. We're just trying to protect your interests."

"You don't know her."

Frank was silent for a moment, staring at the tabletop. His head came up. "I know Dad cut you a check for two hundred thou," he said. He shook his head in disgust, and for a moment, Charlie saw that he was jealous of The Family Weirdo!

But any triumph was short-lived.

"He's equal with us, always," Frank said. "But this time he gave you more. Don't you see it? Don't you get it? Don't you feel any obligation? Don't you feel any responsibility to your family? To Dad? How can you act like it doesn't mean anything?"

"I love Dad," Charlie said, his voice quavering. He let his gaze go back to the hair on his forearm. He was aware that Frank was watching him, but he kept his eyes downward, firm and indignant in his love for his parents.

"We're worried, that's all," Frank said. "Mom's ulcer," he said, "it started acting up again." He paused. "She's been chewing through packets of Tums, Charlie."

"Mom said it was indigestion."

"And you should've seen Dad," Frank said. "Awful. He didn't even sleep for two nights. He said he hasn't had insomnia like that since World War II."

Charlie looked up then. His eyes burned and he had the sudden urge to reach across the table and strangle his brother; at the same time, an overwhelming grief sank into him, and he fought back tears.

In wary observation, Frank's voice took on a gentle, apologetic tone: "Maybe we're wrong, Charlie; maybe we're wrong."

They were silent. A television in the corner of the bar showed images from the O. J. Simpson trial—detective Mark Fuhrman being cross-examined. The day before, Charlie had watched the trial, Fuhrman denying using the word "nigger" in the previous ten years.

Frank noticed Charlie looking at the television and said, "Such a shame. I loved him in those Hertz commercials," and he put his arm out, mimicking O. J. running through the airport as if striding down a football field.

When Charlie didn't respond, he said, "Maybe she's great; maybe she's just great. We haven't even met her yet. Maybe she's just fine."

WHEN CHARLIE ARRIVED back at his apartment, he knew as soon as his hand was on his front doorknob that Esther had left him, because the door was locked. She had saved him the trouble of any confrontations.

He stood for a moment, listening to the birds squawking in a nearby tree; he heard the sounds of traffic and, closer, someone playing a piano—a beginner: *plink plunk plunk.*

The sun was low, but it seemed to be exerting its force one last time, making everything a little brighter, including his arm. He saw the hairs standing like little soldiers, a yellow-blue vein at the inside of his elbow. And then he looked up, to the sky. Strips of peach-colored clouds, long and skinny, were moving quickly. *To hell with her*, he thought. *How could she leave me?*

He found a note on his bedside dresser, propped on his pelican lamp. Her handwriting was small and boxy, in a corner of the paper, as if her words were ashamed and hiding:

Charlie,

The only thing I want you to know for sure, no matter what people tell you, is that I did not have sex with Jim Dunnels or anyone else.

E

He checked the bathroom: Her makeup, even the box of tampons underneath the sink—it was all gone. In the last month, she'd been bringing clothes, leaving them in his closet. He checked there: His clothes were pushed to the far left, and the other half of the closet was full of empty hangers.

In shock, he sat on his bed, closed his eyes. He could still smell her. She had a star-shaped freckle underneath the crease of her left buttock. He could not fathom never seeing it again—he felt its loss like a death.

And then his breath came out, in a long groaning noise. He stretched out on his bed and let himself cry, but even as the tears came, he experienced some relief.

For a long time, he reflected on his conversation with Frank ("Nope, nope, nope, nope"), and then her note. He believed her: She hadn't slept with Jim Dunnels or anyone else. No matter what Frank said. He thought of her breath in his mouth, her hands at his back, as he pushed into her. And he knew.

Yet how had she gotten off those charges? When he'd asked, she hadn't had an answer. And then he'd stopped asking. Why was Eric suddenly out of jail? Why had Sean sent her flowers? That Newport Floral woman had receipts. Marlene's daughter. Who was Marlene? Was she lying? Why would she lie about something like that?

Nothing made sense. He was weary of trying to sort out their relationship; he felt like he'd been examining it for years.

He licked his lips, tasted her mouth. The hard part would be getting her out of his system. Physically, she'd become an extra skin.

Even with her gone, it was like she was reaching inside him and clutching his soul, demanding that he give her more than he was capable of giving, that he believe more than he was capable of believing, and that he trust more than he was capable of trusting.

His legs bent inward, as if to protect his bowels. On the whole, their relationship had been an uneasy business.

Shivering, he pulled the covers over him. He felt around his emotions, like testing his tongue in the region of a sore tooth, but not probing the source directly. Did he want to go after her? Should he try to get her back? He could leave right now. Find her. Demand that she stay. They were in this together. He deserved an explanation. Did he want to hear an explanation? Would it make a difference? He loved her. She loved him.

But something held him back. He took a deep breath, let it out through his nostrils. Three breaths later, he rolled over to his other side, stretched his legs. He let his hand cup his penis, as if comforting it. He scratched his leg, turned again.

As a senior in high school, after his third relationship with a woman, he'd been distraught over their breakup and had stalked his ex for a week; he'd watched her at cheerleading tryouts from underneath the football stands, masturbated to her memory every night. He'd drunkenly relieved his bowels near her parents' rosebushes as a misguided revenge. The porch light had gone on, her mother finding him crouched there. ("Charles Michael Murphy," she'd said, "what are you doing? You should be ashamed of yourself—no better than a dog.") He'd promised never to willingly humiliate himself again.

And yet here he was, cowering in his bed. But the core of him knew that this was different. For a moment, he experienced a desire to find Esther, to catch her in a compromising position with Jim Dunnels. He wanted proof, to expunge his sense of guilt. But it wouldn't work: She wasn't sleeping with anyone else. It would be impossible to catch her. He had to accept that the breakup was his doing, even if she was the one who had instigated it.

He wanted to believe that his motives had a selfless quality, but there was no getting around it: What held him back was not that he had nothing to give. What held him back was the thought of what he might lose.

TWO DAYS OF suffering later, Charlie sat at his desk, near the triage of photographs documenting the phenomenon of Ben Hogan's golf swing, and tried to compose a letter to Esther.

With the pen between his fingertips, his elbow resting on the desk and his cheek in his palm, he directed his eyes to the blank slate of paper. He wouldn't open a possibility for her to come back. His future would be easier without the turbulence that she guaranteed.

And besides, she'd left him.

She'd left him! She'd left him! She was the one who had left!

How was it possible, then, that he felt he owed her an explanation? Such were her powers.

But he felt the lingering responsibilities of a boyfriend to comfort Esther, because her grandmother had passed away, finally, that crazy old bitch.

He saw her staring back at him with the face she made when she was disappointed—an ironic sadness. With Esther, it was one drama after another. There was only so much a man could take. He imagined her fisting her hand and tapping it against her thigh. She leaned her head when she listened, her expression imploring him to slow down, as if she wanted his words to hover over her before they sank inside. She had a soothing voice; she didn't make it go high and girlie, like so many other women he'd been with did.

All these other women—there were many—they'd been crowding into his subconscious these last three days, but Esther rose above the swarm. She was the one who had dug into him, who would leave a permanent mark.

But the pleasures of women would comfort him again; he believed this. He appreciated women. He would find his solace there—it was his guarantee in life.

But for now, in his bedroom, all he felt was an exhausting sense of agony.

"Oh, God," he said, and then he let out a moan.

Enough, he thought, taking a firmer stance. *Courage. I need courage. She might have ruined my life! She might have dragged me down. She's a thief. Her brother's a drug addict. She flirts with other men.*

Jim Dunnels. He owns Fashion Island. No wonder she flirted with him. What else did she do with him? Did she let him see her naked? Mental illness probably runs in her family—no one knows who her real parents are. She's unstable.

Esther,

I wish you only the best.

Esther, Esther, Esther, Esther, Esther

Esther esther Est her Est her

Her her her her

Es es es

He crumpled the page, tossed it. Did she know about his inheritance? How would she have known?

Dear Esther,

You are fearless. You can do anything. Don't give up.

I know you've had a rough life. I don't blame you for anything.

He crumpled the page, tossed it.

Esther,

I will never forget you. Believe me. I will always love you.

Crumple, toss.

Dear Esther,

You are the most beautiful woman ever. Forget me! It's all my fault. Why did I ever know you? How could this have happened? I'm so sorry. Please forget me! The thought of your grief—that I've made you suffer even more—I can't stand it!

Dear Esther,

I'm feeling desperate and sad. More sad. And tired. God, I've done so many things wrong. I don't even know where to begin?

Dear Esther,

You've gone into emotional lockdown mode. You've cut me off.

Dear Esther,

I understand that in life, circumstances take hold and throw you where they will. I feel like that now. Like no matter

> what I want or believe, there is a force at work stronger than anything having to do with me.

He ripped all the papers together, let the pieces fall over his desk, weary of his rationalizations. He felt a longing to be unencumbered by confusion.

The floor beneath the soles of his feet seemed to rise: *I'm here. This is my floor. And my feet are right here.* All the forces of existence washed over him, the extraordinary sensation of being alive.

A feeling of pinpricks was at the back of his head and it moved over his face, to his forehead. He thought again and again and again of his inheritance.

The consolation of $3 million warmed and settled over his broken, raggedy heart. He took the knowledge all the way in, without guilt, like a gust of godlike fresh air in the midst of a polluted shit pile. His shoulders loosened, he leaned back against the chair, and he let go of the pen.

7

ESTHER IMAGINED THAT she was a dog with her tail between her legs. The waitresses avoided her, and she wondered what they were saying about her, since she was outside their circle of rumor and gossip—although, most likely, she was a primary inspiration for it. The disappointment of her life was magnified by the two shots of tequila she'd consumed on the sly, crouched below the bar.

She would eat tonight. A baked potato on her break, maybe a roll with butter. She had trouble getting food down and often had to force her appetite. The surface of the hostess podium was faintly scarred, and she saw gruesome faces in the grainy patterns of wood, with gaping mouths and eyes. Piano music, clinking cutlery, and the endless chattering and laughter of people—all of it blended into one throbbing, disagreeable noise. The small lamp at the podium cast a sharp ray of light over a corner of the black reservation book, opened: Her 9:30 party of six hadn't arrived yet. And the fuckers hadn't canceled, either.

Two stout and unsmiling men entered, and as she showed them to their table (brothers?), she felt their attention on her backside. Men still found her worth a second and third look, but they seemed to sense that she had lost the capacity to care whether they looked or not, and they soon lost interest.

As she passed the men plump menus, she thought that her life had turned out far different than she had ever expected. She wanted to believe that love was everything—and she'd felt that with Charlie. (Rick liked to say, "You have to give everything away in order to keep anything"—or something like that.) But it seemed that with Charlie, the more she gave away, the less of her was left. And she needed to be careful. People were more than willing and ready to take from her—to eat her up without even tasting her.

She stood at the men's table, staring out at the green-black bay water, losing herself in the smeary dark gold on the current, a reflection from the dock light, until one of the men said a harsh thank-you, reminding her to leave.

She had fought against her melancholy tendencies—her trances—for years, but now she willingly lost herself to them. A luxury. There was the intoxicating possibility of slipping clean out of space and time.

A large part of her had been smashed to pieces, and she had trouble recognizing what remained. Or identifying what she believed, as if she'd been dragged through a tunnel—the Charlie Tunnel—and what was left of her was ragged and confused.

Yet she couldn't blame Charlie. Even before their relationship, she'd been unable to follow through on marrying Paul Rice, not to mention the other men: Looking back, it was as if she continually did the wrong things at the right times and the right things at the wrong times.

But she knew better than to engage in self-pity, and she didn't want to go back to the pre-Charlie Esther.

On her way back to her hostess podium, she detoured and walked over to Ted, the bartender, drawn by his salacious stare.

"I've got a rocket in my pocket," he whispered, sidling closer, "and that woman, that one sitting over there, at the end of the—no, no, no, not that one—over there, over there. Hell no, not that one! Over there. Don't stare! Yeah, yeah—her. She's my release."

Esther wasn't sure which woman he was talking about—the one with the piña colada, a pineapple slice perched on her hourglass-shaped goblet, or her Corona-drinking friend—but she didn't really care.

Ted had driven Esther home one night, put a hand on her knee. But he'd handled her rejection well, saying it was standard, nothing personal. He saved neglected cocktails, abandoned bottles of wine, surplus alcohol from his own complicated system, and stored them in a corner of the bar—partitioned off from the restaurant—for the employees.

Staff interactions were often in a fast-forward, intimate, inappropriate, jocular style, and she was getting better at it.

"I'm in trouble," she said.

"Big Boss," Ted agreed, "is not happy."

"Who told him?"

Ted shrugged, and then moved away.

She walked toward her hostess podium, her four feet of an island. She felt a strange safety when she locked into it, with her forearms on the wood surface, her body leaned against it.

She watched Fred Smith strolling from one table to the next. He wore dark slacks and the cuffs of his shirt were folded to his elbows—casually elegant. He mixed amiably in a conversation, a hand on someone's shoulder, his head going back in soft laughter; he made a flattering remark (she saw the delight in the customers' faces), and then moved on to the next table, making his way to the bar.

He'd been avoiding her, so she knew that she was in trouble, even before Ted had confirmed it; she knew that any minute now, Fred would take her to his office and she'd have to endure a meeting.

Fred was listening to two men. The men reminded Esther of peacocks, their chests thrust out, competing for his attention. Then, probably because they bored him, Fred moved away. Before he reached the bar, he sent her a mournful look.

She hated disappointing him, hated that a menial job was proving to be so difficult, hated that she was incompetent, that she had no training or skills. Who would have thought that answering a phone, booking reservations, and seating parties could be so complicated? And all that standing and smiling. People were rude when they were hungry, as if it were her fault!

Last week, she'd booked a party of five at a table that seated only three, and she'd overbooked the eight o'clock slot, causing three parties to leave in anger, rather than wait an extra fifteen minutes. One customer had written a letter (she'd found it on Fred's desk), declaring his new mission to spread the news of The Palms' substandard service, all because of her failure to seat him promptly.

She saw a man with longish hair standing at the bar, talking with passion. He fisted his hand, slapped it in the palm of the other—twice—making a point.

A flare of adrenaline rose up the back of her neck, spreading across her in nebulous alarm. Was that Charlie? Could that be him? Excitement made her wobbly, and she steadied herself against the podium.

But then the man laughed, turned, reached for his margarita, and she saw the whiskers at his cheek, his not-Charlie lips and his not-Charlie nose and his not-Charlie forehead.

And her guts tightened in reprimand, wondering why she kept imagining Charlie, when he was obviously not there. He was probably in Greece or the Caribbean or Spain, with his newfound fortune. A woman latched on to each shoulder. She knew that Charlie had inherited money prematurely from his still-breathing parents, and that he was traveling. Brenda had been all too happy to spread this information to her when Esther had seen her at Grandma Eileen's funeral. But in her sincere effort to forget him (or, at the very least, to forget *about* him), she was daydreaming he was even more present, and it made her crazy and irrational.

She relived details of their relationship and then analyzed its demise. The stupid things she'd said came back to her; Charlie's endless, nervous intellectual banter; how she'd said "I love you" by accident while in the throes of passion.

All these memories and more burned through her with poignancy, making him so near that she felt his legs entwined with hers or his breath at her ear, and she would have to shake herself back into the present.

For a long time, she'd believed that she might get a phone call; there had been weeks when she'd stayed beside the phone, not to miss it. But she understood that what had passed between them made it impossible to go back to how she'd felt originally, and that a phone call might complicate any progress. Besides, she decided, Charles Murphy was an incomplete gathering of ideas and promises; he was bound to develop, most likely in all sorts of directions, but just not toward her.

I'm okay, she told herself. *I'm really okay*. She would repeat it, over and over, carefully, lightly, as she went about her day, trying not to examine this awareness too closely, or lose it with any deeper examination, as if it were a fragile egg she carried in her hand.

Often, she had to seat people she knew, and she could feel them gossiping about her as soon as she turned and left them.

And there was also the shameful anonymity of being ignored completely—unseen. In the beginning, entire shifts had passed without anyone's acknowledging her directly, unless Fred was there, overseeing the restaurant.

Fred had hired her when no one else would. He'd told her that her first month would be hard, that it would take a while to adjust, and that she needed to hang tight.

Month two, and she hadn't experienced much of an improvement.

She appreciated Fred's well-intentioned advice. ("Assholes will always be assholes, no matter what you tell them. They were assholes before you were arrested, and they'll be assholes after, but now it's easier to tell the difference.") But she disliked that he'd done her a favor—that she owed him a debt. It lurked around them, her sense of obligatory constant gratitude, and made her uneasy, unequal.

Most of the waitresses resented her, and she didn't blame them. Her incompetence affected their tables, and therefore their tips. Often she would see them arguing with Fred, probably urging him to fire her.

She shifted the toothpicks in the brass urn, made them crowd to the left. "Where's the bathroom?" a man asked, and without looking up, she pointed in its direction.

"Thanks," he said sarcastically, and she tried reminding herself to be grateful that she had a job. All the same, it could be worse: She had a place to live; she had a job. She had a job. She had a job. Eric (as far as she knew) was sober.

Aunt Lottie had kicked her out, blamed her for everything, including Grandma Eileen's unglamorous finish, but Esther wouldn't let her win. She remembered Mary's look of pitying condescension as she and Rick had carried paper bags full of her things out of Grandma Eileen's house. Aunt Lottie was already practicing her ignore-and-dismiss technique, making Esther disappear mentally before the demand was accomplished physically. But Mary had handed her a note, written on the back of a deposit slip from her checkbook:

> Dear Esther,
>
> This phrase could help.
>
> BELIEVE MORE DEEPLY HOLD YOUR FACE UP TO THE LIGHT!
>
> Please try. Suggestion: more prayer for cleansing. You have so much spiritual healing work to be done. Your behavior has hurt us all. REMEMBER THAT THERE IS NO END AND THERE IS NO BEGINNING THERE IS ONLY NOW. Walk in peace and harmony—less stress for you, too!

And then she'd found a handwritten letter from Mary tucked in one of the paper bags, among her clothes:

> Dear Esther,
>
> Try to understand that none of us (no human) ever hurts another one of us unless he/she has been hurt first, usually and firstly when we are little by some well-meaning but confused adult. And this doesn't even take into account the emotional baggage we carry from our past lives. But I don't want to get into that!
>
> In the best of all worlds, I would just let you tell me all the details of what it was like for you and listen until you felt fully listened to and fully loved and fully understood—until you had cried every last tear and stormed every last bit of rage. That's really what we all want and what we all deserve. This is our true fully human legacy. YOU ARE

COMPLETELY GOOD AND COMPLETELY LOVEABLE—
ALWAYS HAVE BEEN AND ALWAYS WILL BE!

Love,
Mary

If she killed herself, gave up, Mary would throw a party and Aunt Lottie would come early, stay late.

Fred was watching her from across the bar. She pretended not to notice, arranging a stack of menus, smoothing her hand over the podium. He walked past her and she straightened, tried to look alert, but it felt like a cold wind passing.

THE MEETING BETWEEN boss and employee lasted fewer than five minutes. When Fred opened the door and gestured for her to enter, she noted that he looked tired and sorry, and she was crushed.

She sat in a chair before his desk. Fred sat and then cleared his throat. It was obviously tearing him up, whatever he had to say, and she vowed that she would be a better hostess, that she wouldn't put him in this position again. She would smile; she would engage customers in genial conversations; she would make more of an effort with her appearance.

Fred inhaled through his nose and blew air through his lips audibly, his chest rising and falling. He folded his cuffs to his biceps. The window by his desk was open, allowing a slight odor of seaweed and gasoline; small waves murmured and lapped, and every now and then the pier creaked. He bowed his head in reflection, his forearms against his desk. "I know you're under stress," he said, looking up.

Yes, she wanted to tell him. *Keep going. Don't stop. It's okay.*

"I think it might be good for you to take a leave, maybe take it easy for a while. You might feel better. Then you can decide if you want to come back."

"What did I do?"

"Maybe that's not what's relevant," he suggested.

Her face was coloring, she knew, because she felt its heat. She needed the money, and she understood that this was Fred's way of warning her. He wouldn't make her take a leave. But she wanted to know what he'd heard, who had told him. She wanted confirmation. How much did he know? She leaned back and smiled, hoping to look casual, but he didn't smile back and she gave up.

She thought of quitting, saving Fred the trouble of having to fire her. She was no good at her job. But she had all her bills to pay; she owed Rick *something* for letting her stay at his place, no matter what he said. And eventually she wanted to get her own place. No offense to Rick's taste, but his Thomas Kinkade paintings, the teddy bear collection, and all those framed pieces of lace were starting to grate.

And Rick was planning a trip to Europe—Spain and France—with the money he'd stolen from Grandma Eileen. She was going to go with him, but she didn't want him to pay, even though he liked to say, "It's our money."

She'd rather pay her own way.

At least she'd been cured—knock on wood—of stealing. She hadn't stolen since her arrest. Rick said that most of the time people were unwilling to give up their defense mechanisms because they provided people with immediate release and satisfaction. He said that people had to see beyond their fears before they let them go. Strange that the things that hurt her and were self-destructive were the things that gave her relief. She used to believe that she was owed, that life shouldn't be so difficult, and that she should get credit, since she'd been through so much. But she no longer kept score.

Sometimes she tried to add up all her bills—to assess her debt—but the results were staggering: She couldn't believe it. She would try again, but soon she would get confused and frightened. She ended up shoving all the bills in a dresser drawer and trying to forget them. To get cash, she'd sold her clothes, her sunglasses and handbags, most everything of any value, to Moving Up! on Pacific Coast Highway, for the discounted used-clothing rate.

She needed this job. The routine. The money. She'd wasted time. Had she known sooner what was valuable in life—love, education, compassion—she would have prepared herself. She made discoveries every day, most of which were painful, and the majority of which were about her. She sensed that there must be something greater and more meaningful than the world she lived in, but she didn't know what it was. Her job, she believed, anchored her, and the only real answer, she decided, was to continue seeking.

The important thing now was to find out what Fred knew. And then she could assess how much damage she needed to repair. She could invent an excuse, a justification for her conduct.

The night in question—last night—she'd been in the third hour of her shift when the Platt party had arrived, a bridal shower party of ten: the woman with the duck lips (her younger double) and her giggling, fake-breasted friends.

A sense of indignation overcame Esther: She had to serve these women! It seemed that fate was pursuing her, killing her; she felt outraged and humiliated. And right away, she sensed that they were mocking her: two of them whispering while watching her.

She showed them to their table. She tried to hand them their menus while they kissed, touched, and complimented each other. ("Oh, you look so pretty!" "I love your earrings!")

She unfolded the napkins and set them in the laps of the women who were too stupid to do so on their own, as she'd been trained to do. She was disgusted by their brashness, the stupidity of their chatter, and their imbecilic self-satisfaction.

To soften her contempt, she found her nook in the bar and quickly pirated a shot of Absolut peach vodka, and then another, and then one more, fulfilling her quota of three shots per shift.

At first, Ted had questioned her judgment, but whatever he saw in her face had ignited a look of pity in his own, and he'd passed her the bottle without comment. In addition to her earlier consumption of a leftover quarter-full glass of dry zinfandel (on an empty stomach), the result had been like spreading gasoline on a flame, stoking her emotions into a withering, uncontrollable scorn.

A spirit of combat tormented her: She wanted to spit in their faces, to crush them, to strike them down and kill them all.

But she kept her place at the podium—she maintained a semblance of emotional equilibrium, leaned into the wood.

The table was loud and boisterous, and she did her best to disregard the women, avoiding any eye contact.

All might have passed had not one of them shouted, "Excuse me! Hostess! Come here!"

She ignored them.

"Hostess! You!"

She walked toward the table, shaking and furious. She tried to calm down, thinking of what she would say. "How is everything?" she would ask. "Yes, ladies? How can I help you? Can I get you something?"

But when she reached the table, the words died in her mouth.

Sour and malevolent, with tear-rimmed eyes, she stared at each face, going down the table, until her eyes met those of Paul's fiancée.

"Is your name Esther?" she heard, from another woman.

She faced the questioner, blond and young—those ugly clear braces on the bottom row of her teeth.

"We have a bet," the woman next to the braces woman said. "You're Esther, right?"

"I want my five dollars," the braces woman said.

The table broke into laughter, but Paul's intended looked startled. Her hands were under the table and her eyes were wide.

For a second, Esther became her—a transference. She fingered the diamond of her engagement ring under the table, her hands in her lap, and stared at the hostess.

"Is she okay?" she heard.

"Just say your name, so I can get my five bucks."

And then she transferred back into her own raging flesh, and she saw that Paul's intended was sad, her eyes apologetic.

Esther blinked, and blinked again. She felt as if her guts were being pinched. At the same time, welling up was a surge of compassion for Paul's fiancée, which confused her.

"I want my five bucks."

"She didn't say."

"Shut up," Esther said, letting everything release. The faces of the women blended into one pink stretch of skin. "Shut up, shut up, shut up," and her hands went to the table, she leaned her hips against it. A great pressure loosened—it felt so good. "Shut up, shut up, shut up, shut up."

The braces woman flung her arm out, as if to physically stop Esther from speaking. A bread plate clattered to the floor, a bottle of wine dropped. Three of them rose, chairs flung out, to avoid the spillage. Wine spread across the white tablecloth in a ruby-colored blossom.

Esther set her hand in the stain, as if to make a stamp.

"WHAT DID I do?" she asked now.

Fred paused, rubbed the back of his neck with his hand. Then, looking at her as if she should have known better than to ask, he said, "Among other things, it was brought to my attention, by one of our customers, that you were crying last night. In fact, the exact words were 'weeping uncontrollably.'"

She flexed her legs, and her back went stiff against the chair. She had done most of her crying in the walk-in freezer; she hadn't expected this.

Fred clasped his hands, his forefingers pressed together and pointing across the desk. "Three employees corroborated this account," he said.

She looked at his basketball trophies lined up on a shelf behind him, and then down at her lap. She thought of Charlie, and for the first time, he was erased by the crushing weight of reality—she could feel him becoming a memory.

When she looked up, Fred's expression was sympathetic. His kindness made her weak, and she forced her tears back. She felt their weight, lodged in the space behind her eyes and nose. Her sorrow was tangible, like taking a bite of an apple. But at least—unlike last night—she was participating; at least she was active in her grief. It wasn't simply having its way with her.

Fred's face showed concern, his eyes deep and serious. He was letting her know that they were done discussing what had happened, that he wasn't about to fire her, and that he wouldn't put her through any more humiliation.

8

NORA GIVENS HAD experienced a surge of success with Clothing for Change, due mostly to a large donation ($200,000) from an anonymous benefactor. With the extra funds as an incentive, Nora had tried to hire Esther—who she knew was in financial and emotional duress—as an "accessories consultant," but Esther had gracefully declined (fortuitous, since God knew with Esther's reputation, the board of directors would have fought the hire).

"Poor Esther!" she said (although her thoughts were far more complex), when she learned of the breakup and Charlie's subsequent trip around the world.

Who had broken up with whom? There'd been so many nasty rumors. Had Esther slept with Jim Dunnels? Nora didn't know much about the man, except that he owned Fashion Island. But ever since she'd witnessed Esther's open cavity of pain, she no longer passed judgment; it was as if her soul had fused with Esther's, in some kind of empathetic lifelong union.

Sometimes Nora joined in the mirthful gossip, in the most peripheral of ways, by listening. But within minutes of solitary introspection, the full extent of her betrayal would overcome her, and she'd vow not to participate. A challenge, considering Esther was an easy target and a common topic of conversation.

In the six months that had passed, Nora had become occupied with the opening of two more "outlets," and while she hadn't necessarily forgotten about Esther's plight, she didn't think of her as often, and when she did, it was with something like sad curiosity.

Nora's feelings for Charlie didn't have the same grip. She thought of him with a rueful sadness, a resignation, and her disappointment had liberated her from the bondage of fantasy. She felt that she could take him or leave him—it was all the same.

But he kept in contact, sending her postcards from his travels. He'd been promoted to full professor at Orange County Community College, and he continued to travel at every opportunity.

"Poor Esther!" Nora said again, when she heard that Esther had not received money from Eileen's will. "Poor Esther!" Rumor had it that Eileen had been alone at the time of her death, but that relatives had come out of the woodwork for the reading of her will, from Canada and Michigan and Arizona, from all over. Nora imagined them as vultures circling roadkill. But Eileen had left her estate in arrears, and the will was nebulous enough for the relatives to fight, ensuring that much of the money would go to lawyers, and that the battle would continue for years—vultures circling vultures circling roadkill.

Esther had been stonewalled, her disgrace blamed for accelerating Eileen's demise. And there was something about a neglected cat—Esther had a cat?—that had caused Eileen's fall.

Nora had heard that Esther was living with Eileen's former caretaker in an apartment somewhere in Costa Mesa, and that Esther couldn't get a job because no one would hire her. She knew that Esther's brother, Eric, had stayed sober for a long period—but a while ago he'd disappeared, in blatant violation of his parole. No one knew where to, which, Nora believed, didn't bode well for his sobriety.

And it was this very same exclamation ("Poor Esther!") that came to mind when Nora happened to drive past a dark alleyway in Mariner's Mile. She was driving home from an unfortunate blind date (What was she thinking? No more blind dates, ever!) and had made a wrong turn.

Sitting at a curb, a skinnier Esther was smoking a cigarette while two men hosed something that looked to be black and made of rubber—the protective flooring, perhaps, of a restaurant kitchen, the jet of water thudding against it.

Nora slowed her car, turned off her headlights, and pulled over beside a Dumpster. She was disgusted by her voyeurism, but her voyeurism was stronger than her disgust.

There was a keen possibility of being seen, but Esther appeared consumed by her thoughts. Her elbows were at her knees, her legs extended from the curb. She wore a black skirt and blouse, and the skirt was gathered between her legs.

The only light came from a single streetlight and a light above the back doorway, but it was enough to see that her face had become more angular.

Her hair was pulled back in what looked like a loose braid. Her face was pinched in concentration, a heaviness of thought. She appeared to have forgotten about the cigarette. After some time, she stubbed it out on the curb, flicked it into the gutter. The hose was turned off and spray drifted, lingering, a haze of silver. Her head hung down for a long moment, and then she lifted it, said something to the men.

Nora rolled down her window, but it was too late. She'd missed whatever had been said. The men were laughing, in a casual way that suggested they worked together. The surroundings smelled of rotted eggs and ocean, and the odor drifted into her open window with the breeze, settled over her in the moist air.

She watched the men put the flooring down, and they walked to the side of the alley, ready to haul another mat to be cleaned.

And then Esther stood, turned to go through the back door. But before she opened it, she turned around, as if she'd forgotten something. She was looking, and then she found her lighter. She leaned over and picked it up, and when she stood, her gaze came up, hitting Nora directly.

Nora was going to duck, but it was too late and she sat frozen, stared back.

Esther's head came forward—she was peering, making sure. "What are you doing?" she called out, smiling sadly.

Nora gave a small hand wave.

"Are you spying on me?"

Nora tried to ignore the ringing in her ears. Her face composed itself into a false smile. She imagined it looked like a horrified smile, so she let her lips go slack.

With a look of humiliation and defiance, Esther began walking to her. Not only had she lost weight—the folds of her black skirt and blouse clung to her, which made her seem hardened somehow—but also something had changed about her face: A weary sadness that Nora had caught only glimmers of before—weaving in and out of the composed Esther—was displayed openly, nakedly present. Poor Esther!

"What are you doing?" Esther repeated, crouching beside the car door.

Nora didn't know how to respond. She was at a loss, her mouth dry.

After a moment, Esther said, "You look like you've seen a ghost."

Nora made an effort to calm her facial features.

"Why are you here?" Esther asked.

"I had a blind date," Nora said, with a pinch of humiliation, remembering how her date had looked over her shoulder while she had talked, assessing the women at the bar.

Esther's stare became a smile, as if understanding everything that Nora's blind date meant.

Nora could hear the men conversing in a hum of Spanish, the sound of their hose, and the traffic on Pacific Coast Highway. Esther tapped the lighter against the car, as if to break up the tension.

Nora noticed a sapphire ring on Esther's ring finger, and she must have been staring, because Esther said, "Grandma Eileen left it to me." She wondered why Esther didn't sell it for money, but decorum prevented her from asking. They heard a scraping noise. The men were sliding the rubber flooring through the door. The sky was dark and murky with marine clouds, and the streetlight flickered and then went out.

"I miss him," Esther said. Her lips pressed together. "But don't tell me where he is. I don't want to know." She paused, thinking. "I woke up," she said. She looked down for a long second, and when her face came up, she seemed surprised. "There's more space around me," she said, and she looked to her left and then to her right, as if she could see the space.

The heavy back door slammed; the men had gone inside. The light over the doorway made the air look silky and soft.

Esther began to rise, slowly.

"Wait."

Esther leaned her palm against the car door to keep her balance, squatting again.

"I don't know," Nora said. "It's just, I'm wondering if you're okay. I mean, are you happy?" As soon as she asked, she regretted it. "Not happy. That's not what I mean."

Esther was watching her steadily. She looked very serious.

"That's such a stupid word," Nora said. "Is anyone ever happy? I'm just trying to understand, about more space."

Caught in the current of Esther's stare, locked back into an intimacy that she had never expected, Nora saw her answer, and she understood that the kindest thing she could do would be to leave Esther alone.

She waited to start her car, watching while Esther walked slowly to the back door. Because Esther wore black and the streetlight had gone dark, for a second, even before she slipped inside the restaurant, Nora lost her to the night.

Later, sitting in a chair on her balcony, the breeze rattling the palm fronds, the stars invisible, and the only evidence of the moon a dull amber gleam, Nora decided that more space was good, and the view and the sky and her breathing seemed to verify it, as if her consciousness was, in her present awareness, still meeting and connecting with Esther's. Briefly, an airplane twinkled red over the horizon, and then it was gone. And all seemed further confirmed by the dark space of nothing that came when Nora closed her eyes.

ACKNOWLEDGMENTS

My deep gratitude goes to Michael Carlisle, Ethan Bassoff, and Jack Shoemaker. Thank you to these friends for their insight, honesty, and patience: Danzy Senna, Veronica Gonzalez, Dana Johnson, Michael Leone, Michelle Huneven, Natasha Prime, and Holly Stauffer. Also, thanks to Terri Waits-Smith and Debra Albin-Riley for opening their homes when I needed a space to write. Profound thanks as well to my parents and to my brother, and, as always, Chris, Cole, and Ry.

Printed in the United States
by Baker & Taylor Publisher Services